GATE TO KAGOSHIMA

GATE TO KAGOSHIMA

A Novel

Book One of the Ancestor Memories Series

POPPY KUROKI

HARPER PERENNIAL

NEW YORK • LONDON • TORONTO • SYDNEY • NEW DELHI • AUCKLAND

HARPER ● PERENNIAL

Originally published in Great Britain in 2024 by Oneworld Publications.

FIRST US EDITION

Library of Congress Cataloging-in-Publication Data

Names: Kuroki, Poppy, 1993- author.
Title: Gate to Kagoshima : a novel / Poppy Kuroki.
Description: First US edition. | New York : Harper Paperbacks, 2025. |
    Series: Ancestor memories ; book 1
Identifiers: LCCN 2024023649 | ISBN 9780063410879 (trade paperback)
| ISBN
    9780063410893 (ebook)
Subjects: LCGFT: Romance fiction. | Fantasy fiction. | Novels.
Classification: LCC PR6111.U76 G38 2025 | DDC 823/.92--dc23/
eng/20240715
LC record available at https://lccn.loc.gov/2024023649

ISBN 978-0-06-341087-9 (pbk.)

25 26 27 28 29 WOR 10 9 8 7 6 5 4 3 2 1

For Mum, who has always believed in me
And for Jack Valentine, my inspiration

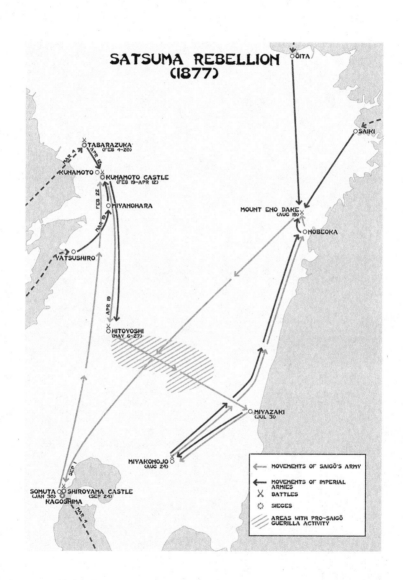

SATSUMA REBELLION
(1877)

ŌITA

SAIKI

TABARAZUKA
(FEB 4-20)

MAR 4

APR 12

KUNAMOTO

KUNAMOTO CASTLE
(FEB 19-APR 12)

FEB 22

MAR 15

MIYANOHARA

MOUNT ENO DAKE
(AUG 19)

NOBEOKA

YATSUSHIRO

APR 19

HITOYOSHI
(MAY 6-27)

MIYAZAKI
(JUL 31)

MIYAKONOJO
(AUG 24)

SOMUTA
(JAN 30)

SHIROYAMA CASTLE
(SEP 24)

SEP 1

MAR 4

KAGOSHIMA

MOVEMENTS OF SAIGŌ'S ARMY
MOVEMENTS OF IMPERIAL ARMIES
X   BATTLES
O   SIEGES
AREAS WITH PRO-SAIGŌ GUERILLA ACTIVITY

MEMORY

Truth is not what you want it to be; it is what it is, and you must bend to its power or live a lie.

Musashi Miyamoto

GATE TO KAGOSHIMA

CHAPTER 1

I'm descended from samurai.

    It sounded like the coolest thing in the world, not that Isla MacKenzie would ever say so aloud.

Finally, after months of planning, she was in Kagoshima. The bustling Japanese city nestled among thick forests and craggy hills, in the shadow of the great active volcano, Mount Sakurajima. A dry winter breeze washed over her, smelling of soil and stone and the river. She inhaled, a smile spreading on her face.

Isla's third-great-grandfather had walked these lands nearly a hundred and thirty years ago. The MacKenzie family lore had it that perhaps he was one of the warriors who had fought alongside Takamori Saigō, the rebel samurai leader who fought to his death against the emperor's army in 1877. He would have been a brave warrior, and maybe even a great hero. Isla liked to think of his blood beating still in her own veins.

She gazed in the direction of the great mountain concealed by winter rain. Mist hid the peak that belched frequent plumes of smoke and rained ash on the city. Today, the volcano remained subdued.

Takamori Saigō was *everywhere*, even in the tiny airport welcoming guests to the city of Kagoshima. His face, round and cartoonish with his signature thick, black eyebrows, could be found on posters, signs, advertisements, and every piece of merchandise in the souvenir shops. Ironic, since in life he had never let anyone take his photograph.

Isla MacKenzie wandered along the river's edge, where loose grass floated lazily down the stream, the surface dancing with scatters of rainfall. She was here on a mission: to find her third-great-grandfather's history. Her grandfather, may he rest in peace, had begun his own research, hoping to discover Hisakichi Kuroki's story, but he had never returned to Japan after his parents shunned him for marrying a foreigner. And with this breaking of ties, any family knowledge concerning the details of the life of his own great-grandfather had faded into obscurity.

The mere memory of her grandad brought an ache that settled into Isla's chest, heavy like a stone. She stopped at the riverbank to unfold his photograph, the centre fold creased to white, lost in memories of sitting on his lap, his scent of vanilla and coffee, and his contagious laugh that would always send anyone in the room into helpless fits of giggles.

'Eye, eye, eye-la,' he would say, tapping her eyebrows and then her nose with each syllable.

'Tom, Tom, Tomo,' she'd giggle back, flicking his ears, then his nose. Isla's grandfather's name had been Yoshitomo, but everyone in Scotland had called him Tom.

I will finish what you started, Grandad.

She would find the truth about Hisakichi Kuroki. Was he a samurai or a lowly peasant? Had he fought alongside one of the most famous Japanese historical figures of all time? Grandad would never know, but Isla would. Part of her wanted to vow she wouldn't return to her university accommodation in Tokyo until she knew for sure. The thought summoned Mum's stern face to her mind. Maybe it would be better to just work fast.

Though she was a quarter Japanese, Isla had inherited the bright red hair of her Scottish father's side, and her fiery locks, feathered into layers, barely brushed her shoulders. She tucked a stray strand behind her ear, checking the time on her flip phone. It was a new Motorola Razr, a gift from Dad just before she started her study-abroad year in Japan. Not that she could do much with it here except take pictures. Isla noted the battery was getting low, and she told herself to remember to charge it once she had made it to the hotel.

Wandering alone along the riverside was peaceful, stones crunching beneath her trainers and the wind cold on her skin. It was healing to be here, away from the drama of home. A sharp pain that had nothing to do with her grandfather joined the melancholy in her heart. Maybe, now she had some time away, she could learn to forget about *him*. Isla scowled and looked out at the faint outline of the city landscape. She would not let her ex-boyfriend ruin this special time for her.

Isla drew close to the Museum of the Meiji Restoration, a modest and unassuming building that was nothing like the towering skyscrapers of Tokyo. Perhaps she would find answers here. Along the way were signposts displaying snippets of the past and details on historical figures. There was even a traditional samurai house of wooden floors, a slate roof and sliding *washi* paper doors, and Isla took a quick look inside.

A bird flitted past and landed on the skeletal branch of a tree, chirping. Though it was a weekend, it was quiet here, away from Tenmonkan Street where people wandered to cafés and walked their dogs among the scent of ramen noodles and sweet rice cakes. January was a perfect time to travel. After the excitement and holidays in the New Year, barely anyone was around. The crowds of Tokyo often made her impatient; everyone moved too slowly for her liking.

Visiting the museum to find information on an obscure person from the past was a long shot, Isla knew. She had found nothing in textbooks or newspaper archives that mentioned her third-great-grandfather. Only the most famous and influential samurai had been mentioned. But it felt important for her to be here, to taste the history, to walk the lands her ancestors had. Grandad's wishes aside, Isla was more than a little curious herself about where she had come from.

She read everything she could in the museum, even struggling through the long passages of Japanese and wishing for the thousandth time she was more practised in kanji, the more complicated alphabet.

She learned about how the samurai tried and failed to take Kumamoto Castle, how they spent months fighting imperial soldiers, and how it all kicked off after the army sent a warship to Kagoshima City – of the Satsuma province, as it was called back then – at the end of that January to confiscate their weapons and ammunition. Someone caught them and raised the alarm, unleashing the rage of Takamori Saigō's samurai. It was an arresting idea, hundreds of angry samurai armed with whatever they could find, chasing off the emperor's soldiers until they fled to the open sea.

The museum displayed the dialect of old Satsuma, which sounded nothing like standard Japanese. Isla's understanding was fractured. Grandad and Mum's help as well as two years studying Japanese at the University of Edinburgh had not prepared her for cultural nuances. A little cartoon of Takamori Saigō and his dog gave the standard form and the Satsuma form, written both in Japanese and in Roman letters. A wee smile played on Isla's lips as she wondered how this historical figure would feel if he knew there were so many goofy cartoon versions of him.

'*Watashi wa anata no koto ga daisuki desu.*' The board gave the standard Japanese of the phrase 'I like you a lot', and then provided the Satsuma version, '*Oi wa omansa ga wazze sujja.*'

Isla studied the script, writing the phrases in her notebook. Her language skills were decent enough, but clearly she still had a long way to go. Her half-Japanese mum would be so proud if she managed to find information on Hisakichi Kuroki.

In a glass case sat a biwa lute, a teardrop-shaped instrument made from mulberry wood, with four silk strings and an intricate carved samurai helmet and sword decorating its centre. Near this display was a sumo game, where you pushed as hard as you could against a cartoonish wrestler painted on the wall. Isla was rather proud of her score of forty-two kilograms.

Things became sombre further along the museum. There was a 3-D model of Saigō kneeling on a mountain, surrounded by his remaining friends, all sitting with their heads bent. Their fists were clenched and their faces bleak. Even while immortalising the moment, the artist had captured the quiet acceptance of their fates. They knew they were about to die.

Isla peered closely at the little figurines. Had Hisakichi Kuroki been among them, knowing the long, gruelling war had come to an end and he would soon draw his last breath? Or did he die early on, in the battle for Kumamoto Castle, perhaps, or one of the many guerrilla attacks that followed?

The only thing Grandad knew about Hisakichi Kuroki was his name and that he was from Kagoshima. Hisakichi Kuroki's wife's name and when he had died were a mystery. Isla wished she had more to go on, something like the birthday of Hisakichi Kuroki's son – Isla's great-great-grandfather – as this would have indicated whether he had died during the Satsuma Rebellion.

Many Japanese people thought of the war's end as romantic. The samurai, battle-worn and half-starved, had run down the mountainside in the morning sun, katana swords in hands, facing their certain deaths with the fearless courage they'd learned and breathed from childhood.

She read about the schools for young boys where they trained in literature and language and martial arts, having their morals set firmly in stone. Thanks to Takamori Saigō, young samurai had places to go to learn and train. Figures of small boys wrestled in their loincloths or sat in rapt attention as they listened to their sensei.

Their mantra was on the information board: *Do not lie. Do not mistreat the weak. And never be defeated.*

Isla thought this a good way to live.

*

A wild boar snuffled on the hillside, snout pushing aside dirt and twigs in the search for food. Hunger made the boar oblivious to two young men crouching nearby.

Maeda Keiichirō and Mori Toramasa squatted low, hidden among the bushes. An icy gust blew, the air dry and carrying the scent of soil and grass.

An ache formed in Keiichirō's back, but he didn't move. The wide, flowing legs of his hakama trousers fluttered in the wind as he remained still, watching the boar as it foraged.

'Steady,' best friend Toramasa whispered, his long fingers curling around the hilt of his sword. The narrow pit trap they had laid for the boar still stood two metres to its left, and the tusked creature didn't show any interest in the bait they had set inside.

Keiichirō's mouth filled with saliva. There was enough meat on that thing to last for days.

The stocky *inoshishi* boar trotted across the forest clearing, its snout quivering. For a moment it seemed it might finally go for the bait. But as the wind washed over them from behind, the boar caught the scent of the hunters. It glanced up and its beady eyes looked straight in their direction.

Before Keiichirō could grab him, Toramasa sprang up. His tall stature cast a shadow onto the boar's back and, with one pull, his katana sword was free. The sun glinted off the blade, a flash of brilliance, before he plunged it into the beast. Crimson spurted onto Toramasa's leg.

But instead of falling dead, the boar squealed and took off, racing through the bush and out of sight, drops of blood marking the twigs and dead leaves.

'*Bakamono*,' Keiichirō admonished, straightening. 'Your first strike must always kill. We should have brought guns.'

'And warned the farmer?' Toramasa snorted. He gave the sword a sharp flick to shake the worst of the blood from the blade, then wiped it on the grass. He slipped it back into his belt beside his shorter wakizashi sword.

Keiichirō looked him in the eyes. 'The farmer?'

Toramasa gave a cheeky smile. It was a look Keiichirō knew only too well. 'You wouldn't have agreed to come.'

'Who's there?' a voice roared from the trees. 'Who's poaching?'

Keiichirō cursed.

The grass whipped their sandals as they ran, Keiichirō clutching his own swords against his left hip. Branches scratched his face and hair as the two of them crashed through the woods.

The bark of a dog sounded behind, and echoed as if there were a dozen hounds among the trees.

'You didn't mention this land belonged to a farmer,' Keiichirō panted, 'or that he had a dog.'

They left the trees and sprinted across scrub, laughing. The dog burst from the foliage, yapping and snarling.

'Run!' Keiichirō shouted.

They didn't stop until they had slipped between the low-roofed buildings of the town and reached a familiar neighbourhood.

On the horizon sat Mount Sakurajima, the mighty volcano on the island for which it was named. On this day, no mist crowned its peak. A thin trail of smoke floated from it to mingle with the clouds.

'Is the dog still there?' Keiichirō imagined snarling jaws snapping at his ankles.

'I don't think so. But still, in here.'

They slipped through an alley between wooden homes, sandals slapping now upon a dirt road. Soon they were passing soba noodle shops and the scent of soy sauce and green onions, *noren* curtains fluttering over the entrances that had speciality dishes painted on them in white or gold.

At last, they came to the riverside.

Toramasa anxiously patted his hair and Keiichirō snorted a laugh.

Women knelt by the water, washing silk kimonos and beating futon mattresses, obi belts tied around their waists to form large bows at their backs. A few glanced up and some of the older ones exchanged looks.

Keiichirō saw why Toramasa had been so eager to smooth his hair.

Ikeda Uhei, an older student of the great Saigō-sama's schools for samurai, which they attended, came towards them, confident and at ease. He had always favoured Toramasa, with his clear, alabaster skin and delicate cheekbones. Girls had always giggled over Toramasa's good looks.

Toramasa swallowed, glancing at Keiichirō as though asking for support, as they bowed low to their senior.

'Good afternoon, Ikeda-san,' said Keiichirō as the silence stretched between the trio.

Ikeda Uhei had the demeanour of an older man, despite only being twenty-six. He regarded the younger students with a small bow of his own, a few strays from his straight hair blowing in the breeze. The corners of his mouth turned upward in a smile that was hard to read. His voice was silk. 'Maeda-san. Mori-san. Not causing mischief, I trust?'

'Not at all, Ikeda-san,' Toramasa squeaked.

Ikeda's gaze lingered for a shade longer before he sauntered away, leaving behind the cool scent of pine needles.

Toramasa let out a long breath as if the encounter had winded him.

'What do we do now?' Keiichirō asked. With an effort, he avoided glancing behind for the pursuing farmer and the dog, even though the back of his neck still prickled. They hadn't made a kill, and now the farmer would know someone was poaching from his land. Keiichirō had been a fool for blindly following Toramasa. Since they were boys, his best friend had always got him into trouble, and he should have known better. 'We still haven't any food. Kana won't be pleased.'

'She'll be right to be upset. Let's go fishing, then.' Toramasa stopped gawping after Ikeda-san and grinned at his friend. 'There's always a way.'

'One that usually gets us into trouble,' Keiichirō muttered, but he went after his friend all the same.

As the sun sank beneath the horizon, sapping the day of the last of its warmth, and the first of the stars pinpricked in a sky the colour of spilled ink, goosebumps stippled Keiichirō's hands and neck as they headed home, three fish in his bag, his spirits high. He, Kana and Yura would eat tonight, and, with the current state of things, this was a blessing. Japan was at war, rice was scarce, and even samurai had to sometimes resort to poaching to feed their families.

A small boy sniffled as he and Toramasa passed, the youngster clutching a fishing rod and an empty bag. He scuffed his feet along the ground, skinny shoulders slumped. He gave a start and then bowed low as they approached, murmuring a greeting.

'Best get home, little one. It's getting dark,' said Toramasa cheerfully, barely sparing the child a glance.

'Here.' Keiichirō took out one of his fish and offered it to the boy.

'I can't.' The child backed away. Something between anxiety and alarm crossed his face as he clenched the bag to his stomach like it embarrassed him.

'Yes, you can.' Keiichirō knelt before the child. 'How old are you?'

'Seven.'

'You received your wakizashi sword already,' said Toramasa, nodding to the blade at the boy's hip.

'*H-hai*. I just got it last week.' The boy's shyness gave way to pride.

'That's deserving of a reward.' Keiichirō took the boy's bag and deposited the fish inside. 'There. You need to eat to be strong and protect your family, *ne?*'

The boy bowed and ran off into the darkness with his prize.

'You'll be hungry tonight,' said Toramasa.

'Yes,' Keiichirō agreed. 'But he won't.'

CHAPTER 2

When Isla left the museum, it was raining. She found a nearby café and ordered a coffee in Japanese, although she had to repeat herself twice.

The young barista apologised profusely with the sort of smile she couldn't help but return. Maybe it was his uniform, or the way his gaze lingered on hers, but her stomach gave a tiny flip as he promised to bring her cinnamon latte over as soon as it was ready.

The tingle of enjoyment was immediately doused by something darker. Isla didn't trust herself any more. Not since... Well, she hadn't deleted her MySpace account and flown halfway across the world for nothing. She had to fulfil her promise to find her ancestors' history, aye, but it didn't hurt that the more miles that lay between Will and herself the better. There was nothing like nursing a broken heart from a failed love affair to make one not want to think about home or those she had left behind.

Isla opened her notebook at a random page to distract herself from damaging thoughts of her relationship; it hadn't been worth saving and she needed to keep thinking of that. Men were going to be off the table for quite some time, Isla just knew, and that was fine with her.

As she'd suspected would be the case, she hadn't found a whisper of Hisakichi Kuroki in the Museum of the Meiji Restoration. But then, only the most well-known samurai had been mentioned there.

It didn't mean he hadn't participated in the rebellion. Thousands of samurai had been present fighting alongside Takamori Saigō, after all.

Before finding the café, she had found the life-sized statue of the fabled leader at the foot of Mount Shiroyama. He was taller than she had expected, although the people of Satsuma had been taller than the average Japanese person because of their meat-rich diet.

Takamori Saigō stood with his dog, Tsun, and he boasted broad shoulders and a dominating figure. The statue depicted him in his Western-style soldier's uniform from his days fighting for the emperor. Could he have known Isla's third-great-grandfather? Did he have any idea back then that his hometown would one day have his face everywhere, a statue erected near the place of his death so he could be remembered as 'the last samurai' for ever?

Did you know a man named Hisakichi Kuroki?

Isla imagined Takamori Saigō turning to her from his frozen place on his stand, smiling as he told her how she had inherited the brown eyes of one of his most courageous soldiers.

Watching her coffee being prepared, Isla decided she would head up Mount Shiroyama in the morning. There was an observatory overlooking the volcano and caves where the samurai hid immediately before their final hours.

If the downpour continued into tomorrow, well, she'd pull her hood up. The Scottish weren't afraid of the rain.

'Thank you for waiting.'

Isla glanced up to see the young barista.

'I'm so sorry about not understanding you before,' he said in slow, simple Japanese, carefully setting down her mug. A heart was drawn on top in foam. He bowed to her. He had sleek black hair tied in a bun. It suited him.

'It's all right,' said Isla. 'No one can understand me. My pronunciation isn't very good.'

He gave a polite laugh and returned to the counter.

She sipped slowly, the milky coffee warming her. She wrote, or more exactly pretended to, as rain beat against the window. The barista greeted every customer with a clear *irasshaimase* to welcome them, his tone professional and friendly as was expected in Japan.

Isla went to the counter again and bought a pastry as she waited for the rain to lessen, and reread her notes until it was nearly three o'clock, the time she could finally check into her hotel. As she rose to leave, backpack in hand, the barista threaded his way through the tables with ease.

'Have you tried *tapioka*?'

'I'm not sure.'

'Let me make you a matcha *tapioka*.'

She sat down again and tapped her pen softly on the table, self-consciously rubbing pastry crumbs from her lips. The barista came back with a clear plastic cup with the café's logo on its side and a wide straw. Dark balls of what Isla assumed to be tapioca filled the bottom half. The drink on top was a deep green.

He placed the cup before Isla, saying, 'No charge.'

She sipped cautiously. Several tapioca balls made their way up the straw, and she found they were soft and slightly chewy. It was a strange sensation but she enjoyed it. It was like having a dessert in a cup.

The barista smiled as she nodded her approval. 'What are you doing in Kagoshima? Are you here on holiday?' he asked.

Isla felt tongue-tied. Most of her Japanese speaking had been with Mum and Grandad or her teacher back at university, not a native speaker who would definitely know if she made a mistake.

'I want to know more about your city,' she said finally. 'I went to the museum and learned the history of the Satsuma Rebellion.'

Painfully aware of the way she stumbled over words and likely used the wrong particle, she hoped she hadn't embarrassed herself too much. She should carry around a disclaimer like a business card, apologising in advance for causing offence by using any wrong letter.

'Did you learn about Saigō Takamori? He's a hero around here. I'm so happy foreigners are interested in him too.'

Isla noticed the barista used the historic figure's surname first. 'Will you join me for a minute?' she asked.

The barista looked around, but all the unoccupied tables were clear of crockery, and nobody was waiting at the counter, and so he sat down.

'You're from Kagoshima?' Isla took another sip of bubble tea.

'Yes. My whole family lives here,' he said proudly.

They chatted some more, and Isla was pleased the rain had turned even heavier. There didn't seem to be many people braving it out on the street, and the counter remained quiet. Nor did she have to make an excuse about why she wasn't leaving just yet.

'What are you doing tomorrow?' she said, surprising herself. 'I would love to see more of Kagoshima and learn more about the rebellion. If you're not busy and you'd like to—' She stopped in embarrassment.

'I finish my shift at one o'clock tomorrow. Would you like to meet me here?' the barista said politely and stood to go back to the counter.

It was only when she had checked in and found her room for the night that Isla realised she hadn't asked his name.

She felt restless and her mind refused to calm in the small simple room of the business hotel.

This was her ancestors' homeland, and she had three days to explore. Distracted and pacing, she smacked her shin on the corner of the bed.

Eyes watering, Isla lowered herself onto the firm mattress and rubbed her hurt leg. A run would set her mind straight. She changed into her running clothes, blue leggings and a hoodie, and headed outside. Looking forward to a hot shower on her return and some dinner at the hotel restaurant, she stepped into the cold street and set off.

The downpour had eased to a light mist. Isla jogged down a side street so she wouldn't have to keep dodging around people clutching umbrellas. After a while she began to enjoy the burn in her muscles as her trainers pounded on the concrete. She wanted to keep up with her fitness as it made her feel so much better. The stereotype of moving to Japan was you lost weight, but there was more to the Japanese diet than miso soup and vegetables, and she had been warned more than once about cheap beer and convenience-store fried chicken. But weight wasn't a concern. Back in Scotland, Isla loved to hike, and her little brother Douglas wouldn't let her hear the end of it if she was left behind, puffing and panting, by her family on one of their walks. It wasn't easy finding hiking trails from central Tokyo – they certainly existed, but it often involved long train journeys – and so running was the best way to keep up her stamina.

Besides, she needed a way to get rid of her odd nervous energy. Maybe it was being here in her ancestors' homeland, or the prospect of a date tomorrow, but she simply didn't want to keep still.

Icy air in her lungs, she pounded past a few more houses, glancing to the rain still running from the sloped roofs and into gutters. A cute shiba inu dog trotted by on a dripping leash, led by a disgruntled old man muttering about the cold.

Isla came to a more traditional side of the town, a narrow hill where the buildings had sloping roofs and bamboo fences. Glows from spherical lanterns lit her way. Her feet were wet, but now her body ached with pleasant fatigue. She made up her mind to go just a little farther and then she'd head back.

Isla soon came to a shrine she hadn't seen before. She slowed, panting as she stared at it. The shrine was unusual, she thought, or at least it had captured her attention in a way that other shrines hadn't so far. A red torii gate separated the city street from a stone path, where chimes clinked and a new surge of raindrops plinked on metal and rock. Stone statues of lions snarled either side of the path leading to a slope-roofed, elegant building. A rope hung from a large bell at the entrance, which was flanked with wooden Japanese lanterns painted red. It was a slice of the past within the city.

Isla had to see more. Back in Scotland she had always enjoyed looking at pictures of shrines and temples, views of Mount Fuji and cherry blossoms. It was the same deep love she held for the mountains of her homeland, with its sweeping fields of heather and mountains of black and gold. It wasn't something she could put into words, just like she couldn't explain why she was wandering into shrine grounds she didn't know despite the weather suddenly becoming heavy and inhospitable.

The inclement weather swept over her like an icy curtain and drenched her hair anew, as freezing droplets ran down her neck and made her wince. One quick look around, and then she'd head back and for that well-deserved shower, she told herself.

But as Isla looked around she couldn't deny there was something immensely intriguing about this little shrine. Stone figures hazy in the deluge, curious statues and old stone lanterns and skeletal trees. For a moment, it was easy to forget she was in the middle of a city and, unbidden, a wave of excitement washed over her, and Isla felt a deep love for what seemed to be history surrounding her.

She approached the shrine itself, but each step brought fiercer wind and heavier rain. But Isla barely noticed as the wind howled and raged like an abrupt, out-of-season typhoon. Rain lashed the shrine and wrenched the hanging rope this way and that in the windy gusts. The bell sounded an ominous, low note as the statues were pelted with new-found violence. Isla's hoodie clung to her, her bobbed hair glued to her scalp. For a moment she thought that it was as if the weather was trying to make her stay away, to protect the shrine's secrets.

Isla jammed her hands into her armpits, hugging herself as grey engulfed her. She turned and marched down the path from which she had come, but almost collided with a solid wall.

Confusion fluttered through her.

Wasn't this the exit?

She had just wandered up this path. How was there a wall here now when there hadn't been before?

She swivelled her head in every direction, searching for the way out, disliking this more and more, as a seed of fear began to take root.

But there was nothing but white around her now, like thick fog had fallen on the city. The wind howled and whipped at her clothes, pushing her body left and right.

'I'm going!' she shouted as thick rain engulfed her from every direction. *If only I can work out how.* What had seemed so compelling mere minutes ago now seemed sinister and Isla wanted nothing more than to escape this place.

Up until now she had believed that typhoons in Tokyo were little more than a regular day in Scotland. There had been one a week after she'd arrived in Japan in September, and though they were mentioned in the news, to Isla they felt little more than a bit of wind and rain.

In any case, it was now the wrong time of year. January was traditionally well past typhoon season here.

Something was wrong.

Increasingly desperate, Isla stumbled past graves and statues in a ferocious storm, but as her hair was whipped into her eyes she couldn't find the way out. The more she tried to retrace her original steps inside the shrine, the more it made no sense to her.

You idiot, Isla told herself as she forced herself to be calm and think rationally. But it was no good. She felt panic wash through her as the shrine's grounds looked nightmarish, with an endless stone path at her feet and everything similar, with the wind chimes singing in all directions, mocking her despair. Now and then a shape would emerge from the non-stop deluge, but it would be just another lion statue or a grave. Offerings – cans of sake, packets of sweets, flowers – lay scattered, blown around by the wind, and sometimes Isla felt something wet whip her as the wind lifted this debris and tossed it around.

The cold set deep beneath Isla's skin and shakes racked her body. She *had* to find her way back to the road or she might suffer symptoms of exposure. While there wouldn't be any cars out – people's phones would be beeping with weather warnings of the sudden storm – Isla promised herself that once on the road she could find shelter. She couldn't even tell where the shrine building was.

Blinded now with heavier rain, her outstretched fingers found a wall. Exhausted, she stood there with her head bowed, but the stone wall offered no protection from the weather. Isla stepped close to the wall and rested her forehead against it. She didn't know how long she'd been lost in the rainfall. It could be hours – it felt like hours, certainly – but it might only be minutes. The wet had sunk deep into her trainers, soaking her socks. Her clothes clung to her skin and she could barely feel her freezing fingers.

Perhaps it would be better to hunker down here and wait it out. This typhoon or storm, whatever it was, lashed at her clothes, blowing her off balance, a fierce and sudden maelstrom in the middle of a city.

She had never experienced anything like it.

She wished she had worn more than her leggings and hoodie. She wished she had stayed in the hotel. She wished she was anywhere but here.

Isla pulled out her phone and flipped it open. It was dead, fat droplets splashing on to the screen reflecting her scared face. Her breath ragged, she pulled her hood over her head.

The wind wailed above like she was stuck somewhere in the mountains, not in a city. A beast raged in the clouds, roaring like a battle of gods.

Isla squinted into the grey. The murk was clearing in one particular space. There! A white torii gate. A back entrance to the shrine grounds, maybe?

It didn't matter, as long as she could get out of here. In twenty minutes, Isla promised herself, she'd be in her hotel about to step into a scalding shower, and tomorrow she'd be back at the café to see the friendly barista, regaling him with her tale of getting lost in the rain.

But as she headed towards the torii gate, things felt more wrong.

Her fingers tingled, pins and needles prickling her digits. Dizziness assaulted her, a wave of what felt like drunkenness, and she stumbled. She fell against a stone wall as rain thrashed her face once more.

What was happening?

Isla clutched the wall, breathing hard. Where was she? She needed to reach, well, somewhere. She had a vague sense of a hotel, the scent of coffee, a smiling young man…

Whispers surrounded her and she cowered, wondering if she were hallucinating. Her head turned as she searched for where the voices came from. But, try as she might, Isla couldn't make out what they were saying. What she could hear felt like murmurs from beyond the veil, encouraging her, yet also mocking.

'What?' she croaked, forcing herself upright. She took several staggering steps forward. The weather was disorientating her, making her doubt herself.

She wanted to see cars, people with umbrellas being whipped away by the wind, the glow of streetlights. But everywhere was greyish white. The mist was strange, an otherworldly fog that had no business here among this heavy deluge. Isla made her way forward, her steps dragging. She had to find civilisation soon. Wasn't that why she was here? She couldn't quite remember.

The tingling intensified, spreading across all her limbs. A voice whispered, making her start. She struggled to think. The rain was ice on her skin, or was this because of who was talking to her?

The shape of a tree emerged like a mirage in the fog. Isla huddled beneath it and curled into a ball, confusion and desperation mingling as one in her petrified heart.

The wind chimes jangled, a requiem of dread.

She must have slept.

When she opened her eyes orange streaked the sky, setting the clouds aflame as the sun sank beneath the horizon. Isla was stiff and uncomfortable, chill and damp still deep in her skin. She pulled herself to her feet. Every movement felt sluggish and exhaustion settled in her bones.

Isla shuddered in the winter air. She badly needed to get back to her hotel, peel off her clothes, and take a long, hot shower. That had been no normal storm, but at least it was over.

She looked around her. The lion statues stared back, frozen scowls on their carved faces, as she tried to make up her mind which direction she needed to go. She couldn't see the buildings from earlier, though that was likely because it was getting dark.

Isla felt confused but wasn't at first sure why. Then she realised there were no streetlights or lights from buildings in sight, nor the sound of traffic. But why? She was in a built-up area.

Isla picked her way through the rapidly falling darkness, searching for a light, a voice, a car engine. Anything.

Fear pricked her skin. She felt more alone than she ever had done in her life.

Had she passed out? Had she been blown away? Had the typhoon caused so much damage it had knocked out the city's power? Yes, that was likely.

But she found herself hurrying forward all the same.

The clouds cleared, their retreat so rapid it was almost unnatural. Stars glinted above, lighting her way. And there was the wall of the shrine. For a moment, she was pleased to see something she recognised.

Isla's fingers grazed the stone, her breathing loud in her ears. Her hair stuck to her neck, her soaked hoodie doing little to ward off the chill. She pulled down her hood and raked fingers through her red locks as a new sensation flooded her.

As long as she lived, she never wanted to see this shrine again. She glanced at the building, to where the rope gently swung. Along the roof were painted symbols, a vertical cross within a circle.

She turned her back on the building and rubbed her hands together.

Ahead, there was nothing. No road, no concrete path. Before her was a cinder track and grass and starlight.

Long grass caressed her shins. None of this made sense. Kagoshima was full of cafés, roads and shops, with a bright, twenty-four-hour convenience store every fifty feet.

All there was now in the starlight was a hill and a bamboo forest ahead, its stalks pale. A half-moon emerged from behind a cloud, bathing her surroundings in silver.

A movement in a nearby group of trees caught her eye. A woman emerged from the shadows, wearing a kimono and obi belt, both grey in the darkness, for the faint moonlight sucked the colour from the world. Isla's heart lifted. The woman had a youthful face with her hair in a bun at the back of her head. She looked like somebody on her way to a festival, her straw sandals silent in the grass. Her short steps were careful and delicate, as though she was trying not to be seen. Was she lost, too?

The girl jumped violently when she saw Isla, her eyes wide.

'Excuse me,' said Isla in her limited Japanese. 'Do you know how to get to—'

The girl shrieked, almost falling as she backed away. Her tight kimono skirt hindered her as she pushed her way into the trees, screaming a single word.

'*Yōkai!*'

CHAPTER 3

Keiichirō and Toramasa had nearly reached the street where the Mori household resided when they heard the scream. It took Keiichirō a moment to realise it wasn't the playful squeals of children but a woman in a panic, crying that she had seen a demon.

'*Ndamoshitan!* What's going on?' said Toramasa, looking around.

Keiichirō's gaze snapped back towards the dirt road they'd just walked down. Sloped roofs flanked it with some windows aglow with lantern light. It all looked so ordinary that encountering a real *yōkai* seemed unlikely, although something had obviously terrified the woman. Perhaps it was ronin, masterless samurai who had come from the east to stir up mischief.

Toramasa put a hand to his sword and Keiichirō did the same, their feet in a fighting stance.

The woman, now sobbing, ran towards them with difficulty, holding her kimono skirt. Some strands of her midnight hair were loose, sticking to her face.

The friends recognised her and relaxed a little. Hirayama Aiko halted before them, a delicate, pale hand fluttering to her chest.

'Hirayama-san. What's wrong?' asked Toramasa.

Other footsteps smacked the road as several men appeared, some with swords drawn, alerted by Aiko's scream.

'There's a *yōkai* in the forest. I saw it!' Aiko cried. She nodded towards the west, at the hill near the bamboo woods.

'A *yōkai*?' The men who'd just arrived sheathed their swords, exchanging dubious looks.

Toramasa looked at Keiichirō. *Yōkai*, spirit creatures who wandered the earth, were a source of scepticism to most, and Aiko was unhurt.

'We should check,' said Toramasa all the same. 'Just in case.'

Aiko's pained expression melted into relief. 'Oh, thank you for your kindness, Mori-san.' She bowed low.

'I'll come, too,' said Taguchi Hanzō. 'Lead the way, Aiko-chan.' He was a square-jawed man with a thin moustache that reminded Keiichirō of a tiny, furry caterpillar. Their eyes locked and Taguchi's face twisted in disgust.

Keiichirō stared until Taguchi lowered his gaze, and Keiichirō had to swallow the urge to laugh.

Hirayama Aiko led them to where she'd seen the monster, ignoring those she passed who were bringing in clothes or cooking dinner for the night, filling the air with the scent of fish and meat. Keiichirō ignored the longing in his empty stomach.

'It had bright red hair, like fire,' Aiko said, her voice thick. 'And long claws. Blue legs. It was over there, near the old shrine.'

This didn't sound like any *yōkai* Keiichirō had heard of. There were *ittan-momen*, white-sheet monsters, which tried to suffocate you if you stayed out too late, and *utan*, which lived in the walls of abandoned homes. But no one went near the shrine if they could help it. The elderly ladies in town said it was evil, and everyone believed them.

'Over there?' asked Taguchi as they took a path between the bamboo forest and a copse of trees. The sky was clear of clouds, the hill bathed in starlight as an owl hooted.

Aiko stopped at the edge of the bamboo forest, fervently shaking her head. 'I can't go any farther.'

Keiichirō told her to return home. 'Come on,' he grunted to the others once she was gone. 'Let's get this over with.'

He didn't for a moment believe they would find a monster. But then, moving towards the trees up ahead was a shape.

Toramasa inhaled sharply. 'Over there. It's going into the farmer's woods.'

*

Isla's confusion grew. She still hadn't seen any sign of the city, and the woman she had seen had fled into a bamboo forest. Isla hadn't tried to follow her through the whispering stalks that clattered in the darkness. She didn't know what had spooked her, but it wasn't exactly reassuring.

Isla hugged herself, clenching her teeth to stop them chattering. She was still damp and cold, her toes icy in her sopping trainers. She must keep going – if she walked in a straight line, she had to find civilisation.

Then an odd rustling sound ahead made her shiver.

Slits of moonlight shone through the gaps in the branches above her head, but it was almost pitch black. Isla suddenly found herself in a hidden clearing.

She took a step forward and tumbled into nothingness.

She yelped in fear as her stomach lurched. She hit the ground with a thump, legs crumpling beneath her as pain shot up her ankle. In the inky dark, she thought she might be looking at muddy walls around her. But this made even less sense than everything else had since she had set off on her run.

She tried to stand, putting her weight on her good leg, but her injured ankle had no strength. Isla had to set her teeth against the painful sensation of a thousand knives stabbing the strained tendons, and she fought a wave of nausea.

She hissed every swear word she knew, clutching her leg.

Then against the dark sky she saw silhouettes of heads above her, shown in relief against the starlight. There were three men, all with topknots, staring at her.

'What are you doing? Let me out!' she cried in English. Realisation fell on her. She had fallen into a pit.

She winced as her ankle gave a painful throb. She tried to put weight on it and her face twisted in pain. Then anger overtook her. She had fallen into this stupid hole, she was cold and exhausted, and now these men were looking at her like she was an animal in a zoo.

The men muttered something, their words so rapid and quiet Isla couldn't make them out, although their tone didn't sound aggressive.

Isla grabbed the muddy sides of the strange hole and tried to climb out, but her trainers slipped and she landed once more in a heap at the bottom of the pit. Someone above tried to smother a laugh.

She switched to Japanese. 'I want to get out. Now!'

One man recoiled like she'd slapped him. '*Nihongo wakaru.*'

Fuck yes, I do speak Japanese, she thought, although she only glowered.

One of her onlookers knelt with a rustle of clothes and reached towards her. She flinched, but his empty palm faced upwards, inches from her face.

Was this a lifeline? Surely taking it was better than being left in this pit. She grabbed the man's warm forearm, and he hers, and he pulled her out with remarkable strength.

She sank to the forest floor and caught her breath, clutching her sore ankle as she glared at them all. She was a mess, drenched from the rain, covered in leaves and muck, and with her running gear ripped on one knee. Two of the men were in jackets and waist-high, wide trousers with wrapping for belts. The glint of katana sword handles flashed at their hips.

Perfect. How typical that on the day she met a man who seemed nice, it was then going to be snatched away. Screw this, she thought, furious. She didn't think that she maybe ought to have been intimidated.

'You must be cold,' said the man who had lifted her out of the hole. His voice was rich and smooth, and strangely calming. There was a freckle near his mouth, and, as a cloud scudded away from the moon, Isla could see serious eyes and sharp cheekbones. He shrugged off the outer layer of his kimono, a *haori* jacket, and placed it over her shoulders.

She stared at him in silence, convinced now she was in the midst of a particularly vivid dream.

'What are you doing?' barked one of the men. He was square-jawed and moustached, and frowned at her like she was something disgusting he had stepped in. 'We need to kill it.'

'This isn't a *yōkai*,' said Isla's rescuer, to a snort of disagreement from the man with the moustache. But her saviour ignored his companion, saying firmly, 'She is a woman. We have to help her.'

There was an even firmer huff of anger.

The jacket was heavy on her shoulders, and she noticed a white crest stitched on the front: a circle with a vertical cross inside. It was the same symbol as at the shrine.

If she was in trouble, Isla was glad it would happen while she was wearing this warm jacket.

*

'Why did Hirayama-san think she was a *yōkai*?' said Toramasa as he and Keiichirō guided the woman to the town, each with a hand on her arm, not that it seemed she could run away. For this obviously foreign girl with the deep red hair walked with a limp, gasping in pain now and again when she put weight on her left foot.

Keiichirō had expected an enormous creature with ugly, twisted features and the face of a demon, not a frightened woman. Though *yōkai* could be tricky, so he'd heard. Perhaps it had taken the form of a foreigner.

Even the idea made heat crawl up his neck. He looked at her again, and decided it was a silly thought – if this was a monster, it was a feeble one and not the least bit frightening. 'Let's take her to the academy. Kirino-san will know what to do,' Keiichirō said.

Kirino-san, an ex-general of the imperial army and one of Saigō-sama's close friends, wasn't impressed at being called upon in the evening. The narrow-eyed, strong-jawed man ordered them to put the girl in one of the back rooms. Even at night, the scent of cologne wreathed him. There was a running joke among the *shi-gakkō* school students that you could always smell Kirino-san coming.

'Shouldn't we tell Saigō-sama?' asked Toramasa.

'Don't be silly. We won't bother him. You brought a gaijin woman here, of all things, and he will not want to hear this,' Kirino-san snapped at no one in particular.

Keiichirō bowed to Kirino-san and took the trembling girl into the back room by the arm to await her fate. She still wore his *haori* jacket. She looked at him with frightened eyes as she slipped off her shoes at the entrance with a wince and half fell into the tatami mat room, still clutching her wounded ankle.

He went to get some bandages, and bumped into Kirino-san's wife, Hisa. She had a proud face and a confident, straight-backed posture worthy of a samurai's wife. She looked beyond her years, motherly and wise, despite her being only a few years older than Keiichirō.

'Maeda Keiichirō-san. You're too thin.' Her eyes, dark as a new moon, glanced up and down Keiichirō's form. 'Have you eaten?'

'Not today, Kirino-san.'

'Wait here then.'

She reappeared a few moments later with a bag in her hand, heavy with rice. She pressed it into his hands. Keiichirō swallowed a groan of delight; it had been so long since he'd eaten rice. 'This came from traders yesterday. Make sure your little Yura has a full belly, too.'

'*Arigatou gozaimasu.*' He thanked her and bowed. He wouldn't decline such a welcome and unexpected gift in these days of never feeling there was enough food on the table. Kirino Hisa would want Keiichirō's family to enjoy her kindness.

'You have been asked to take care of the foreigner until they decide what to do with her,' said Kirino-san. 'Killing her would be unwise for any of us. You must make sure she comes to no harm.'

'*Hai.*' Keiichirō bowed low to Kirino-san and left, slipping his socked feet into the straw sandals waiting at the entrance.

He needed to see the foreigner once more. He had the feeling this couldn't wait until morning. He burned with curiosity about the flame-headed creature.

Keiichirō grabbed some bandages from the *shi-gakkō*'s stockroom and returned to where the gaijin, the foreigner, waited.

Isla jumped away from the door as he entered, a defiant look hardening her eyes as she glared at him. At least they were normal, a soft brown. He had heard of foreigners having strange eyes. Someone had described a Dutch trader as having eyes like the sky in summer.

She folded her arms, jaw tightening as she stood with her weight on her good leg. Unsure whether to be amused or exasperated, Keiichirō held up the bandages and knelt before her, watching until she understood that her bad leg needed wrapping. She winced with pain as she moved, and sat with both legs stretched in front of her, gazing sadly at her swollen ankle.

Aiko's words flashed through his mind. What if this stranger was a *yōkai*, a monster from the dark, and her gentle attitude had lulled him into a mistaken security? But the way she moved was the same as any woman here, even if her clothes and hair were strange. She breathed hard, real fear in her face as she looked up at him.

'Do you speak Japanese?' he asked, taking comfort all the same that his swords were at his hip like always, just in case she sprang to attack.

'*Hai, chotto*,' she said. *A little.*

Keiichirō offered the bandage in invitation. She took it from him and wound it around her ankle herself, pain flitting across her face. It wasn't done very well, and Keiichirō could have done it better. But he liked watching her. She had a dainty nose, full lips, and skin as pale as the moon. Lantern light from outside caught in her leaf-strewn hair, the colour of a sunset. He had never seen anything like that, and it made her seem otherworldly. He thought her fascinating as he watched her in silence.

When she had finished with her ankle, he gestured for her to follow, resting a hand on the hilt of his sword. She limped beside him, her hair hiding her face as she looked down to make sure there was nothing she would bump into. He could see the nape of her neck and his cheeks warmed at seeing such a private part of her body.

He made himself look away, and then Keiichirō led her past the sloping stone walls of the academy and the ruins of the castle that had burned down three years prior.

'Kana,' he called as they came to the sliding door of his home. Though it was night, this couldn't wait. The foreigner looked cold even though she was still wearing his warm jacket. Gaijin or not, clearly she felt winter's chill in her bones just like they all did.

'*Hai, hai,* what is it?' Kana stepped out in a kimono, her long hair down loose, not expecting a visitor. She gasped when her eyes fell on the woman beside him, and tightened her robe. 'What's that? Why is it wearing your *haori?*'

'I will tell you about it later, but Kirino-san has asked us to take care of this foreign woman. Can you give her a bath and some food?' He handed Kana the remaining fish he had caught earlier and the bag of rice from Kirino Hisa.

Kana snatched them from him, her lips pursed.

The foreign woman kicked off the strange things on her feet without anyone indicating this was what she should do. Then she hobbled over to the steps to the sliding door, nodding as she approached Kana. Kana flinched like the newcomer was a cockroach and ignored the gaijin's bandaged ankle. Keiichirō prickled at her rudeness.

Kana wasn't done yet. 'It's late,' she hissed. 'She'll wake Yura. Whatever were you thinking?'

'I had no choice,' he said. 'Nobody is at the *onsen* now. And this is our duty. What else would you have me do?'

Kana gave a huff of disapproval, but she opened the sliding door for Isla to go through.

Keiichirō felt strange. He hadn't asked their visitor a single question yet, but he had the feeling she had been through a lot. How had she appeared here in Satsuma? And what might it mean?

*

Every moment that passed was more and more confusing.

Somehow, Isla had been swept away by the typhoon and had landed in a peculiar, traditional village. Here, they wore kimonos and hakama trousers, carried swords, and cooked over fires. Isla had had no idea such communities still existed, and she felt as if she had ended up in some kind of Japanese version of an Amish town. Her mobile phone was dead. She was definitely going to need access to a landline telephone if she was going to find her way back to her hotel.

She was lucky she had only suffered a sprained ankle through this whole ordeal. She let the man's wife, Kana, guide her through the small rooms that held the scent of cooked sweet potatoes and woodchips. Kana went before her, sighing and muttering to herself, and Isla was left in no doubt that she was in this household under immense sufferance. They made their way through what Isla assumed was a living area, with a sunken hearth surrounded by square cushions in the middle of dark wooden floors. Kana lit an oil lantern and took Isla through a tatami mat room and through another sliding wooden door that opened on to a garden, Isla's sprained ankle complaining with every step. Isla shivered as they went down a narrow path, the air icy now. Even with the young man's *haori* jacket, it was freezing. The lantern bobbed along in front, casting a shuddering yellow light from the rhythm of Kana's steps.

Then, unexpectedly, there was a shaft of warmth, and they came to a natural hot spring. It was the most welcome sight Isla had seen since she'd stepped into the shrine grounds. Steam rose from the pool and warmed the air around them. Kana said something Isla didn't understand and placed the lantern on the grass. With the tiniest of bows, Kana shuffled off. Isla didn't know if she was supposed to get in or not, but what was the worst that could happen? Kana would only tell her to get out again.

Carefully, she took off the *haori* and then the bandage around her ankle. She peeled off her still-damp workout clothes and slipped into the water, steam rising all around. The transition from the cold air to the hot spring water was divine.

The steam caressed her face and her body sank into bliss as her heartbeat slowed and her muscles relaxed. The water was a touch too hot, but it was heaven, soothing her throbbing ankle. The mud and grime from the storm and that horrible pitfall trap washed away as she dunked her head, loving the sensation of her scalp being warmed in the water. As the tension loosened across her body, Isla felt as if almost nothing mattered except this ecstasy.

But, of course, eventually she had to climb out, her skin pink, the steam providing a bubble of warmth. The clothes she had unceremoniously scattered on the grass were gone, she found, and in their place was a neatly folded simple robe and black obi belt, a fresh bandage curled on top. Kana reappeared and handed Isla a towel. Her expression was unreadable, though she didn't seem to care that Isla was naked. When Isla had patted herself dry, Kana helped her dress.

It felt strange and intimate, and there was a painful awkwardness between them. Isla couldn't conjure the words in Japanese to apologise, nor to explain how or why she was here and had appeared in the middle of the night with the woman's husband.

Kana folded the kimono over Isla's chest, her mouth a straight, tight line. But back in the house she gave Isla a bowl of warm rice and guided her to a room, closing the sliding door after she had nodded towards a futon mattress. Though it was dark, moonlight shone through the square *washi* walls of the room, which faced out. Isla perched on the edge of the mattress and ate quickly. The rice was bitter yet also bland, but she was so hungry that it didn't matter. After everything, it felt like one of the best meals she had ever eaten.

Thank goodness they hadn't sent her back to that cold little room where she had first been held. The men who had brought her there had spoken too fast for her to follow, and her sprained ankle had been hurting too much to do much more than follow them blindly through the darkness. As cold as Kana was being, at least she had given her a room, and had taken care of her.

Isla lay down, her bones heavy with drowsiness. A lantern, extinguished, sat in the corner, although the room still held the trace of burning oil. Though the bath had diffused the tension in her muscles and warmed her to the core, fresh anxiety spiked in Isla as she realised there was no smoke alarm, security camera or plug socket in this little room. There was no electricity.

Would anyone notice she was missing? She was due back in Tokyo in a few days. What would happen when they realised she wasn't there if she couldn't alert anyone to her predicament before then? Would Mum panic when she didn't call her at the weekend? How long would it take for anyone to realise if she stayed missing? Would her friends in the international students' apartment building notice she hadn't returned from Kagoshima, or would no one take note of her absence until classes resumed later in January?

It hardly bore thinking about, and panic washed across her, fast and powerful as a tidal wave. Isla clutched the bedsheets, the air suddenly thick, the room too small.

Calm down, she tried to tell herself. She wouldn't be gone that long, and she was safe and warm and fed. First thing in the morning, she would be able to find a phone. Everything would work out. The strangers had been stand-offish but had given her a place to stay.

Isla bunched up the covers and propped up her sore ankle, shifting until she was comfortable, and closed her eyes.

Things would be okay, she thought. Well, she hoped they would.

Somehow, despite the fizz of her unsettled mind, Isla fell into a deep and dreamless sleep.

CHAPTER 4

Sunrise came with the sounds of voices Isla didn't understand and smells she didn't know. Sunlight glowed in the square paper walls. The futon was hard beneath her, and she slowly opened her eyes. A toddler, a little girl with short hair and chubby little arms, stood above her, staring. Isla blinked back, not sure what to do.

'Yura,' Kana whispered from the sliding door, which was open a crack. The little girl tottered to her, and Isla could see the strong resemblance that told her Kana was Yura's mother.

'Good morning.' Isla bowed her head with as much dignity as she could muster from the futon. 'Thank you for your hospitality.'

'Your accent is strange.' Kana's gaze flicked down, like she was judging every inch of Isla. Kana had long hair, dark locks resting on one shoulder and reaching past the obi belt at her waist. Isla tried not to wither beneath her gaze. 'You sound like you're from the east,' Kana said after a while.

Isla's brow furrowed. She spoke standard Japanese – as best she could, at least. She supposed the east must refer to Tokyo.

Isla eyed the tray of food the woman had brought in. A bowl full of chopped sweet potato. Soup with cubes of tofu and seaweed. A slice of fish. A salty, savoury scent that suddenly made Isla's stomach ache with hunger.

The toddler grabbed a fistful of her mother's kimono, her fingers in her mouth. She glanced backwards as she was ushered outside. When Kana slid closed the door, Isla sighed, looking around.

Washi walls, made from squares of Japanese paper, shielded the room against the sunlight. It was much warmer in the daytime. A new kimono was folded nearby, a brown square on top. Her stomach lurched as she scrambled over to snatch it up. Her wallet. Beside it was her phone, dead of course.

Her pulse quickening, Isla opened her wallet. Nothing was missing, not her student ID nor the several 1,000-yen notes. She would have to offer some to the woman and man who had helped her. Her ankle still stung, and she remembered the pitfall trap with a strange mingle of embarrassment and the desire to laugh. What would Mum say when she told her about that?

Isla pulled on the simple robe, leaving the futon folded as neatly as she could make it. She had been so tired last night she had let Kana help her, but she was sure she had figured it out by herself.

She paused, glancing around the room. As she'd thought, there were no electric sockets in the walls, no smoke alarms or light switches. She hoped Kana would at least know someone who had a phone. These people would need to communicate with the outside world sometimes.

Now the shock was wearing off, it was rather exciting being here, right in the middle of a traditional village.

Isla supposed there would be a hot spring resort nearby, or maybe this society was walled off from modern Japan. Whatever the case, she hadn't heard of this place.

She slid open the door with a dull rasp to find just outside a small garden, grass and stones and the scent of winter flora. To her surprise she saw a river that rushed by, startlingly like the Kotsuki River she had walked by just a day ago on her way to the museum. Perhaps she was a little farther along it. There was no safety railing here.

A cold, smoky breeze lifted her hair as she looked beyond.

Sloping roofs greeted her, and then trees and hills as far as she could see. There wasn't a skyscraper in sight, and no sign of any of the buildings of the vibrant and bustling Kagoshima City she had been exploring. It was disorientating.

Isla felt like Dorothy, swept off to Oz.

Confused and suspecting a concussion, gingerly she touched her head, expecting to find a painful lump. There was nothing there.

Her stomach rumbled loudly. She had to eat.

Her breakfast was hearty but mild, and she ate it where the doorway connected her room and the porch.

A chilly wind washed over her as she slipped her feet into a pair of straw sandals waiting outside. She once more tested her weight on her bad ankle. It was less swollen than the night before thanks to the bandage, but still tender.

She shuffled clumsily along, the kimono restricting the movement of her legs. She felt a bit foolish, but Kana hadn't given her clothes back and Isla was worried that refusing to wear the robe might come across as ungrateful. In any case, she was pleased for the extra warmth of the kimono.

The sandals whisked against the stone beneath her soles. She had never been patient, and the urge to get home felt strong. What was the point in sitting around? Isla comforted herself with the thought that she'd be back in her hotel room in a few hours.

She didn't see the young man who'd helped her until she was almost upon him, and she jumped for the second time that morning.

In the daylight, she could make out more of his face. Narrow eyes, a warm light brown. High cheekbones and a straight, serious mouth. His hair, with a widow's peak hairline, was tied in a neat topknot at the top of his head. With his black robe and swords at his left hip, it was like he'd walked straight out of a historical drama.

'Good morning.' He bowed to her.

She returned the gesture and the words. Those, at least, she understood.

His eyes flicked down to her chest and she crossed her arms, annoyed. Her lips had parted to remind him where his eyes had strayed to, but he said, 'Your robe is on wrong.'

'What?'

'Left over right.' He gestured putting on a robe. 'Right over left is... bad luck. It's for someone who has died.'

Isla swallowed a groan. She'd known that, she *knew*, she had just forgotten.

He turned away, and Isla went back to her room to fix her mistake. *Left over right*. At least she'd been corrected before anyone else saw.

His expression was respectful when she went back to him for a second time. He wore his *haori* jacket, probably the one he had lent her, the wide sleeves now blowing behind him like wings. His swords looked like real samurai swords, the same as the ones she had seen in museums and textbooks. She tried not to stare.

'Follow.'

'Is there a telephone box nearby?' she asked, limping a bit more now as she tried to keep up. He didn't answer. Were her words incorrect?

The man slowed and looked at her seriously. He was taller than her, a few strands of his black hair loose now in the breeze. He looked a bit like the café barista from the day before, Isla thought, if he'd been dressed as a samurai.

She was supposed to meet the barista at one o'clock. Isla felt a pang at letting him down. He'd think her rude. She didn't even know his name – she should have asked it.

'I'm taking you to our leader.' Her host's words interrupted these thoughts as they made their way along the riverside. Isla saw people walking around, some of the men carrying sheaves of hay or workmen's tools, and there was an industrious sense to them that told of self-sufficiency. 'He's back from a fishing trip and wants to see you,' her companion added.

Good, thought Isla. This had to be positive.

Then she noticed people were staring at her.

Isla swallowed, her throat tight. They seemed to think her strange, and she didn't like this.

She didn't like anything that was happening. When she'd headed for the museum, the riverside had had a fence, a neat stone path winding through the grass, and signposts with historic notes. But all around her now by the water was raw and wild, and any buildings she saw were low-rise with sloped roofs and wooden construction. Isla didn't see anyone not wearing kimonos or without their hair in buns and topknots. Two children, no older than eight, wrestled wearing only their undergarments, thin strips of white cloth tied around their waists and between their legs. An old man gutted a fish, yellowed teeth bared as he yanked out bones. They passed a home where the strong scent of green tea reached them, a faint murmuring coming from within. It all seemed basic and rural, a bit like a place that time had forgotten. Isla was all for immersive experiences, but this one was proving far too heady.

The winter sky was brilliant blue. Across the river was a familiar shape, and Isla's heart lifted a little.

'Mount Sakurajima,' said the young man, as if reading her thoughts. 'We are lucky. No ash rains from the volcano today.'

This was the volcano she had seen from Kagoshima. They couldn't be far from the city, then. Still, something felt wrong to Isla, some unknown detail niggling at her she couldn't quite fathom, even though she could see what felt like so *much*. Without the huge buildings and lights and roads, what lay before her now was the river winding between small houses and shrines, the scent of cedarwood, incense and miso on the wind.

They turned from the river and passed the ruins of a castle, a blackened skeleton that was a sad remainder of what it used to be. There was something familiar about this place, but Isla couldn't pinpoint what. They came to a busier road with horses and trundling carriages, and as they left the ruin Isla noticed that one or two people glanced at the moat and sloping stone walls with sad shakes of their heads, and wondered if the castle had burned down recently. She would have asked her companion but he seemed to be distracted.

'What is your name?' he asked.

'*Eye-ra*.' She adjusted the pronunciation to the Japanese version, as close to the original as possible while avoiding the tricky 'L' sound.

'*Eye-ra*,' he said as if he were tasting it with his tongue. He stopped and turned towards her, adding, 'Isla-san. I am Maeda Keiichirō.' He had introduced himself with the family name first, as was custom. He bowed low.

She didn't know what else to do, so she used the phrase she knew for 'Nice to meet you', and bowed back.

They moved on and, although Isla saw people whispering about her, somehow this didn't make her as uncomfortable now.

Isla didn't see any young people wearing jeans or band t-shirts, any businessmen in suits, clutching briefcases. This wasn't the Japan she had found, all trendy young people and ambitious office workers. There was no rattle of a passing train, nor a convenience store in sight. She'd heard about authentic-style amusement parks and wondered if Kagoshima was home to one and this was where she was. But there was something not quite right. An amusement park was run by staff, staff who went home at night. Yet she had been given a bed, and nobody had dropped the act to ask why a tourist had wandered inside. And the looks she got were not of polite curiosity, but of suspicion. The talk of gaijin, foreigner, twitched the back of her neck.

Keiichirō's pace slowed as they approached the square-jawed man who had accompanied them yesterday. He stood before them with his arms crossed, glaring as they passed.

Keiichirō ignored him, and Isla tried to do the same, which wasn't easy with her bad ankle. It wasn't as bad as before, the hot spring water having soothed it, but each step still twinged.

'Is he angry about something?' Isla asked when they were out of earshot. She thought she had seen hatred in the man's face, a stiffness to the way he stood with his arms crossed, and such uncloaked loathing made her uneasy.

'Perhaps.'

'Will he do anything?' Isla glanced behind her and saw the man's hand resting on one of his swords.

Keiichirō said, 'He won't.'

'Are you certain?'

'Yes, Isla-san. I never lie.'

It wasn't reassuring. The tone of Keiichirō's voice was much more tentative than his words suggested.

*

At a grand building, wide and one-storeyed, they slipped off their sandals and stepped on to the *engawa* porch. Isla gazed around in fascination at the garden, every bonsai tree and rock perfectly placed to be harmonious with the low stone wall and wooden surroundings.

Keiichirō had been here only once before, and anticipation rose as he escorted Isla to where Beppu-san was waiting, dressed smartly in a kimono and wide hakama trousers, the Shimazu clan crest stitched on each side of the chest.

Beppu Shinsuke was around thirty years old and had thick hair and a goatee. He looked at them briefly and then gave a sharp jerk of his head towards the door. He led them inside.

'Saigō-sama,' said Keiichirō as the sliding door opened with a quiet rasp. Behind him, Isla's breath caught, and he realised she was nervous. 'I'm here about the woman we found. A foreigner. But she speaks a little of our language.'

He glanced at Isla, who lingered in the doorway, looking out of place even with the kimono Kana had lent her. Her hair, short for a woman's, was a tangle. And the colour of fire in a shaft of sunlight. Keiichirō could see it was no wonder Hirayama Aiko had mistaken her for an otherworldly creature. If it weren't for the few foreign teachers Keiichirō had met in the school, the girl would mightily unnerve him.

'Enter, Maeda-kun.' Saigō-sama's use of *kun*, the affectionate honorific, was pleasant and Keiichirō relaxed a little. It was a tatami mat room that carried the scent of wood and rush grass.

Saigō-sama always made Keiichirō want to stop and gaze in awe. He was a huge man with enormous shoulders and thick eyebrows, a heavy-set face and large, powerful hands. It was claimed Saigō-sama was unbeaten in sumo training since he was a child, and he had fought alongside the emperor, bringing Japan into a new age after toppling the Tokugawa Shogunate. He had retired shortly afterwards and established the *shi-gakkō* academies to train samurai. Saigō-sama was a true leader, and the samurai would rather have had no one else as head of the schools. It was thanks to Saigō-sama that men like Keiichirō had a place to go and things to do. It wasn't easy for a young samurai to try to make a living by making umbrellas or working in the fields.

But two hundred years of peace in Japan meant the traditional ways of the samurai had long since ended.

It was something Keiichirō's father, Maeda Ujio, had always lamented, longing for the days when the samurai would clad themselves in lamellar armour and die gloriously in battle, or commit seppuku, ritual suicide, in the face of defeat. Ujio always held a nostalgic ache for what he called the better days. He had fought against the Tokugawa Shogunate under Saigō-sama, something that gave him a sense of purpose after the death of Keiichirō's mother.

This unrest, however, left a bitter taste in many veterans' mouths. Some samurai clans had been forced to submit to the emperor and now there were rumours of disdain in Satsuma for the new *shinseifu* government and the way they had abandoned centuries-long traditions. Since the Americans had arrived in Japan and forced open the country's borders, the emperor had been so eager to become powerful in the world that he had dismantled the samurai's power and discarded centuries of tradition.

And now the once-mighty warrior class struggled to survive.

Recently the emperor had banned the public wearing of swords, and those in government were cutting their hair short and wearing Western clothing.

Keiichirō's fingers brushed the swords at his hip. The people of Satsuma were proud of their heritage and traditions. They would not easily bow to the whims of the new *shinseifu* government. The way of the samurai was still strong here.

Silence swirled in the room. Saigō-sama was looking at Isla, and slowly his expression became warm.

'Good morning, *oneesan*,' said Saigō-sama, gracing her with a small bow. He sat with his legs crossed. His sword, a pale tassel hanging from the handle, and his gun lay against the wall nearby, along with his fishing gear. 'I trust you're finding your stay comfortable?'

Keiichirō wondered if all foreigners were the same. He could read every emotion that flickered across Isla's face, and it was as though she was laying her heart out in an open book. But now confusion flashed across her expression as she glanced to Keiichirō.

She doesn't understand.

'I'm afraid her Japanese is limited, Saigō-sama.' Keiichirō paused, then decided not to mention Isla falling into the trap, saying instead, 'A village girl saw her. We found her in the woods on the outskirts of the town, near the old shrine. Her name is Isla.'

Saigō-sama's voice was slow and kind as he asked more questions.

Isla stuttered, her accent a strange mix of Tokyo dialect and the clumsy tripping up of a foreigner's tongue, and some strange vocabulary he didn't recognise.

Keiichirō had heard non-native Japanese before, of course, for in the *shi-gakkō* they had foreign teachers for Chinese and Dutch studies. His neck warmed. He should have asked Isla these questions before bringing her here. He hadn't even known her name until a few minutes earlier.

He watched and listened, hoping the senior men would find out why Isla had come to their community.

CHAPTER 5

Isla had been ready to ask for the nearest plug socket, but that rushed from her mind when she set eyes upon the man Keiichirō had called Saigō-sama.

She had seen drawings, cartoon images, stickers, manga adaptations, statues and endless souvenirs with Takamori Saigō's face on them. Friendly, happy, thick-eyebrowed and strong, he was recognisable to everyone in Kyushu, perhaps all of Japan.

Seeing him now was the most surreal thing she had ever experienced.

His skin was leathery and the faint scent of perspiration came from the kimono he wore loosely, almost casually, on his stocky frame. As intense as he was, though, there was a friendliness to him.

Isla tried to remind herself that Takamori Saigō died one hundred and twenty-eight years ago, along with the rest of the last samurai, but knowing this didn't make the man she was staring at seem either a fluke or trick.

For all the world it seemed as if the leader of the Satsuma samurai was before her, looking politely interested as she knelt beside Keiichirō, her insides quickly turning to water.

The lack of electricity, the traditional clothes. Kana's suspicion at her accent. The samurai swords. The river and the view of Mount Sakurajima void of buildings and cars.

Isla breathed in sharply, and she could *smell* age and heritage and tradition and old-fashioned ways of making furniture and cloth.

It was impossible. But there it was.

In a flash Isla understood with every beat of her heart that she had travelled back through time, all the way to nineteenth-century Japan. She had no idea how or why, she just knew it had happened.

And now one of the most famous historical figures in samurai culture was sitting right before her, his gun and his sword behind him, asking her questions.

It was dizzying, and she turned to Keiichirō for some sort of reassurance; but, before he could look at her, Isla heard Saigō asking for a second time with a tone of impatience now in his voice, 'Where are you from, young lady?'

Isla just opened and shut her mouth. What on earth could she say that wasn't going to make her precarious situation worse?

Her pulse raced as she recognised the danger she was in.

'Scotland,' she said finally, voice quivering. The samurai hated lies. But how could she be truthful, without seeming a liar? Or worse, an enemy, or a spy?

'What are you doing here?'

She hesitated.

They'd never believe that in 2005 she was caught in a typhoon in the nearby shrine and then she woke up here. They'd assume she was lying, and that in itself would get her into trouble even though it was the truth.

'I think I hit my head,' was the best Isla could come up with. 'I don't remember.'

The three samurai exchanged looks.

Her words weren't good enough.

'How did you come to Japan?' said Saigō.

Oh, God. Were planes invented yet?

'Um, by ship?' Her chest was tight and her anxious voice high. She needed to breathe.

She'd seen a statue of her interrogator just a day previously. Now, watching him move and speak was too much, and the room around Isla began to tilt.

'What about your family?' said the younger man beside Saigō. He had a pinched, serious face and narrow eyes. A thick goatee adorned his upper lip and chin, and when he looked at her he did not smile.

Isla couldn't help but think of Mum, her younger brother Douglas and her father. Would they be looking for her? Did her timeline still exist parallel to this one, or had they ceased to be when she had stepped through time? Unbidden tears came and Isla suppressed a sniffle.

The men watched her, Saigō slowly blinking as he waited.

'We were separated,' she said as she tried to concentrate on the question rather than the faint feeling threatening to overwhelm her. 'I'm sorry. I don't remember much else.'

She winced at the feeble lie. The tension intensified as doubt flickered across Saigō's face and the other man glanced at him, opening his mouth.

A playful yap jerked their gazes to a nearby door, breaking the tense moment.

A little dog squeezed through the slightly open sliding door. It had a smiley mouth and a rich brown coat. Its ears flopped as it bounded over to Saigō, who chuckled. It was a rumble deep in the barrel of his chest, his great body moving as he petted the small creature.

Isla had seen a statue of this dog just a day ago. A Satsuma inu, similar to a shiba, with its charming, intelligent face. It sniffed at Saigō's robe and then looked at Isla before looking back at its master.

'Tsun doesn't usually like strangers, but he's not barked. And so you may stay here until you find your family,' said Saigō, petting the dog behind the ears. 'Maeda-kun, you'll take care of her.' It didn't sound like a request.

If Keiichirō felt displeased, he didn't show it. '*Hai*, Saigō-sama,' he replied and leaned forward in a low bow, forehead almost touching the tatami mat beneath them.

Isla hardly dared breathe until they were back outside and heading back to Keiichirō's home.

'I didn't expect the dog,' said an amused Keiichirō.

'I didn't expect any of it.'

Keiichirō glanced at Isla, as her voice was serious.

'Keiichirō-san? Can I ask you something?' she said.

He slowed. 'Am I going too fast for you?'

'It's not that,' she said, though she was grateful their pace had eased. 'I'm a little confused. What is the date?'

He gave her a look she couldn't quite interpret, and then Keiichirō said, 'I suppose you use the new calendar. It's the fifth of January.'

It was consistent. Isla had arrived in Kagoshima on the morning of the fourth.

'And the year?'

'Meiji 10. 1877. Of course.'

Isla's chest felt as if she'd been pierced with shards of broken glass. Something roared in her ears.

'Isla-san?' Keiichirō's voice was full of concern now.

'I need to sit down.'

She staggered, but a hand took her forearm, steadying her as her knees lost their strength, and he helped her to a wall.

Isla clung to Keiichirō's obi belt, looking up at him.

She couldn't explain, so instead they sat quietly and she let him guide her back to his home.

'Go and rest,' said Keiichirō when at last they reached his wooden home by the river.

'Why are you looking at me like that?' Isla asked. 'Why were you told to look after me? There must be hundreds of others who could have done so.'

Keiichirō replied, 'It is my duty. Because my family's honour needs to be redeemed.'

Isla didn't know what to say to that.

Keiichirō bowed to her and had words with Kana before leaving the two women. Isla spent the rest of the day watching the little girl, Yura, run around the garden while her mother occasionally sniffed and glared in Isla's direction while she was washing clothes in a wooden bucket or cutting vegetables. She waved away all of Isla's offers to help.

It felt like a very long day.

That night, Isla sneaked into the cold night air, intent on finding the shrine. She did not belong here, and she felt it was only at the shrine that she might be able to find some sort of answer to her predicament.

They had eaten sparingly today, and it was hard not to notice the rotting beams that held up the porch, how frayed their robes were. Isla wanted to be gone from their hospitality as soon as she could. The family's resources were clearly stretched tight, although Yura looked well cared for, the little girl smiling happily at their visitor when offered a portion of Isla's rice. Isla was a burden Keiichirō and Kana didn't need.

Though the stars were out, Isla wasn't used to such darkness. No streetlights or the glow of surrounding buildings cast comforting light. But that meant nobody would see her, either, and that was how she wanted it. One good thing, too, about hours of sitting around was that her ankle felt much better.

Isla was fully dressed in her own clothes, which Kana had finally returned, now smelling faintly of river water.

She had waited until the house was asleep. Keiichirō had returned after sunset, bags beneath his eyes and rubbing his forearm. He'd looked exhausted, and Yura had only fallen silent after wailing for a long while. Even though she wasn't sleepy, Isla made herself rest on her futon until the house was totally still. She counted the minutes, one after the other, listening out for sounds, before finally she slipped out, wincing at every scrape of the sliding wooden door.

At the strange shrine, she hoped to find the white torii gate. The more she thought about it, the more it seemed that going through it was how she had ended up here. It was the only thing she could think of.

Her breath fogged before her, the icy air a far cry from the cosy warmth of the Maeda household. For a moment she wanted to be there again, snug in her futon.

But she told herself she must go back to her world, that of busy buildings in Kagoshima, and the cute guy in the coffee shop.

Isla reached a part she recognised, near the riverside farther upstream. Aye, there was the bamboo forest where the young woman had seen her. A smile crept onto Isla's face; the poor girl's panic made so much more sense now. How many foreigners had visited this town before? Probably very few in the middle of the night drenched to their skin.

Ignoring the odd spasm in her ankle, Isla made for the stalks of bamboo, entering the forest near where she'd plunged into that hateful pitfall trap. Away from Kana's serious gaze, she felt increasingly confident.

Isla almost screamed when a creature that looked somewhere between a goat and an antelope appeared from some nearby bushes. It gave a startled chitter, as surprised as she was, and ran off into the trees.

At last the shrine emerged from the darkness, a regular red torii gate marking the entrance to a stone pathway leading to the inner building.

Isla paused, listening to the stir of the trees. Snarling statues of lions sat frozen on slabs of stone, flanking the red torii gate. A thick rope hung above the entrance, wooden steps leading to its interior. Even now, apparently over a century earlier than when she had first seen it, the shrine looked decrepit and unused.

Now she must find the white torii gate. Stepping through the red one had done nothing.

She shivered, the chill air stinging her face.

Isla longed for a shower, for a telephone so she could call her parents and hear their voices.

Those who had found her here would search for her a while, then give up, putting it down to strange happenings that would eventually be forgotten. She hoped, though, that Keiichirō and Kana wouldn't get blamed in any way for her absence – she hadn't thought of that before. Isla was sad she'd not been able to say goodbye to Keiichirō, or Kana and Yura, either.

She shook herself. She couldn't worry about that now. No one would care in a couple of days.

Carefully, Isla searched the whole shrine, her desperation mounting with each minute that passed. But it was no good. There was no sign of any white torii gate anywhere. The shrine was a lonely place, overgrown with weeds. No offerings sat at the statues. It was like this place was frozen and unkempt, as if people hardly knew it was there.

Even when Isla returned to the tree, the very place she was certain she had awoken, there was nothing but a path of stones. Her sigh was carried away by the icy wind as bitter disappointment surged through her. What was it that she was missing?

She looked up at the stars. The winter's night was clear and cold and, though the moon was nowhere to be seen tonight, a glittering radiance bathed her. If she had been at peace, she would have enjoyed the spectacle of stars above her, spread across a black canvas like spilled sugar.

A movement behind her made her swivel around. Before she could react, crunching footsteps assaulted the shrine's gravel pathway and a cold hand clamped over her mouth.

Isla struggled, terror piercing her as she tried to bite into the palm.

'Shh,' said a voice in her ear. 'It's only me.'

Isla recognised the voice and, once she had relaxed slightly, Keiichirō removed his hand.

'What are you doing?' Isla hissed through clenched teeth, her heart still beating furiously, a fist in her chest punching against her ribcage. 'You almost...' She paused, realising telling Keiichirō he'd almost given her a heart attack might not translate well. She sighed in exasperation and then said lamely, 'You scared me.'

'Why did you run away?' He took her arm. 'There are wild animals here. Boars, wolves. Bandits sometimes roam these lands. You could get hurt. We will go home now.'

Isla sulked as Keiichirō took her back to the village. But she couldn't stay cross for long. He was right, she was lucky she hadn't come across any dangerous beasts. The torii gate wasn't here. And she had been stupid to come out here alone at night. Her impatience had clouded her judgement.

Keiichirō's expression seemed to say he had just about had enough of her. For a second she was reminded of the other young samurai who'd glared at her so piercingly that morning without a scrap of kindness in his hard face.

It was lucky it was Keiichirō who'd found her. Her memory was still of the strength with which he'd held her steady when she'd felt as if she might pass out. Combined with his intention now of making sure no harm came to her, it made her feel safe.

She looked again at Keiichirō, at the starlight reflected in his topknot, messy as if he'd tied it in haste. Now and again, she caught whiffs of sandalwood and dried seaweed and the fragrances of the town. Gradually, his firm grip on her arm loosened, though not enough for her to pull away, making her flesh warm beneath his touch. He glanced at her, and then they walked in silence, the grass sighing beneath their feet.

Without warning Keiichirō froze, his hand releasing her wrist to land on his sword. Barely seeming to breathe, he scanned the bamboo around them with sharp eyes, listening to the darkness. Isla stilled, too, not sure if she should be ready to run or seek somewhere to hide. After a moment, Keiichirō straightened and gave her a small nod.

Isla let out a breath that fogged before her. 'Listen,' she said as they left the woods, the dark silhouette of Mount Sakurajima a black giant over the town. 'I'm sorry, Keiichirō. I was trying to get back.'

'Get back?' Keiichirō asked. 'The port is the other way. If you need a ship back to Scotland, I'm sure there we can find someone who can help you.'

Isla blinked. 'Back to Scotland?'

'Isn't that what you want, Isla?' Keiichirō stood still. 'Your family must be looking for you. Well, unless you're a *kanchō*.'

She didn't understand that word. 'A what?'

'*Kanchō*. Coming here in secret to watch us, learn things about us and then report everything you see to your people.'

Kanchō must mean spy. Isla was horrified.

Keiichirō added, 'Saigō-sama said I'm to take care of you, until we've found out the truth. But seeing you run off suggests you have much to hide.'

'I was trying to get home!'

'In the old shrine? Hard to believe.'

'Yes, the old shrine. Look, Keiichirō, I don't know how I got here, I don't know why I'm here, and I don't know how to find what I do know. I'm more confused than you are. I was by the shrine, and it was in the city – and there was a storm, and when I woke up, I was here. And I fell in that stupid trap and now I don't know how to get home! All I do know is that I shouldn't be here. And you've been decent to me.' Isla heard the wail in her voice.

Keiichirō was looking at her with deep suspicion. Was he remembering the frightened woman's words of *yōkai* and spirits?

Dejected, Isla leaned against a tree and massaged her swollen ankle. 'I am from Scotland, but the rest is too complicated to explain. But the most important thing is I don't know how I got here. I'm still trying to figure that part out for myself.'

'You're not making any sense.' Keiichirō stepped towards her again and, before she could move, took her arm. 'Part of me wants to cut you down right here and forget about you. Whoever you are, you're trouble for me and my family. You might be a spy for the imperial army or for some foreign—'

Keiichirō's eyes widened as the brush beside them rustled. He cursed softly as a samurai emerged from the undergrowth.

Isla's stomach twisted with unease when she saw it was the square-jawed man who had regarded them with disgust that morning.

'What's going on here, Maeda?' he said.

CHAPTER 6

'Taguchi,' said Keiichirō, his voice tight. 'What are you doing here?'

Taguchi snorted in disdain. He was not as tall as Keiichirō, but he made up for it in swagger. His swords sat at his hip and a smug look grew on his face as he approached them. 'My, my! Why are you both out here, late at night? With your responsibilities at home, too.'

With difficulty, Keiichirō resisted the urge to curl his fingers around his sword hilt. 'We're just going home.'

A lascivious sneer twisted Taguchi's mouth as he glanced at Isla, and then he said, 'You wouldn't want to give Saigō-sama another reason to mistrust you, would you, Maeda? Your situation being as precarious as it is.'

Keiichirō stood tall. 'This visitor to our town is under my protection, and she is none of your business.'

'It *is* my business if you're keeping a spy in your household.' Taguchi's fingers were around his sword hilt now, the other hand clenched to a fist at his side. He let out a low, challenging click of his tongue, and both Keiichirō and

Isla could smell alcohol on his breath. 'I'd hate to see Kana or little Yura left on their own.'

Rage swept through Keiichirō like a storm, but he reined it in. It bubbled at the surface, not reaching his icy exterior. Taguchi's eyes travelled over his face, the steady rise and fall of his chest, searching for weakness.

'You're to go home. Now,' said Keiichirō. 'You're turning into a bully, Taguchi, just like your brother, and that is not the samurai way.'

Taguchi's fist crashed into Keiichirō's jaw and he stumbled. He lurched forward in retaliation and grabbed Taguchi around his waist, tackling him to the ground. They scratched and punched, snarling their fury in growled insults.

There was no grace to their rage-fuelled fight and, after several seconds of rolling in the dirt, his jaw throbbing, Keiichirō scrambled to his feet.

'*Bakamono*. She's gone!'

Isla stumbled through the trees, ignoring the stabbing pain in her sore ankle. She needed to get away. If they thought she was a spy, who knew what would happen? There would be nothing and no one to protect her from harm if they decided to interrogate her.

She had been naive, she thought as she ran through the brush, too scared to try to be quiet. The care Kana and the others had given her had been out of politeness, not kindness. They could never trust a foreigner who appeared from nowhere, especially now this had happened.

She would lie low somewhere. There had been a storm when she had come here, like the tornado that took Dorothy to Oz. That's what she was missing. And there had to be another typhoon sometime. Then the white torii gate would reappear and she could go home.

What she would do until then was unclear. Right now, all Isla wanted was to get away from those two samurai and their swords.

She gave a panicked scream as something crashed into her from behind. She landed hard in the mud and had to spit out a mouthful of leaves.

Someone hauled her back to her feet.

Taguchi, his nose bloodied, grimaced down at her. His topknot had come loose, locks of hair framing his face. She struggled, but his fingers held on to her arm with bruising force.

'Stop it!' Keiichirō roared as he shoved Taguchi away from her.

They had chased her, and now the samurai squared off against each other once more, hands on sword handles, glaring.

'Are you going to kill me, Maeda? Become a murderer like your father?' taunted Taguchi.

Isla expected Keiichirō to yank out his sword and spill blood.

Instead he straightened, a mask of dignity on his face.

'Have you forgotten what you've learned?' Keiichirō stepped before Isla, shielding her from Taguchi's greedy gaze. 'To never mistreat the weak? You dare assault a woman!'

Isla knew there would once, before all this, have been a time when she'd have shouted that she wasn't weak. But today was not that time.

'She's going back to Saigō-sama.' Taguchi jerked his head in Isla's direction, but the last thing Isla wanted was to be left at the mercy of Taguchi. 'Or I will.'

Keiichirō looked at Isla in the moonlight in such a way that she knew he had a plan, a plan that also meant she must keep quiet and trust him, and so this was exactly what she did.

It must have been past midnight.

Exhaustion battled terror as Isla focused on putting one foot in front of the other while Keiichirō half-guided, half-supported her back down to town, making sure to keep Taguchi in clear sight ahead.

Now and then, the shorter man would glance back and smirk. When he did, Keiichirō's grip tightened slightly on Isla's arm, though not enough to hurt.

She shivered, and told herself not to cry, even though she felt tears threaten. To weep in front of Keiichirō would confirm his opinion that she was a weak person.

Why do I care what he thinks of me? she thought.

Because he's all you've got, replied an answering voice in her mind.

Takamori Saigō's house loomed into view, sloped roofs beyond the stone wall. The gate was closed, and two guards shot them suspicious looks as they approached.

'We're here to see Saigō-sama,' boasted Taguchi.

'He's not here.' The nearest guard's close-set eyes studied the trio with an unchanging expression. 'But Murata-san is still awake.'

Isla felt verging on the delirious as they entered a tatami-clad room. She barely registered kicking off her trainers.

Keiichirō glanced at her with a silent reminder to say nothing.

'An unusual time for a visit,' said a deep voice, and through the door stepped another face Isla recognised.

It was Shinpachi Murata, who she had also seen in the museum. He was a close friend of Takamori Saigō and a powerful samurai. He was tall and rugged, with a moustache that led around his cheeks to his sideburns. Even Taguchi wilted before his penetrating gaze.

Murata sat before them and crossed his legs. Behind him was an accordion that had not been in the room when Keiichirō and Isla had been here last.

'So sorry to disturb you, Murata-san,' said Taguchi, his voice small and much less confident now.

'No matter. Tell me why you're here.'

Isla let the men's rapid Japanese that followed, too quick for her to understand, wash over her as she stared at the same spot on the wall. She had to trust Keiichirō to get them out of this. Taguchi and Keiichirō were each eager to tell their side of the story and Murata listened intently.

'And I heard Maeda say he thinks the girl is a spy,' said Taguchi.

Isla recognised these words. 'I'm not,' she interrupted. '*Kanchō janai!* I'm not a spy.'

Murata raised his large hand and the room fell silent and still.

'Why were you out in the late evening?' asked Murata, looking at her with his unflinching gaze. 'If you are not a spy, why did you leave Maeda's home?'

Isla could see Taguchi's triumphant expression in her peripheral vision and longed to slap him. Her mind raced.

She couldn't claim to have gone looking for white torii gates in the old shrine.

'She was out with me,' said Keiichirō.

'Doing what?'

Keiichirō remained silent.

'He was interrogating her,' Taguchi cried. 'He said she was a spy.'

'Control yourself, Taguchi,' Murata rumbled. 'Maeda. Saigō-sama put you in charge of this young woman. Do you believe she is a spy from Tokyo? From foreign forces, perhaps? Should we keep her here, or in the school, and interrogate her? Or are you willing to take responsibility and question her yourself?'

Keiichirō gave a low bow. 'I will take responsibility for this. I'm sorry to have shamed myself, Murata-san.'

'Young lady, you will work with the other women from tomorrow,' said Murata. 'We have spread the word that we have you among our British contacts.'

Isla didn't know if this was good news, or not.

'I will talk to Saigō-sama when he's back. Now,' Shinpachi Murata rose to his feet, 'you must all go home.'

Isla didn't dare look up for a long time as she and Keiichirō walked home. As they left the guards Taguchi had glared at them and then slipped off into the shadows. Though it seemed unlikely he would come back, Isla's neck remained tense.

Fish hopped from the water as they walked along the riverside, creating ripples across the dark surface.

'Did he hurt you?' Keiichirō said suddenly as he stood in front of her.

'No, he didn't have the time, you were there so quickly. I'm all right. But thank you for saving me. Again.'

They walked on. Another fish leapt, making a loud splash.

'Why do they do that?' she asked. 'Why do the fish jump like that?'

'Maybe they're trying to escape the kappa,' said Keiichirō. 'You know, water demons who live in the river. My father always said we mustn't swim in the river in case one grabbed us. They're excellent at sumo wrestling, apparently.'

Perhaps Isla was simply exhausted, but his words made her giggle. 'We don't have kappa where I come from.'

'And what do you have, Isla-san?'

Keiichirō turned to look at her again, and a flicker of warmth ran through her. His question was so innocent, yet Isla saw that it held the promise of interest, of Keiichirō wanting to know more about her. And she saw, too, that she liked that feeling.

But they were going home to his wife and child, Isla reminded herself, and she had caused him enough problems already.

This jerk back to reality was almost physically unpleasant.

Isla snapped her gaze away from Keiichirō, shame burning through her. He was married, she kept saying to herself. *Married.*

She marched ahead of him, not caring that her weak ankle protested.

Then she remembered Taguchi's words. *Are you going to kill me, Maeda? Become a murderer like your father?* Did Keiichirō have dark secrets of his own?

The door slid open at their approach. Golden light from an oil lamp fell on them, stark against the night. Kana stood on the threshold, her long hair down, a dark robe on her shoulders. Isla stopped short, a fresh flush of shame coursing through her as Keiichirō appeared at her side.

'Where were you?' Kana's voice was hushed.

Isla went to say something, but Kana was looking at Keiichirō.

He muttered something Isla didn't catch, and they both took off their shoes and stepped into the warmth. Kana disappeared into their bedroom and Keiichirō guided Isla back to hers, ignoring her weak protests. Perhaps he still didn't trust her not to run.

'Get some sleep,' he said as she knelt beside the futon. He stood at the doorway like he wanted to say more.

'I won't run away again,' she whispered. 'I just wanted to find a way home.'

They glanced quickly at each other, and then Keiichirō said, 'We have a busy day tomorrow. Try to sleep, Isla-san.'

'I'm sorry,' she said as the door slid across.

Keiichirō paused when it was a couple of inches from closing, then slid it back open.

'If I made your wife uncomfortable,' Isla elaborated. She could only imagine what Kana must have thought when she saw them return alone in the middle of the night.

'My wife?' Keiichirō laughed.

Isla nodded, feeling awkward although she wasn't sure why.

'Kana is my sister.' He shut the door.

She supposed she would lie awake fretting until morning, the events of the night making her heart awash with emotions. Her failed return to the shrine, Taguchi's strange hatred, the suspicion she was a spy for God knew who. And Keiichirō's father maybe being a murderer – whatever might *that* mean? Was that what made Keiichirō in ill favour with Saigō-sama and the others? If that was the case, would there be repercussions for her?

However, Isla was so exhausted she fell asleep almost at once, and she dreamed of mountains, wild animals and elusive torii gates.

CHAPTER 7

Isla awoke to the sounds of a stringed instrument.

It was a haunting sound she knew from Japanese theatres and TV shows. Not quite music, it involved strummed notes that made Isla think of legends and mysteries of the untamed countryside, forgotten battles and the changing of seasons.

She rose and went to see what was going on, her skin pimpling with gooseflesh. Keiichirō was on the porch of the house, a cool wind blowing his kimono, his hair loose and flowing to the middle of his back. It was just before dawn, the sky with a milky whiteness creeping across from the east. He gripped a mulberry wood instrument that resembled a lute, a pick poised on the strings. It was a biwa lute. Isla had seen one in the museum.

Each pluck of the strings brought another poignant twang. It was as if Keiichirō was trying to pierce the spirit world, and Isla thought she could feel magic flowing over her with each haunting note.

She didn't want to disturb him, so she sat where she was and allowed the notes to wash over her. The music mingled with everything that surrounded them, things she had not taken the time to notice before. Dry leaves blowing along the dirt road, the creak of the sloping roof above their heads, the faint rushing of the river.

The spell shattered when two men appeared around the corner, both young and wearing kimonos and hakama trousers, long hair in topknots. Keiichirō glanced up, his hand falling from the biwa lute. The music ended. Isla returned to reality, her bottom numb from sitting on the wooden porch, a shiver trembling across her body.

'Kei-chan, *ohayou*.' The stockier man gave Keiichirō a wave.

'Good morning, Tacchan, Mori.' Keiichirō placed the lute beside him. 'How's my cousin?'

'Learning to fight.' The man puffed out his chest proudly. 'My Jin is a menace.'

'Tatsuzō was just telling me about *another* dream he had,' said Mori. He gave the briefest of nods to Isla, who nervously nodded back. Not a hair was out of place, and there was an almost feminine beauty to him. Of course; he was the third man who had found her in the pitfall trap. She squashed the flush of embarrassment at the memory and straightened her back.

'They're almost daily now,' said Tatsuzō. 'Well, nightly, I suppose.'

'And what did you dream this time?' Keiichirō asked.

'Another battle. Lots of blood,' Tatsuzō said.

'Isla-san,' Keiichirō called as Isla was about to slip back into her room. 'This is my cousin, Maeda Tatsuzō. And this is Mori Toramasa, the bane of my existence.'

Toramasa playfully smacked Keiichirō around the head, knocking his topknot. 'And here I thought you were starting to enjoy my company.'

'Isla-san, was it?' said the larger man, Tatsuzō. The only resemblance between Tatsuzō and Keiichirō that Isla could see was the widow's-peak hairline. Where Keiichirō was serious-looking, Tatsuzō's face held a hint of humour. He had a wide, large mouth and a thick neck.

'Kirino-san will be here soon. She said she had some work for you to do,' said Tatsuzō with a nod at Isla to show he was speaking to her.

'I understand,' she replied.

Keiichirō turned to face her. 'Is your ankle all right?' he asked, and she nodded.

As the three walked away, Toramasa Mori said something that made Keiichirō shove him with a barking laugh.

A stern-looking woman appeared a moment later.

Hisa Kirino was athletic and slim, and had a no-nonsense air about her. Though she was perhaps only in her thirties, she walked with the air of an older, wise woman. And after Isla had dressed and breakfasted, Kirino-san bustled her out of the house a bit like she would shoo a chicken, saying she was taking her to where the unmarried women spent their days.

They walked in silence to a different part of the village, where many young women washed clothes and carried water. Some, to Isla's surprise, sparred with wooden sticks, wearing wide trousers similar to those she had seen men wearing. Isla watched with fascination and then awe at the skill with which these women fought, grunting and skin glistening with perspiration.

The rest of the women murmured to each other, some glancing over to stare at Isla. She wished they wouldn't, but she could understand their curiosity.

Kirino-san beckoned over a round-faced young woman, who came to stand on Isla's other side, holding a bundle of clothes in her arms.

'Good morning,' she said.

'Hello,' said Isla.

She was probably around Isla's age and she bowed stiffly, which made Isla wonder if she had been tasked with showing the new girl the ropes and was unhappy about it. But she passed the clothes she was holding to Isla, indicating that she should put them on.

Isla thanked her, and the girl helped her dress in the wide trousers and a short kimono-like robe that folded across her chest – left over right – and a warm *haori* jacket that bore the same white vertical cross inside a circle. Isla's finger traced the stitching.

'It's the crest of the Shimazu clan. And I am Nakamura Nene.'

'MacKenzie Isla.'

Isla decided that Nene was reserved but not unfriendly.

'They say you're from across the ocean,' Nene said later as they carried baskets of linens to the river, which rushed fast and cold that morning. 'From Scotland. Where is that?'

Isla swallowed the laugh that crawled up her throat. The world was a lot bigger before planes and phones. She gasped as they dumped the clothes into the river. It was like plunging her hands into ice.

She explained to the best of her ability, not helped by being unable to remember if Scotland was part of Europe in the nineteenth century. 'It's a country north of England, part of what is called the British Isles.'

'There was a war here between the British and our people a couple of years ago.'

Isla groaned inwardly. Of course there was, and this might be part of why she was being treated generally with such suspicion. 'Some Scots don't think much of being termed as British,' she replied in a way she hoped would help Nene understand that Isla didn't personally have a grudge against Japan.

'We were only children at the time,' Nene said as she grabbed a man's kimono and thrust it into the running water, perhaps splashing more roughly than necessary. She didn't say anything else for a while, and so Isla copied her and the other women as best she could, as her fingers quickly lost all feeling.

After a while she looked up. The sky was cloudless now, without a chance of another typhoon anytime soon.

The more she thought about it, the more she was sure the storm had been the key that connected the present – Isla's time – and the past. She was away from her home and her family, and longed for what she knew and could take for certain.

She turned to where Mount Sakurajima lay on the horizon. A thin trail of smoke drifted from the volcano, and Isla could smell the scent of ash on the air.

'That's Mount Sakurajima, and sometimes ash coats the town,' Nene said, and Isla didn't feel she could tell her that she already knew this. She glanced at Nene, who gave Isla a tiny smile. The shadow of a dimple appeared on her cheek. 'Does your country have volcanoes?' Nene asked.

Thinking of Scotland brought an ache. Isla described the scars of volcanoes that erupted many hundreds of years earlier, and the striking, untamed landscapes and dramatic cliffs, the fields of heather that bloomed in summertime and the scent of burning peat and dog hair and the sea.

As she spoke, Isla realised that when she had been back in Scotland (and not too occupied with Will in her heady first days of being in love), she had been so engrossed in thoughts of her third-great-grandfather, Hisakichi Kuroki, after her beloved grandfather Tom had died, that when she and Will broke up she hadn't been able to wait to come to Japan. But now she was here, she felt homesick.

As Nene stopped washing the clothes to listen, Isla looked around as she spoke. Nothing marred the forget-me-not blue of the sky above them as, void of aircraft and their contrails, the sky looked empty. And Isla wondered what her home country would be like at this time. There was a strange comfort in knowing that, whatever was going on across the sea in 1870s Scotland, its mountains and cliffs would be unchanged.

When the washing was done, Kirino-san let everybody, other than Isla, spar with wooden sticks. Kirino-san barked orders and instructions, reminding Isla of a bossy older sister. Grunts and the clacking of sticks filled the air and Isla watched for a while until, to her surprise, she was invited to join in.

A tall young woman said something Isla couldn't catch, making the others laugh, although Kirino shot them a glance worthy of a mother disciplining a rowdy toddler, and instantly they all became serious.

Isla was paired with a nervous-looking young woman, both of them holding thick bokken sticks.

'Remember, girls, not all fighters are men,' said Kirino-san. 'And everyone has the right to protect their families.'

Isla didn't have a clue what to do, and simply tried to keep up with the others.

The nervous girl's face hardened in a way Isla didn't like. She seemed much less nervous now as she swung her training stick, long sleeves flying. It landed hard on Isla's shoulder, sending a thrill of pain along her collarbone.

'Ow!' Isla rubbed the spot and scowled. 'Wait, wait, do that again. More slowly.'

An hour later, sweat-soaked, every bit of her aching, and with fresh bruises on her shoulders and forearms, Isla sat down to eat lunch by the river with the young women, who were all wearing the same sort of loose trousers that she was.

It felt otherworldly to sit eating sweet potato and fish with chipped chopsticks, with no one checking their make-up or tapping in a text on their mobile phone.

Was it better? Isla couldn't quite decide. It was certainly different. Simpler. And companionable, somehow. She let their chatter wash over her for a while.

'Excuse me.'

The young woman who had screamed when she saw Isla in the forest that night was crouching beside her, offering a lacquered bowl of steaming soup. '*Dōzo*,' she whispered, shy.

Isla smiled at her and took it with thanks. A moment passed between them and then Nene said, 'This is Hirayama Aiko. Aiko, meet MacKenzie Isla.'

Isla returned the bow and greeting and took a sip of soup. It was salty and tasty, with wakame seaweed and cubes of soft tofu floating in the hot broth. 'Thank you, it's delicious.'

'I'm sorry I called you a *yōkai*,' Aiko said. 'It was rude.'

Isla laughed. 'It's really all right. It didn't seem that way at all.'

Villagers murmured about the foreign girl as they passed. If the others noticed, they said nothing about it. Isla didn't understand most of what they said. The Satsuma dialect was unfamiliar, words or whole sentences different to what she was used to. It made her head ache. She hadn't heard English aloud in what felt like ages.

The sound of a biwa lute travelled on the wind, its haunting notes giving Isla goosebumps that had nothing to do with the chill.

'Everyone has a lute in their home,' said Nene. 'You should listen to Nakahara-san. His playing is wonderful, but he doesn't let me listen much. He said people might think it's strange to see us together because we aren't courting.'

Isla had no idea who Nakahara-san was, but she decided that Nene was a natural chatterbox who didn't seem to need more from Isla at this moment than vague nods and the occasional grunt.

But Nene's mention of courting turned Isla's thoughts towards Keiichirō and she wondered what he was doing right at that moment at Takamori Saigō's *shi-gakkō* school. Perhaps Chinese studies or swordplay training.

The sun was well towards the horizon when the women carried their bundles away from the river and towards the hillside.

'We've got your towel, MacKenzie-san,' said Aiko.

'Where are we going?'

'The *onsen*. The hot springs. Do you have those in your country?'

Isla could tell Aiko was making polite conversation, but she wished they wouldn't make her feel like such a foreigner. However, courteously she replied, 'Maybe we did once, but none of the volcanoes are alive any more.' She didn't know how to say 'active'. Aiko giggled at what was sure to be a mistake, but Isla found she didn't mind.

They passed shopkeepers shouting for passers-by to look at their wares. These were older workers with towels tied around their heads and they turned to stare at Isla's hair. There were a few women, holding woven baskets or bags in their arms as they spoke with friends. Isla eyed their modest kimono robes and their silver-streaked hair.

Their clothing and hairstyles were a relatively rare sight in modern-day Japan, but Isla liked seeing that gossiping wasn't new at all. People weren't all that different, even across eras.

Isla was about to ask Nene how much farther they had to go when they arrived at a private *onsen* that smelled faintly of sulphur. Everyone took off their robes and folded them carefully, and Isla made sure she did likewise.

The prospect of a dip in a bath was wonderful after the hard day they'd had, and Isla wasn't going to draw further attention to herself by acting shy. Staying behind Aiko and Nene when she could, she wriggled out of the borrowed hakama trousers and the robe underneath. The steam from the natural hot spring looked so tempting that Isla could barely wait to slip into the hot water and soak herself. She went to the edge of the spring and dipped her toe into the water.

'MacKenzie-san!' Aiko's voice was shocked.

'What?' she hissed back through clenched teeth. It wasn't fun being naked, and Aiko's call had turned several heads in their direction.

Nene came to the rescue, saying, 'You have to wash yourself first.'

Crap! 'Ah,' said Isla, and meekly went to where Nene and Aiko were scrubbing themselves with cloths and well water. Isla's cheeks burned. She hadn't washed before she had sunk herself into the hot spring near Keiichirō's house when she first arrived. Had she left a bunch of dirt and grime in the hot water there? Kana must think her such an idiot.

She followed Nene and Aiko into the steaming water. Though Isla would have preferred to be alone in the natural spring, after a few minutes she couldn't deny there was something nice about sitting in the hot water with a dozen other women, their limbs wiry and toned from their physical work, faces and hands browned by the sun. They now took little notice of Isla as they spoke with each other, though she caught one or two of them glancing with interest at her breasts.

Resisting the urge to cover herself, Isla sat with Nene and Aiko at the edge closest to where they had laid the towels.

'*Onsen* in winter are wonderful, *ne*?' Aiko let out a relaxed sigh, leaning her head back. Her cheeks were pinking from the hot water. 'Satsuma has the best hot springs in Japan, I'm sure. MacKenzie-san, you've met Mori Toramasa, haven't you?'

'Briefly,' said Isla, thinking of the time with the pitfall trap and their formal introduction just this morning.

'Has he said anything about me?' Aiko tried but failed to make her voice sound casual.

Isla saw Nene hiding a smile.

'Not yet. But I've hardly spoken to him,' Isla replied.

Aiko looked disappointed, and the trio sat in silence for a while.

Isla hadn't been to a public bath in Tokyo, and so had made the embarrassing mistake of forgetting to wash first. Now she was surrounded by people who regarded her as an outsider at best and an enemy at worst. The water was wonderfully warming, and, though Isla had a sense of anxiety that would never quite go away, it was wonderful to be cosy right down to her toes. She didn't much want to return to the house, where Kana would give her strange looks, and of course wandering off on her own was now no longer an option.

As they carried their damp towels back to the town, which was now aglow with lanterns, Kirino-san called Isla to her side.

'For your work.' She pressed a bag into Isla's hands. Inside were two sweet potatoes, several apples, some meat wrapped carefully in cloth, and a ceramic bottle of what Isla supposed was a spirit.

'Thank you.' Isla bowed, hoping that being able to bring home some food for Keiichirō's family would make Kana think more kindly of her. Trying not to think about her embarrassing cultural mistake, she kept her head down and found her way back to the Maeda household, all too aware of the talk that resumed when her back was turned.

Kana was immensely pleased with the food Isla gave her, and waved Isla away and told her to rest while she got on with preparing their evening meal.

Isla kept hold of the ceramic bottle and went to her room. But away from whispers and curious eyes, she was surprised to find herself breaking down, and giving in to a volley of sobs.

Desperation wrapped around her heart. She had tried her hardest to stay strong, but misery swamped her. She had been here for days, and her parents would be frantic. And to make things worse, today marked four years since her grandfather, the reason she had come to Japan in the first place, had passed away. Tears slid down Isla's cheeks, hot and fast, and she covered her face, unable to quell the flood of despair.

She didn't hear the door slide open, didn't notice Keiichirō's presence until he asked, 'Did someone hurt you?'

'My grandfather died four years ago today,' Isla said, unable to explain the rest of it. 'And I miss him.'

Keiichirō crouched before her, and she told him that this was the first year she hadn't been able to put flowers on his grave. Not that she would have been able to do it this year anyway, but it hurt to know his grave didn't even exist here. There was nothing of Yoshitomo Kuroki yet, nothing except an ancestor she was nowhere close to finding out about.

'We can make a shrine for him in the morning.' Keiichirō rose to his feet. 'We'll make do with what we have. And it will mean you have something of your grandfather here.'

Unable to think of what to say to this kindness, Isla stood up too and passed Keiichirō the ceramic bottle. Its top was still sealed with wax.

He smiled, and said, 'You must have worked hard, Isla. This is *shōchū*, a spirit made from sweet potatoes. We'll drink some tomorrow in memory of your grandfather.'

And so the next afternoon, Isla and Keiichirō gathered river stones outside and built a shrine by its banks. It was nothing special really, but Isla was touched by the way Keiichirō insisted they find similar-looking stones and a pleasant place by the river.

'What did you call him?' Keiichirō asked.

'Tom.'

'Then Tom-san shall be remembered here.' Keiichirō placed the stone with careful precision on top of two others. They cleared the dry dirt around it and gathered some sticks. It was not like a grave or shrine Isla had ever seen, but something warm blossomed in her chest to see him work, not minding that the dirt got under his fingernails or on his hakama trousers.

'This is perfect,' he said, sounding pleased, when they found a longer slab of stone. He placed it in the middle of the others. 'Usually we'd write something here, but I don't have the tools.' He sucked his lip, looking so worried it made Isla giggle.

'It's enough,' she assured him. There was something sweet about that fact that, although her grandfather technically hadn't lived here yet, his grave was here, beside the river. It was a peaceful place.

Once Keiichirō had left her, Isla found another stone, on which she used a small chalky pebble she had found to scratch in wobbly letters *KUROKI* in Japanese, the kanji character for black and the kanji character for tree. Then she stood in contemplation for a few minutes, finally saying, 'I hope you think this is a good spot. And I will get back home to Scotland, Grandad, I promise.'

Back in the house, Keiichirō was waiting with the bottle of *shōchū*. 'This was my father's favourite cup.' He held up a small and delicate ceramic cup. 'See how the dark blue fades to white? It's supposed to look like the early morning sky. He always drank from it.' Keiichirō held the cup as carefully as though it were a baby bird. He must have loved his father very much.

Carefully Isla poured some *shōchū* into the blue cup. 'Is that enough?'

'A little more. Make sure it's nearly full. *Sou, sou.* That's right.'

Keiichirō filled another cup with the clear spirit for her, and, as Isla watched the sleeve of his robe rise above his wrist, she felt that them each pouring the other's drinks was peculiarly intimate. 'Let's drink to both Tom and your father,' she offered.

'*Kanpai.*' And so they toasted and drank to a man who hadn't been born yet.

*

Weeks passed, and every day Keiichirō grew more used to the foreign girl living in his home.

Isla made sure to work hard to give Kana any vegetables and wrapped meat Kirino-san gave for her toil. Kana still regarded the visitor with disdain, and worked with pursed lips, her expression sour when Isla was in her vicinity. Isla took care always to eat in her room and to try to be as unobtrusive as possible in the household.

Under Murata-san's instruction, Keiichirō watched for Isla sending letters, just in case she really was a spy. But although Isla spent nearly all the time at his house in her room, Keiichirō never heard her request ink or paper.

'I have asked the traders to spread word of the MacKenzie girl,' Kirino-san assured him one chilly morning at the *shigakkō* school. 'And of course you will let me know if she does anything suspicious?'

'*Hai*, Kirino-san.'

An hour later, a breeze ruffled against Keiichirō's hair as he watched Toramasa swing his sword, a fine katana passed down through his father's family. The blades clashed with a ring that echoed around the field and the sparring partners grunted with each swing. Toramasa's opponent, the quiet and fierce Nakahara Hisao, fought with a ferocity Keiichirō hadn't before seen in training. They usually trained with bokken sticks, but today Nakahara had insisted on trying with real blades.

'Why?' Keiichirō had asked when the soft-spoken older man had asked to practise with katanas. 'The bokken ensure we don't injure each other.'

'I'll do it. I'm not scared,' Toramasa said, and stood with a swagger as he unsheathed his katana. 'You're right, Nakahara-san. We need to know how to use blades, too.'

As he watched them, every clash of steel made Keiichirō flinch, not that he allowed anyone to see. Toramasa stepped and pivoted as he had been taught, while Keiichirō and their swordplay senior, Ikeda Uhei, watched from the sidelines. Though Keiichirō was supposed to watch and study his friend's footwork, his mind wandered to the redheaded girl.

Few trusted her, but somehow he did even though he was at a loss to explain why. He decided there was a sweetness and fragility about her that needed protection. That wasn't to say Isla didn't have an inner strength that set her apart from other women he knew. The way she had run off during his foolish fight with Taguchi and her honesty when asked her thoughts or opinions testified to this. It was so un-Japanese, yet he sensed in Isla a determination that mirrored his own, a strength of mind that mirrored that of the samurai spirit.

He had felt her presence when she had watched him practise on his grandfather's lute. Her breath, her scent of pine and earth, the way she watched him.

The way the pulse in her wrist had fluttered beneath his fingertips.

Toramasa gasped and blood spurted from his hand. He stumbled back, gripping his wrist, the katana falling to the grass with a soft thud.

'Enough,' said Ikeda. A cut had severed Toramasa's skin, a line of red dripping onto the grass at their feet.

'*Bakamono*,' Keiichirō muttered, and thought he heard Ikeda stifle a laugh. 'You all right, Mori?' Keiichirō asked Toramasa, who straightened and bowed to his opponent.

'Nakahara-san, you fought well, but with your emotions. This is not good even though you bested your opponent this time.' Ikeda, regal and elegant, stepped forward, his hakama trousers rustling about his ankles. 'Are you angry with Mori-san?'

'I'm not angry,' Nakahara insisted. Everyone looked at the blood on Toramasa's hand.

You let your guard down, thought Keiichirō. *As I would have. If I had been sparring with a sword while thinking about Isla, I'd have lost my whole hand.*

'If I fought better, I would have avoided getting my hand cut,' said Toramasa, and he bowed low to Nakahara. 'I'm glad you are on our side, Nakahara-san. Thank you for this lesson.'

For a moment, Nakahara looked confused. He was a pinch-faced man, his hair brushing his shoulders. He was perhaps a few years older than Ikeda, with a darkness behind his eyes Keiichirō couldn't read. Nakahara finally bowed back, his movements stiff, and strode across the grass past the other sparring pairs.

'Where are you going?' Toramasa called after him, perhaps stung. 'Off to write? You're always writing.'

Nakahara ignored him, back straight as he headed back to the *shi-gakkō* school.

Ikeda took Toramasa's wrist in his long, delicate fingers. The younger man's cheeks blazed plum-blossom-red. 'You were distracted. Do you see what happens when you don't fight as well as you should?'

Embarrassment flushed through Keiichirō on his best friend's behalf. He watched as Toramasa met Ikeda's eyes, and the older man said, 'Concentrate more next time. But for now, go and get that wound dressed. Keiichirō, your sister can tend to him, yes?'

'*Hai.*'

Keiichirō headed home with Toramasa at his side. He had expected that his friend would find a reason to stay with Ikeda so he could spar with someone else. But Ikeda was correct to teach them the lesson that wounds to the hands were dangerous. They could affect fighting skills, as well as the ability to work. And the cut on Toramasa's left hand was deeper than it had first looked.

'Do you think Nakahara Hisao fights with too much emotion?' Toramasa asked as they crossed a stone bridge over the river.

'Perhaps. Or you don't fight with enough skill.' Keiichirō laughed and had to dodge a swipe from Toramasa's uninjured hand. 'Kana will see your injury won't affect you getting revenge on Nakahara. Did he seek to cut you, do you think?'

Toramasa looked skyward, sighing. 'Who knows. Anyway, isn't it time you married? Then you'll have a wife to take care of your injuries. Mine, too.' He chuckled.

Keiichirō gave him a scalding look. 'You're one to speak. You're not married, either, and we're the same age.'

'Doomed to die alone if we don't take a wife each before next summer. Alas' – Toramasa gripped his jacket as if to clutch at his heart – 'I'm yet to find a woman who is worthy of Mori Toramasa.'

Keiichirō snorted and smacked his best friend around the head.

CHAPTER 8

Isla was readying for bed when an unusual dull clunk and what might have been the rustle of cloth caught her attention. She slid open the door to her room to peer into the tatami room.

Keiichirō was there, wearing a simple dark robe, his hair loose. He was kneeling before an alcove, and he looked at her.

'Sorry. I didn't mean to disturb you,' she said, feeling bad for interrupting a private moment.

But to her surprise Keiichirō asked her to join him.

She went to his side, aware of his sleepy warmth, the scent of the cotton of his kimono. His presence was like a mountain, silent and regal. For many beats of silence they looked at the samurai armour sitting on a stand, well used judging by its chips and signs of use and the edges of the red lamellar armour rusted to brown. Beside it was an urn that was simple, dark and polished to a shine, with the now familiar crest of the Shimazu clan painted on it in white, the cross inside a circle Isla had seen many times since she arrived.

'Who is in the urn?' As soon as the words left her mouth, Isla wanted to wince. She should be respecting the quiet of the moment, and not blurting things out.

Keiichirō didn't seem to have heard. Then, in a far-away voice, he said, 'My father. He died two years ago.'

Keiichirō prepared some incense to offer before his father's urn, and Isla helped him as best she could.

'How did he die?'

'He killed someone who hurt Kana. There was a young samurai from the village who forced himself on my sister. My father killed him for it, but it was the wrong sort of punishment. He slit the man's throat in his sleep, the type of murder only a coward would do. So my father committed seppuku to win back his family's honour.'

Seppuku, ritual sacrifice. Sinking a blade into one's own belly to disembowel oneself, a painful death.

Isla wondered who had done this to Kana, and her gaze turned in the direction of the door behind which Keiichirō's sister and her daughter Yura slept.

'She was pregnant with Yura when she told him,' Keiichirō added. 'It's not Yura's fault, of course, but when she was a newborn, I couldn't touch her, couldn't look at her. She looks too much like Kana's attacker. My mother died when I was six and Kana was four. Father was all we had, and, because of *him*, we no longer have a father.'

Isla felt Keiichirō had to force his voice to remain calm; a tremor, like an earthquake deep beneath the ocean, gave away the extent of his emotion. And no wonder.

'I'm so sorry, Keiichirō.'

Isla had no words strong enough, not in English nor in Japanese, to tell Keiichirō how horrible it all was. To know your sister was raped, then to lose your father so soon after.

Keiichirō closed his eyes as he bowed his head. Then he straightened his back.

'Tell me about him,' asked Isla, as the smoke of the incense wreathed them. 'I'd like to know more.'

Keiichirō answered that his father had been called Ujio, and he had had a great talent for playing the biwa lute as well as unwavering nostalgia for the glory days of the fighting samurai. 'He loved *shōchū*. You remember his cup? He had a few small cups, but the blue one you saw was his favourite, the one he would drink *shōchū* from.'

'My grandfather Tom was partial to whisky,' Isla said, and told Keiichirō some of the history of Scottish whisky. She tried to describe the woody, peaty taste of Scotland's favourite spirit. 'I think Tom and Ujio would have liked each other.'

Keiichirō made Isla and himself some tea. 'My father loved to play pranks. I remember when I was young, perhaps around five, I complained I had a stone in my sandal. He took a huge rock and hid it behind his back, then when he shook out the stone, he dropped the rock onto the ground. He always said I just gaped at him, looking between him and the ground. I thought it had come from my sandal.' They laughed at this. 'I got him back, eventually. I'm scared of cockroaches, but my father was always afraid of worms. I once put one on his face while he was asleep. He screamed so loudly my mother thought there were bandits in the house.'

Isla laughed again, just as the door slid open. Kana came through, her hair mussed and with a sleepy Yura in her arms. She glanced at them both and then moved into the next room.

Isla realised dawn had broken and it was a new day. Somehow daylight had come while they were talking.

Their talk seemed to have put Keiichirō in a better mood. 'Shall we catch some fish for breakfast?'

'I've never fished before,' Isla admitted.

'Then I'll show you how.'

Isla dressed in yesterday's clothes. The robe and hakama trousers were becoming easier to don by the day. Five minutes later, she and Keiichirō were heading towards the river, a simple rod and tackle in Keiichirō's hand.

'How about your father?' he asked as they sat watching the river, waiting for a fish to nibble the line. 'And your mother?'

Isla had tried not to think about her family since the realisation that she had stepped through time. Hearing someone else ask about them, even in another language, brought a deep loneliness.

'You never did tell me. Did you come to Japan with them?' Keiichirō kept his eyes on the river as he spoke.

Was Keiichirō still trying to find out about her after all? And if so, who could blame him?

Isla wanted to confess everything. To explain she came from the twenty-first century and to tell him about all its mayhem, and that a broken heart had been a large part of the reason she had come to Japan, and increasingly she was thinking about her third-great-grandfather Hisakichi Kuroki and whether he had been a renowned samurai as her family lore claimed.

Isla imagined those soft brown eyes that were now looking at her blinking in confusion, his features wrinkling into puzzlement. There was no way Keiichirō could understand any bit of the truth. But what other answer could she possibly give? The samurai hated liars, and Isla didn't want to make something up. She liked Keiichirō too much, and he would think less of her if he caught her in a lie. Well, for now he had simply asked about her parents, she reminded herself.

'I came to Satsuma alone,' she said eventually, noting the slight rise of Keiichirō's eyebrows. 'I was looking for information on Kuroki Hisakichi. Have you heard of him?'

'Kuroki?' Keiichirō fiddled with the line, then glanced at her. 'Here in Kagoshima?'

'Maybe,' she said. A thrill of excitement ran through her. 'Do you think you could find him? He might go to your *shi-gakkō*.'

There was a jerk on the fishing line and Keiichirō reeled it in. He held up a squirming silver fish. 'Barely enough for a mouthful.' He glanced skyward. 'Let's go inside.'

Keiichirō folded his unused futon, a sharpness deep in his chest. It was a feeling he didn't like.

Jealousy.

Kuroki Hisakichi, Isla had said, was someone she was looking for. Someone she thought might be a samurai at one of Saigō-sama's *shi-gakkō* schools. But how could that be? If she had stepped foot in the Satsuma province before that night in early January, he would have known about it. No gaijin with hair that red could have remained hidden for so

long. The gossip about Isla currently flying around his school
was a testament to that.

'I'll check and see if anyone knows him,' he had promised
her. He had managed to keep putting one foot in front
of another and his expression stoic until he had slid the
door closed and was alone with his thoughts and gathering
daylight.

Kuroki...

He had no right to be jealous. Isla was not his wife.

The reminder didn't help.

At the *shi-gakkō* later, Keiichirō asked anyone he could
about Kuroki Hisakichi. But there were thousands of
students in dozens of academies all over Satsuma territory,
so it was unsurprising that the name was unfamiliar.
Toramasa hadn't heard of him, and neither had Keiichirō's
cousin, Tatsuzō.

Keiichirō tried not to think about why MacKenzie Isla
might be looking for a Satsuma samurai. There was no reason
he could think of that was not upsetting.

Still, Keiichirō greeted his friend Murakami near a soba
noodle shop on a street overlooking the bay. 'I'm looking for
someone, and I hear he might be a student at the *shi-gakkō*.
Kuroki Hisakichi. Do you know him?'

'Can't say I do,' said Murakami, scratching the stubble on
his cheeks.

Something smashed behind Keiichirō, making them both
glance around.

Nakamura Nene and Hirayama Aiko were fussing around
a broken pot that had smashed to bits on the road.

'Is everything all right, Nene-chan?' called Keiichirō.

'Hm? Oh, yes, Maeda-san. Everything's fine.' Nene's round cheeks pinked as she and Aiko hurried off, the broken bits of pottery in their hands.

*

Isla ate alone in her room. Working with Nene and the others tending to the fields, or washing and cleaning, made eating a meal in the evening merely a quick prelude to falling into bed. It was a simple life, one she did not belong to. Isla missed chocolate and coffee, texting and showers. She longed to wear different clothes every day, to be able to brush the tangles out of her hair and properly clean her teeth. She missed electric lights, video games and refrigerators more than she would ever have thought possible. But it was her family and friends she missed most.

The people she had met in Satsuma so far were reserved and private. This made it easier not to betray her emotions too much, and she got on with her tasks with quiet toil, every day and night, always keeping on the lookout for gathering storms that might lead her home.

Increasingly, though, Isla thought of how Satsuma's history was presented in tours and museums. How would the people she now knew personally, the people intent on eking out a living and following Takamori Saigō in the fight to preserve their way of life, feel if they knew that a century into the future it had all been for nothing, and that people would enjoy reading and watching their history and learning about their beliefs and passions merely as entertainment? The tawdry souvenir stickers and the badges bearing the

Shimazu clan crest reduced these life-and-death times to a fun day out.

Isla supposed the same could be said for any time period. Even in this old Satsuma she was experiencing, people enjoyed theatre plays of stories and samurai warriors from long ago.

*

'MacKenzie-san?' called Nene Nakamura one chilly morning in late January.

Mount Sakurajima had erupted the day before, covering the town in ash. Kana and Isla had spent most of the morning sweeping the porch, but it was a losing battle.

'Nakamura-san, *ohayou gozaimasu*,' Kana greeted Nene as Isla stepped outside. 'You missed Keiichirō. He just left.'

'Nana!' cried Yura from the porch, waving happily at Nene.

She giggled and waved back. 'Hello, Yura-chan! Ah, MacKenzie-san, *ohayou*. Kirino-san is waiting for us.'

'Call me Isla,' she said.

The ash had left a grey coat over everything, and down it still fluttered from trees, like dirty snowflakes.

'Then please call me Nene.' Nene rubbed her scalp, looking up at the nearest tree. 'This ash is so unpleasant.'

Weeks here in the nineteenth century, and not a drop of rain had fallen.

Nene explained that the volcano's eruption meant the working women would need to collect falling ash that day, packing it into sacks that would be already sitting on the back of a wagon. Otherwise the ash would further damage the crops, which were already scarce and a cause for concern.

'People are always worried about the volcano,' Nene sighed as they shovelled ash. 'Sometimes I think one day it will erupt and destroy the whole town, taking everyone here with it.'

'It won't,' said Isla before she could stop herself. She quickly tried to backtrack. 'It's a dangerous volcano. But it won't bury the town, I'm sure.'

Nene gave her a strange look that made Isla's insides drop. She had meant her words to sound reassuring, but all she had done was to make Nene wonder anew about her.

Isla decided the best thing for her to do would be to work hard at helping clear the ash. She struggled to keep up with the others. It seemed everyone else could carry twice as much as she could in half the time. But Isla made sure not to show she was tired. She had to take one day, one task, at a time, and try not to panic. She had been here for weeks already; surely it couldn't be for much longer.

'Everyone,' called Kirino-san, gathering the women together as they kept an eye on the skies for more ash. 'Come. We've done as much as we can do with the ash today. It's time for some sparring.'

Wearing the now familiar wide trousers and holding a bokken stick of her own, Isla was paired with a slender woman who looked unsure how hard to try to beat her. Isla responded by wildly swinging her stick, forcing the girl to raise her own bokken just in time. A wild giggle burst from Isla's lips as they sparred, parts of her body bruised. Kirino-san even offered her tips, showing her how to stand and how to swing properly.

She had been sparring for a while with the women now, and although she was hardly an expert, she felt more comfortable than before with a weapon in her hand. In fact, it was fast coming to feel as if her bokken was something of a friend.

The slender woman smacked her in the ribs, and Isla gasped and lowered her stick. Embarrassment flushed through her, followed by a familiar wave of anger. Her bokken fell on the grass while her opponent straightened, satisfied.

Isla snatched up the weapon with more force than necessary and squared up to her opponent once more. But her flush of temper died immediately when the sound of horses' hooves reached them, accompanied by voices with a timbre very different to the usual Japanese. Isla glanced over the field, just as everyone else did.

Men – Caucasian men – sat in a horse-drawn carriage. It was clear they were looking over at the sparring women.

Kirino-san made sure, Isla noted, to place herself between these men and the young women, like a lioness protecting her cubs.

The voices grew more distinct as the carriage drew near, and Isla caught snippets of syllables on the wind. They weren't speaking in English.

'Ow!' Isla dropped her stick as pain exploded across her fingers. She shook her hand as the girl stood before her looking shocked. 'Ugh. Good game. I wasn't concentrating.' She gave a hasty bow and retreated to Kirino-san and, as the carriage proceeded past the group of women, Isla asked, 'Who are they?'

Kirino-san's glare at the now retreating men could have melted steel, and for a moment Isla appreciated how tolerant

Hisa Kirino had been of Isla's own presence. Then Kirino-san said, 'They are traders from Nagasaki. Dutch, from the community of Holland nationals on Dejima Island.' Then in a loud voice she added, 'That's enough gawping, everyone. Back to sparring.'

Isla paired herself with Nene.

'Don't hold back,' she said, even though her side and fingers were throbbing.

'You, either.' Nene gave a hard swing, wood cracking close to Isla's head as she blocked.

They all swapped partners again and again, and with each round Isla picked up more of the way the best opponents moved and were able to second-guess her own moves, how they swung the bokken sticks in ways that aimed at weak points like the neck, and how they rose their weapons to block a coming attack.

Isla put her frustration into her attacks, sometimes hitting harder than necessary. But she loved the rush of satisfaction she felt whenever she landed a hit, even if it wasn't the most graceful way of achieving it.

'MacKenzie-san, you got me.' Aiko Hirayama rubbed her shoulder and gave a low bow.

'You got me twice,' Isla said back with a grin. She was breathing hard, relishing the feeling of hard exercise. It kept some of her ever-present anxiety at bay. She even enjoyed the bruises already forming on her skin, evidence that she wasn't afraid to come in close to the other person's bokken. Isla would have hated it if anybody accused her of being weak or timid.

She ended the session being paired with Nene once more, Kirino-san circling them all and observing carefully. Nervous at being under such pressure, Isla didn't anticipate a hard hit in the side of her head that made her shout out in pain, clutching her ear.

'Block like this.' Hisa Kirino raised her own stick and urged Nene to hit again like before. Her ear throbbing, Isla watched the older woman dodge and block, and for a moment she felt embarrassed that she hadn't been able to react in this adept way. But Kirino-san wasn't trying to humiliate her but to teach her, and what she had to be was patient as well as open to learning.

'Do that move again,' said Isla, standing in front of Nene. The girl's plump cheeks were flushed, and, when she swung for Isla's head again in exactly the same way as before, this time Isla was able to block with a loud clack. She grinned with satisfaction.

When Kirino-san called a halt, they were covered in sweat and ash, and flopped onto a nearby stretch of grass, where they passed around water.

'You're getting better,' acknowledged Nene, although she didn't look especially happy about this.

'Thank you for helping me,' said Isla. 'You'd prefer to be paired with someone else.'

'Not at all, Isla-san. We have to look out for each other,' answered Nene, and Isla tried to concentrate on the words, rather than the slight pause before Nene had said them.

CHAPTER 9

'I'm sorry. I looked everywhere and asked everyone I thought may be able to help, but I couldn't find anything about Kuroki Hisakichi.'

Isla looked up at Keiichirō from where she was bent over a bucketful of water, washing the bowls and chopsticks they had used for dinner. 'You checked for me? I didn't expect you to do that.'

Keiichirō had spent a long time going through school ledgers. He'd asked as many teachers as he could about the man Isla was seeking, but there was nobody called Kuroki at the school. He had drawn a blank; it was as if a man with the name of Kuroki had never existed. 'Why are you interested in him? Do you think he will help you find your way home?' he asked, not wholly convinced he wanted to know Isla's answers to these questions.

'Not exactly, but I would like to find him before I go home. *If* I can get home, that is.'

'You mustn't feel trapped here, Isla,' said Keiichirō quietly. 'You're not a prisoner. I don't care if the others are suspicious, I believe you are not a spy.'

Isla didn't say anything as she patted her hands dry on a towel and brushed an errant lock of hair from her face. Her emotions, so easy to read, thought Keiichirō again, flickered between wistful and touched.

'Tell me about your home. Tell me about Scotland.' Keiichirō helped her dry the bowls, neatly wipe off the chopsticks and set them on a tray.

He listened to her talk, and once she began she barely paused for breath.

After a matter of weeks, Isla was speaking Japanese with more confidence and fluidity, and not tripping up on the syllables so much. She described mountains and rivers and waterfalls, and men wearing a garment she called a kilt.

Keiichirō couldn't imagine much of what she said, but he liked listening to her, the music in her voice. They sat on the grass overlooking the river.

'I have to ask,' Keiichirō said, 'this Kuroki Hisakichi…'

She glanced over at him, her warm brown eyes darting between his. Her gaze travelled over his face, landing on his lips for the briefest of breath-stealing moments before she looked back over at the river. When she said nothing, he finished his sentence. 'Does he mean something to you? Is he a friend?'

'No, he's not a friend. I've never even met him.' Isla sighed, her head leaning back as she put her weight on her hands behind her. 'He's an acquaintance of my family.'

'Your family?' Trepidation trod on the warm feeling that had settled on Keiichirō like a blanket at sitting here with Isla. 'You have a husband?'

A laugh burst from Isla's lips. 'No, no husband.'

But although this was what he'd hoped to hear, Keiichirō couldn't avoid noticing a sad look in Isla's eyes. She remained as much of a mystery to him as she had been on the very first day they had met, a person who had more of what she was trying to conceal exposed with every question of his that she answered. Deep in thought, he stared at the riverbank across from them.

'Is everything all right, Kei?' she asked.

'Kei?'

'Easier to say than Keiichirō.'

He smiled. It's what his mother had called him.

*

The next day, Isla was out working with the women, and was straightening out a crick in her back when something wonderful happened.

Rain began to fall.

Everyone cried out as a great torrent fell in moments, soaking the ground and drenching their clothes.

But while the others looked unhappy at their unexpected dousing, Isla laughed up at the bleak sky, raindrops that tasted faintly of ash splashing her face. Her hair stuck to her scalp, the rain falling in what felt a beautiful downpour, and her fingers were crossed for the wind to pick up. Today was the day; suddenly she was sure. The day when the white torii gate would reappear and, with a bit of luck, she would escape this bad dream.

Kirino-san called to the women to pack up the supplies. But the moment her back was turned, Isla slunk away, and then ran off as fast as she could when she was sure no one was watching.

She had to be quick.

For all she knew, this might be her only chance to reach the shrine. She wasn't going to miss a moment of opportunity if she could help it.

Keiichirō's face crossed her mind, but she couldn't entertain any thoughts about him. No matter the spark she sensed between them, her place was not here. And so she pushed Keiichirō from her thoughts. She needed to get back to her time, to her family. She had not found Hisakichi Kuroki, but that no longer mattered. Whatever the cost to her or anybody else, she just needed to get home.

She hurried past people rushing to cover their stalls or their wheelbarrows, shouting to each other. No one tried to stop the foreign girl, moving awkwardly through the puddles in sandalled feet, half-blind in the heavy rain. Thunder rumbled in the distance and her heart lifted even more. If luck were on her side, soon she'd be back to normality, to her own time, to showers and air conditioning and all the food she missed, to her parents, to her brother Douglas and their darling border collie, Whisky, telling them of her wild adventure.

She reached the edge of town and searched for the bamboo trees and the forest beside it. The rain fell in a musical patter, and Isla thought it the most wonderful sound she had ever heard. In a gust of icy air, she pushed into the woods and stepped on soggy leaves and twigs, keeping an eye out for pitfall traps.

As she headed in the direction of the shrine, she didn't care that every part of her was slick with rain. Her hakama trousers flew behind her as she brushed hair from her eyes. There it was, the shrine. All she had to do was find the white gate and she'd be home.

Rain fell on the shrine building, the statues and the unlit lanterns. She ran through the grounds, seeking the pale gate, waiting for the thick mist to descend like it had before.

Eventually Isla had to slow, her heart racing. She shivered. Her excitement faltered as she looked around. The bell rang, wind chimes singing to her. It seemed like last time, but…

Something was wrong.

'No!' Isla yelled, refusing to believe what she saw before her, searching the shrine again and again, ever more frantically. She checked every corner, ran her fingers along the slick walls, and even stepped into the shrine building itself in case the gate had somehow manifested itself inside.

But there was no sign of it.

'No!' she screamed as the rain began to lessen, the downpour turning softer and the sky lighter. She stopped in the centre of the shrine grounds, her head whipping about as she looked. There was the forest, the tree she had crouched beneath, the shrine building, the regular red torii gate. She even ran through it, hoping beyond hope she would find her prize on the other side.

Nothing happened. And there was no prize.

As Isla let out a final shriek of frustration, the rain stopped.

She was left freezing cold, and with her clothes soaked through. Worst of all, she was still stuck in 1877.

'What am I doing wrong?' she sobbed, sinking to her knees.

As a weak sun burst through a gap in the heavy clouds, there wasn't even the tiniest answer from a ringing bell.

If Isla had thought previously she had plumbed the pits of despair, it was nothing to the wretchedness she felt now.

*

The racket of gunfire made Keiichirō's skull rattle. He stood on the dusty ground of the training ring, a square of dirt surrounded by wooden walls and sliding doors. Before him and his fellow samurai were a dozen targets made of hay, littered with holes. The air smelled unpleasantly of gunpowder and sweat.

He aimed the rifle at a target and fired, standing firm to stop the recoil from throwing him off his feet. An explosion and the strong scent of gunpowder assaulted his nose. On his left his cousin Tatsuzō was swearing beneath his breath at having taken such a poor shot. 'Your father always said guns were dishonourable,' he muttered to Keiichirō.

'We can't deny that guns have won many battles,' Keiichirō said as he reloaded, not that the artillery practice was his favourite part of *shi-gakkō* classes.

The irony was not lost on Keiichirō that the warriors of Japan had benefited from weapons imported from overseas. Many Japanese people rejected the *shinseifu* government's new policies of sharing more with the West, while simultaneously enjoying the positive side of trading with foreigners.

His jaw set, Keiichirō lifted the heavy gun back onto his shoulder and aimed at the target.

Nakahara Hisao, the student who'd cut Toramasa's hand, came in with a bow and an apology to the sensei for being late. He flexed ink-stained fingers and hurried to snatch up his own rifle, bidding a hasty good morning to his classmates. Taguchi stood at the far end, as far away from Keiichirō as possible. They had avoided each other since their embarrassing brawl, and Keiichirō was just fine with that.

Keiichirō's finger pressed the trigger as a shape appeared at the door to their right. He braced for the brain-shaking explosion, then glanced over.

'Maeda,' called the man at the door. Kirino Toshiaki stood waiting.

Keiichirō and Tatsuzō looked at each other, unsure who was being referred to by their mutual family name.

Kirino-san's cologne reached Keiichirō's nose long before he did. 'Yes, the both of you will do,' Kirino-san said, and then he asked Tatsuzō, 'You have met the foreigner?'

'Yes. Briefly, Kirino-san,' said Tatsuzō, taken aback.

Keiichirō's stomach plummeted. He had not reported back on anything to do with Isla to Murata-san and the others who claimed an interest in her.

They left behind the gunshots and went through the *shi-gakkō* and outside into the cold air. It was already past noon. The sloping walls outside the school were still dripping with water as they trudged across the wet grass. The gunfire had been so loud that Keiichirō hadn't noticed the rain.

'I need to talk to you both about the foreigner.'

'MacKenzie Isla,' said Keiichirō. He owed it to Isla to make it clear she had a name.

Kirino-san gave a sharp nod. '*Hai*. You must know her best, Maeda-san.' His piercing gaze, eyes surrounded by crow's feet and holding a mountain's worth of wisdom, bored into

Keiichirō's. 'Tell me, has this MacKenzie written letters that you know of?'

'Foreign women can read and write?' Tatsuzō seemed surprised.

Keiichirō ignored him. 'Not a single letter, Kirino-san. She hasn't asked me or my sister for a brush or paper.'

'I see,' said Kirino-san.

They walked along the *shi-gakkō* walls, where the grunts of younger students practising martial arts could be heard. The damp grass smelled sharp and fresh; drops of water fell from nearby trees. 'Good. My wife says she has been working hard with the others, but we can't help but wonder why she is here. Her family must surely be searching for her.'

'Everything suggests that she came alone, and that nobody knows she is here,' said Keiichirō.

'A woman, sailing to Japan without even an escort?' Kirino-san snorted in disbelief. Even Tatsuzō chuckled.

Keiichirō didn't want to believe Isla had lied to him. She always seemed so lost and unmoored. If she were an actor, then she was convincing. Every day, she was here exactly as she should be, sometimes playing with Yura, or helping Nakamura Nene and the others, or being quietly by herself. It didn't add up to the behaviour of a spy or an enemy, Keiichirō was certain. And the time they'd shared together, that felt too real, too authentic to be built upon a lie. But what could he say that wouldn't sound suspicious, that wouldn't make him sound as though he was being played for a fool? If Keiichirō tried to explain any of this, all that would happen would be that he would make the situation worse.

'Saigō-sama has informed me there are Dutch traders staying in town until tonight,' said Kirino-san. 'They may be willing to take the girl to Nagasaki, where they can help her. There are British sailors there who will be able to take her home. She does not belong here. We need her gone.'

The thought of Isla leaving brought a terrible emptiness he could not fathom, but Kirino-san was right – Satsuma was not Isla's home. She had tried to leave before, and she stayed at the Maeda household only because she had no other choice.

Keiichirō had, for the first time, a moment of clarity. He wanted to beg Isla to stay in Satsuma. To stay with him, at his side. Every cell in his body compelled him to open his mouth and speak these words. They had never touched unless by accident, or talked about deeply personal things, or even stared into each other's eyes. And yet Keiichirō knew his life would be less if Isla wasn't there, and her absence would be like draining all the colour from the world. He just *knew*.

No matter.

He knew too that he wouldn't say a word to Isla of his feelings. He cared for her too much to stand in the way of her returning to the place where she felt happy.

And in that moment of clarity his heart broke.

*

Isla should have gone back to Kirino-san and Nene, but she was so disappointed over her failure to find the white gate that she was willing to endure whatever punishment awaited her for not rejoining the women's work. After that, she would go to the hot spring, clear her head, and come up with another plan.

When she reached the Maeda household, however, to her surprise Keiichirō was waiting for her, his face statue-like in its firmness. His broad-shouldered cousin was there, too, looking out across the water, as well as an older man Isla recognised. He was the man who'd ordered Keiichirō and his friends to take her to the school the night she arrived.

'Ah, MacKenzie-san,' the older man said. He gave a short bow, and Isla awkwardly mirrored him.

She could see Keiichirō staring at her, and she thought he was probably wondering why she was in wet clothing.

The man who had bowed to her said, 'I am Kirino Toshiaki. My wife tells me you've been working hard. We have some good news. But, ah, perhaps first you'd like to change?'

'I'll get Kana to make some tea,' said Keiichirō after Isla nodded that she would appreciate the chance to put on a clean outfit. Kana busied herself with a kettle.

Isla was glad to step into the relative privacy of her room. Keiichirō slid open the door and murmured, 'Where were you? Did you fall into the river?'

She ignored the question, asking instead, 'What's that Kirino guy doing here?'

Keiichirō thrust a towel at her. 'He might be able to get you home.' He backed out and slid the door closed.

Confused, Isla was left staring at the closed door for a few seconds. Then, with no dry Japanese clothes to her name, she dressed in her present-day clothes. Her hair still damp, she joined Kirino-san, Keiichirō and Tatsuzō and listened with increasing dread as Kirino-san told her about a group of Dutch traders who planned to head back to Nagasaki that evening.

'They'll be willing to take you with them,' said Kirino-san as they perched uncomfortably on the porch, hot tea in their hands. 'They will be able to find British sailors who can take you on their ship.'

Isla stared, unseeing, in front of her. If they took her to Nagasaki, or even on a ship to Britain, how would she ever get back to her own time? But it might be what she needed to do, as shown by her latest visit to the shrine being so fruitless.

Isla looked at Keiichirō as if that might help her. His expression was blank, and she couldn't work out what he thought.

'The Dutch might even know your family,' added Kirino-san. 'Murata-san is explaining your situation to them right now. They'll take good care of you.'

Isla's thoughts were racing. She was being sent away. What should she do? What could she do? Stay here and hope that somehow the white torii gate would return, or venture into the unknown? And what about Keiichirō?

As Hisa Kirino arrived Isla glanced at Keiichirō, her heart aching. Although he wasn't looking at her but straight ahead, Isla felt as if her world was collapsing into nothing. She wasn't supposed to be here, but now she couldn't bear to leave.

'We'll be back before sunset,' Kirino-san promised. 'Go back to the others and get some work done. We'll pick you up later.'

Isla looked at Keiichirō, and he smiled. Her heart leapt, and she almost smiled back. But as he turned and left, his katana swords at his hip, long black hair blowing in a wind still occasionally flecked with raindrops, she could have screamed in anguish.

It was torture, especially as Nene kept asking Isla if she were scared to leave on her own with the Dutch traders. And when Isla didn't reply, Nene strayed too close to the truth when she asked if Isla would find it hard to manage without Keiichirō, seeing as how he'd been so devoted in offering her sanctuary while also being her protector.

Isla didn't reply, but Nene may have spied a tear under her lashes.

'Oh no, not Keiichirō. You know that can't ever happen, don't you?' Nene's words made Isla look up. There was a strange expression on Nene's face as she said, 'I thought everyone knew he was betrothed.'

Isla frowned as she tried to work out if she had misunderstood.

'He's going to be married. We all thought it was strange enough, you staying there. And Kana says you and Keiichirō go off together all the time and sit and talk for hours. He shouldn't be doing that. He's promised.'

'Kana's confused, and she's exaggerating. We've never done anything wrong,' said Isla, her despair giving way to fury. 'Anyway, I don't for a moment believe he is betrothed. He would have told me.'

'I am not wrong, I assure you,' Nene said with more than a hint of gloat thickening her voice. 'I know this without a doubt. You see, he's betrothed to *me*.'

CHAPTER 10

Isla wished the downpour was back. Compared to this, there had been comfort in a falling sheet of heavy rain, muffling sounds and banishing people from the streets.

But now Isla felt people stare as she ran from Nene Nakamura, thinking how they would be gossiping about her.

Of course Keiichirō wouldn't be unattached. He was handsome and kind, and treated women well, all highly prized qualities.

Isla felt so stupid. She'd let her foolish, gullible heart catch feelings for a good-looking face, let his gentle, caring ways ignite a small flame deep within as they brought something alive in her heart.

But it was just another trick.

All men were the same.

Kirino-san had said he'd pick her up from where the women were, but Isla couldn't bear to be near Nene for a moment longer. No wonder she had been stand-offish and suspicious. Isla's heart lurched. Nene must have been assigned, as Keiichirō and Kana had, to look out for her, as she would be considered an extension of Keiichirō's family.

None of them would have wanted to be involved but, once they had been instructed to take care of her, they had all made sure to do their duty.

Stupid, Isla berated herself, and so humiliating, too.

She sighed. She was so tired of it all. Being in Satsuma in the wrong time, feeling as if she had no purpose, being shunned and distrusted everywhere and by everyone simply for being a gaijin. It was a world she didn't understand and didn't seem to make headway in. And she had had enough of it.

Would going with the Dutch traders help her situation or would it be a mistake? Who knew. But it probably wasn't going to make anything worse.

Isla glanced behind to see if anybody had followed.

She wasn't looking where she was going, and bumped into someone. She stumbled back from the solid figure with a short gasp. 'I'm so sorry. Please excuse me,' she said quickly.

As she spoke, she realised she had walked straight into Takamori Saigō as he stood on the riverbank. Heat crept up Isla's neck as she stared at Kagoshima's most famous historical figure, his thick eyebrows raised slightly in surprise. This was her second time meeting him, and she felt just as much awe at simply being in his presence.

'Get away from Saigō-sama, gaijin,' snarled a bearded man Isla recognised as Shinpachi Murata, the man Taguchi had reported her to. He didn't seem to care that they'd spoken before, and he kept on shielding his leader with a narrow, suspicious glare. Saigō was surrounded by several important-looking samurai, all in regal wear and with their katana swords at their left hips.

'It's all right, Murata-san.' Saigō seemed friendly enough, as he said then, 'Well, MacKenzie-san, have you decided whether you'd like to join the Dutch traders?' They'll be leaving soon and I was about to send for you.'

Isla was touched by Saigō speaking slowly so that she could understand without trouble.

She told him, her eyes downcast, 'I have, Saigō-sama. I've decided to go with them. I must thank you for your hospitality.'

'Very well, *oneesan*.' Saigō used the term for 'young woman', and she appreciated the effort he was making. 'Do you have everything?' he added.

'Not yet, Saigō-sama. I was on my way to collect what I need.'

The whole group of samurai accompanied her, in a silence that felt serious, to Keiichirō's house, where Isla hoped he wasn't waiting. Thankfully, he wasn't.

She slid open the door to her room and discovered the futon was more neatly made than she had left it, with her towel folded tidily on top. Kana may not be married, but she certainly acted like a housewife, and Isla thought that she would no doubt be another person glad to see the back of her.

Kana came up to the house with a basket in her arms, her daughter Yura tottering behind her. She gasped at the sight of the samurai, the basket slipping from her fingers. She prostrated herself on the ground, bowing to them all.

'Maeda-san, we shan't keep you,' said Saigō as Isla came outside with her wallet and her flip phone tucked into the pockets of her running leggings, and wearing her trainers. Yura, oblivious to her mother's bowing, ran over and wrapped her pudgy arms around Isla's leg.

Isla was touched by the little girl's affection. She knelt to her level and gave her a hug.

'Goodbye, little one. And thank you, Kana,' she said. Kana gave her a stiff nod.

'I'm ready,' Isla announced to the samurai.

The carriage smelled of sweat and horses; the traders spoke in rapid Dutch as they threw curious glances at Isla. One, who had a tooth missing, sat beside her on the wagon. Isla thought he was probably no more than fourteen years old.

'Hello,' he said in English.

It had been so long since Isla heard her native language that for a moment it didn't register.

'Hello,' she answered eventually, and heard the relief in her own voice. 'You speak English?'

'A little.'

The sun was setting as they clopped along the road that carried them through the outskirts of the town of Kagoshima.

Isla let her anger fuel her against any fears she had about the future. Keiichirō had said nothing about his engagement to Nene. She had thought they'd shared a moment. Several moments. Had it meant nothing?

The town was bathed in orange light, making it look almost a dreamscape. Mount Sakurajima stood proud and high to one side of the carriage, a silent guardian over the town. Lanterns glowed, the darkening water beyond scattered with boats.

Isla pushed the complicated feelings she had about Keiichirō out of her mind and straightened. *Boats.*

'What's the date?' she asked the boy.

'Today? It's the twenty-ninth of January.'

A memory stirred, and then she felt a shiver down her spine.

For, at the end of the month, the Japanese government would send a naval ship to confiscate the Shimazu clan's weapons and ammunition. She had seen a display about this in the museum.

Why hadn't she thought of this earlier, or its significance? She'd been so fixated on the year, and getting home, that she hadn't thought deeply enough about what happened in the January of that year. There'd been so much to take in that was new and disorientating, and of course she'd spent time with Keiichirō. Her mind had been occupied with other, more personal thoughts.

What if this was why she found herself now here? Was it possible that it wasn't a coincidence that she'd arrived weeks before the beginning of the infamous Satsuma Rebellion, the war that would ultimately end the way of the samurai forever?

This town, the people she had got to know, the hard-working men who worked and lived here, who carried swords at their hips. By September, they'd all be dead. And where would that leave the women she had come to know as she toiled alongside them in recent weeks? How many of them would lose brothers, husbands, sons?

But none of this had happened yet.

And in a surging beat of her heart Isla knew what she must do.

She stood up and rudely pushed past the boy sitting next to her.

'Where are you going? Miss!' he shouted in English as Isla jumped from the carriage, landing in the dirt, and the carriage abruptly came to a halt.

'I changed my mind!' she shouted over her shoulder as she began to race back the way they had just come.

The town lit up at the bottom of the hill, flanked by forests. She ran, trainers pounding on the road, freezing air in her lungs. She had to warn the samurai that the imperial soldiers were mustering. The event that kicked off the whole war might be turned around if she could get them to move the weapons before they could be stolen. With more weapons and ammunition, was there a chance the tide of fortune could be skewed in their favour?

'MacKenzie-san?' said a voice, and she skidded to a halt. It was Keiichirō's friend, the tall one. 'Mori Toramasa.' He patted his chest as he reminded her of his name.

'I need to speak to Keiichirō,' she said, 'it's urgent.'

He was the most likely person in Kagoshima to believe her.

Toramasa nodded and said he would find him. Isla was to wait where she was.

Isla paced anxiously in the gathering dark. Then there were quick footsteps and at last Keiichirō was there, his chest heaving, his eyes strangely wide.

'We need to talk,' said Isla.

'Is this about Nakamura Nene?' Keiichirō asked, his voice low.

'It's not, but we need somewhere private to talk.'

They headed to the harbour, where Mount Sakurajima was barely visible, merely a black silhouette against the sky now.

'I'm glad you came back,' said Keiichirō. 'I don't trust those traders, or like the idea of you on a ship alone with a bunch of barbarians.'

Isla bristled. 'I've come back to warn you. The imperial army are on their way to steal Satsuma weapons.' She said it all in one breath, before Keiichirō could interrupt her.

'Eh?' He frowned in disbelief.

'There's a ship on its way right now!' she almost shouted.

'How do you know?' he asked.

Isla had hoped this question wouldn't come up so soon, but she should have known it was obvious it would. 'If I told you, you wouldn't believe me,' she said after a pause. 'Just trust me, please.'

Keiichirō was looking, transfixed, over her shoulder.

Isla turned towards the water, and as if she had magicked it, there was a ship emerging out of the shadow of the volcano. Isla's pulse raced. This was really happening.

'There's no time,' she screamed. 'That's them!'

*

Keiichirō ran through the darkness until he found the Mori household. Toramasa lived with his elderly mother on a quiet street on the east side of the town.

'Mori-san!'

The lined face of Toramasa's mother looked out of a window, accompanied by the scent of yuzu fruits. 'Maeda-san? What is it?'

'Toramasa must come,' Keiichirō cried. 'We have intruders!'

Next he ran and hammered on his cousin Tatsuzō's door. At the word 'intruder', his cousin made haste. It wasn't long before they had rallied all their *shi-gakkō* friends, and they dispersed to other homes to fetch them.

Full darkness had fallen by the time they ran to the bay and the ominous ship.

'They're taking our weapons,' Toramasa whispered.

As they watched, men carried boxes to small craft tied up on the quay while the ship waited in deeper water and a hissed voice ordered the thieves to go faster. The thieves wore Western-style uniforms, their hair cut short and moustaches oiled.

Traitors. Instruments of the Western invasion.

As the samurai had hastened to the harbour, they had agreed not to spill blood. If they did, it would be seen as provocation of war.

Instead, they'd gathered whatever they could find – bamboo swords and sticks used for training, cooking utensils. Weapons to hurt, but not to kill. Their classmate Murakami wielded an enormous mallet used for pounding rice into *mochi* cakes.

More and more samurai appeared, over a dozen, then fifty or more, moving as silently as shadows, and carefully they all surrounded the oblivious thieves.

Even those who had caught wind of the attack but who didn't belong to the academies wanted to help, and came with improvised weapons of their own, and nobody stopped them.

'Now!' Keiichirō said, and the samurai rose as one. Shouting like maddened dogs, they burst from the shadows, waving weapons above their heads.

The looters started, eyes widening in terror as the might of the Satsuma samurai encircled them.

Toramasa smacked a thief on the back with a bokken stick. Shouts and screams from both sides filled the air as Tatsuzō yelled, 'This is Saigō-sama's property!'

One soldier pulled out a sword, sliding into a fighting stance to spill blood. Murakami tackled him to the ground. They struggled for a moment, until Murakami overpowered him and hauled him to his feet by the scruff of his neck.

Keiichirō revelled in the chaos of their counter-attack, thinking how easily spooked were the men of the imperial army who had ambushed Kagoshima in the night. Boxes thudded to the ground, a welcome sound.

'This is government property!' one of the imperial soldiers spluttered. But the others fled, clambering into their rowing boats, now cleared of their booty, and making haste back to the ship.

'Not so brave or so clever now, *ne?*' shouted Keiichirō to their retreating backs.

'Nakahara!' Toramasa raged as he realised he was grappling with one of their own, moonlight illuminating his face. 'Traitor!'

Murakami gave Nakahara Hisao a violent shake as he pulled him away from Toramasa, and took his swords away. 'You're coming with us. You will have to explain your actions, the actions not worthy of a Satsuma samurai.'

Nakahara Hisao began to beg for leniency, saying he had made a terrible mistake but he hadn't meant to do anything wrong. The men roared at him, disgusted by his cowardice.

'Where are Beppu-san and Kirino-san?' Murakami barked. 'Tell them we've caught a spy.'

Once it had quietened down, the samurai did an inventory of the Satsuma arsenal. The building had been forced open, and crates and boxes were missing, grooves in the dirt where they'd been dragged out in haste.

Even though Keiichirō and the others had fought bravely, over half of their weapons and supplies were gone.

Keiichirō glanced up the hill to where Isla was hidden. She had warned him of this, and at this moment he didn't care how she knew. Thanks to her, he thought, they had saved half of their supplies.

*

Far above Keiichirō, Isla crouched in a secluded spot where the vegetation gave her good cover as she watched the action unfold.

As she'd seen in the museum, hundreds of samurai had descended upon the imperial thieves, creating a racket and scaring the soldiers away.

It had happened exactly like the history books promised, with hundreds of samurai preventing the imperial navy stealing from the weapons depot.

What happened next? Isla wished she knew more about this. She'd been so engrossed in finding information about her third-great-grandfather that she hadn't paid enough attention, and she felt that, in this, she had failed the Satsuma samurai.

CHAPTER 11

'Wake up.'

Nakahara, his hands tied behind him with rope, coughed and spluttered as ice-cold water startled him back to consciousness.

Kono, a student in his middle years, stood breathing hard with the now empty bucket in his hands.

Nakahara hung his head in hopeless acceptance.

Disgust shot through Keiichirō, disgust with both himself and his fellow samurai. Nobody had seen what should have been obvious in their fellow team member.

Now it seemed the fact that Nakahara often wrote letters should have aroused suspicions. He must have been reporting back detailed facts about the Satsuma samurai to his superiors in Tokyo, the eastern capital.

But although Keiichirō hated this, what he hated even more was that there was no fight in the spy, not a single spark. As Nakahara Hisao looked at him with meek acquiescence, all Keiichirō could see before him was a detestable coward.

It was almost morning when the screams stopped. Kono's knuckles were bloody and he had tried every trick he knew to make their captive speak.

So far Nakahara Hisao had confessed that, as they had already surmised, the imperial navy had come to take the Satsuma weapons to Osaka, a city nine hundred kilometres away. But he refused to be drawn on what the purpose of this manoeuvre might be, or whether it was the start of an offensive designed to cripple the samurai's power further.

Kono emerged from the house, squinting as though he had never encountered sunlight before. Dried droplets of blood lay browning on his kimono.

'Any news, Kono-san?' Keiichirō straightened from the beam he'd been leaning against.

'It looks as if there are many more spies in the school. Maybe as many as fifty,' said Kono.

'Fifty!' exclaimed Keiichirō. How would they find out who they were?

'He'll talk.' Kono flexed his fingers, and stared at the drying blood, flakes of rust-red fluttering to the ground. 'He *will* speak.'

Another scream from behind Kono made Keiichirō want to flinch, but he made himself stand strong. 'I must tell Beppu-san what's happened here.'

Beppu Shinsuke was a close friend of Saigō-sama. Sharp-faced with a goatee, he radiated power.

After Keiichirō's report, he burst into the prison where they kept the spies and knelt by Nakahara. His voice was gentle. 'Tell us why you were here. What you want. If you do, I'll tend to your wounds.'

Keiichirō, looking from the doorway, forced himself not to look away. The place stank of sweat and blood. Nakahara sat slumped, hair hanging over his face. The ropes around his wrists were dyed with old blood, his face bruised, tear tracks running through the dirt on his cheeks.

Beppu-san's soft-spoken words were more threatening than those of his torturers. Nakahara began to sob like a child, his body shaking. It was uncomfortable to watch, like beholding something ugly, naked, too intimate and shaming. Finally, Nakahara whispered, 'We were sent to assassinate Saigō Takamori.'

This was bolder and more shocking than anyone had expected. The words struck Keiichirō like a slap. Beppu-san's shoulders tensed. Keiichirō wondered if he might strike the young man, or perhaps unsheathe his katana sword and behead him.

'I see.' The older samurai gained his feet. 'You have infiltrated our community, spied on our people, and insulted us to the vilest degree.'

Keiichirō realised the full implication of Nakahara's dreadful confession, and it wasn't good in any way. His stomach roiled to know that innocently he had spent many, many days alongside spies in the *shi-gakkō*, the academies Saigō-sama had built to give the young samurai something to do, something to live for.

Now, however, it was clear that not only did the new government despise Satsuma being independent and want to crush their spirit, but they wanted Saigō-sama dead, and all his followers. Everything Saigō-sama had done, supporting and fighting for the emperor and helping to bring him to power, was not enough. All his honourable actions had done was to convince the emperor that he, and all that he stood for, must be eradicated. Permanently.

It was an insult of the highest degree, Keiichirō thought. The imperial army wanted the last of the samurai dead and gone, starting with their great leader.

'Maeda, fetch the foreigner,' said Beppu-san.

It was as if Beppu-san had stolen Keiichirō's very worst thought. With the reality of spies being in their midst, Isla was now in the gravest danger.

Beppu-san's words made Keiichirō go cold, but as a dutiful samurai he had to obey.

Feeling a traitor, he found Isla on top of the hill, dozing propped against a tree. She was waiting for him just as he had told her to do.

Keiichirō told her quickly the events of the night, and Nakahara's claims, and that Beppu-san had demanded to see her.

Isla looked at him, and he could see she'd grasped the precarious situation she was in. And then she rose to her feet, exhaustion tightening her face, and with shoulders squared she followed him without a word. Keiichirō felt a rush of pride.

Keiichirō took her to Beppu-san in the interrogation chamber. The older man grabbed her by the arm, making her gasp. A sharp intake of breath escaped Keiichirō at Beppu-san's roughness, and Beppu-san and Isla both looked at him.

Keiichirō wilted beneath Beppu-san's glare, and bowed his head in apology. He hated himself for doing so, but this was what the code of the samurai demanded.

'Do you know this woman?' Beppu-san asked, thrusting Isla before Nakahara.

Nakahara lifted a bloody head, and Keiichirō saw Isla wince at the sight of his wounds. 'It's the foreign girl who came to Satsuma,' said the spy, his voice croaky.

'Did she help you deliver letters? Is she a fellow spy?'

Silence. Then Nakahara grunted a no.

'Tell the truth. We'll find out if you don't.'

'I don't know her!' Nakahara shouted, and he struggled against his bonds. 'We are a league of police officers from Tokyo. Kagoshima is my hometown, that's why I was chosen. That foreign woman has nothing to do with it. As far as I know – I never heard mention of her. Why would the emperor use a gaijin? And a woman? It makes no sense.'

Beppu-san stepped close to Nakahara, dragging Isla with him, and spent a long time looking intently from Nakahara to Isla and back again.

At last, Beppu-san released Isla's arm and pushed her roughly away in dismissal.

Rubbing her wrist, she ran past Keiichirō and out of the interrogation chamber. Keiichirō released a slow breath.

He had been sure that Isla was not a spy or an enemy of Satsuma. After all, it was she who had alerted him to the advancing army. If it weren't for her, they would have lost many more weapons in the fight.

But this wouldn't have mattered if Beppu-san had believed she was, and Keiichirō hated to think of the consequences if that had been the case. To see Nakahara deny her involvement, too, so fervently, insisting that Isla was not part of a Tokyo master plan, brought a wonderful sense of relief. 'May I be excused, sir?'

Beppu-san waved Keiichirō away, his eyes fixed on Nakahara, who hung his head in acceptance of the fate that awaited him, his certain death.

Keiichirō breathed deeply outside in the crisp morning air, glad to clear his lungs of the fetid atmosphere he'd just been in.

He saw Isla standing between some houses, arms wrapped around herself. 'You must be cold. You didn't have to wait all night.'

'I did what you asked of me.' Isla's voice was serious. She glanced towards the bay and suppressed a shiver.

'We need something to eat. Kana will feed us,' said Keiichirō. And together they walked to his house, Keiichirō making sure Isla walked at his side and not behind.

*

Toramasa's face shone with excitement as Ikeda stood at his side. They had mapped out known locations of government arsenals, and a main one was the Somuta arsenal. 'Let's go in there and take everything we can,' Toramasa said.

'They took our stipends, our power, and now they try to cripple us from the inside,' said Ikeda, his long fingers spread on the map before them.

Over a thousand *shi-gakkō* students were angry. Their great leader had been insulted, and they hated the depletion of their weapon stores.

Though the young samurai were fierce and brave, their response wasn't a coordinated attack. However, by sunset they had retrieved spoils from the imperial arsenals, some young boys and women having joined the samurai in this offensive.

'Look at this!' Toramasa jeered at the end of the day, holding up an enormous rifle almost longer than he was tall. Kono stood beside him, his own gun in his hand.

And the samurai shouted and cheered as they paraded their spoils around the town for everyone to see, the Satsuma police turning a blind eye, hiding smiles behind hands.

*

Keiichirō, Toramasa, Tatsuzō, Ikeda, Murakami and the other samurai were summoned to the school three days later, on a cold February morning. Despite his friends at his side, Keiichirō felt a flicker of nerves as they gathered in the lobby, everyone sitting straight-backed beneath the wooden beams that held up the building as they settled themselves onto faded tatami mats.

Saigō-sama had not joined them in their strategic responses.

Now Keiichirō thought over what had happened in the past couple of days, he felt concerned. Everything had occurred so quickly and there hadn't been enough time to think things through and weigh up their actions. But had anyone actually asked for Saigō-sama's thoughts before repelling the invaders, and then stealing imperial-owned weapons and ammunition from the depots? Keiichirō thought not, and he didn't like that the samurai hadn't behaved in the proper way and respected the opinions and guidance of authority.

A hush fell over the young men as the door opened and Saigō-sama stepped before them, his face showing none of his usual gentle charm.

Keiichirō swallowed, feeling like there was a pebble in his throat. Did that mean he was against them? Was he angry at their behaviour? Their parades around town with the stolen weapons and ammunition now seemed tawdry and unbecoming.

Beppu-san followed Saigō-sama. Standing together, they looked awe-inspiring and fearsome, worthy leaders of all the Satsuma samurai.

If he and the others were about to be punished for their hasty actions, thought Keiichirō, they would have deserved it. The two men before them would have carefully considered their position.

'Men of Satsuma,' Saigō announced, his voice a deep rumble. 'I cannot fight against the emperor.'

At this unexpected beginning, Keiichirō felt the creep of unease spread across those seated alongside him.

Saigō-sama paused to let the samurai think about what he had just said.

'It is not the emperor who is our enemy,' said Beppu-san after Keiichirō's ears had almost begun to hurt, the silence having become so intense. 'It is the corrupt Tokyo government. Is that not so?'

The room came alive. Keiichirō's shouts joined those of his peers. 'Yes!' they bellowed. 'That's right!'

It was the government, the men behind the figurehead, who had pulled the strings of power. Someone in the government had sent the spies, not the emperor. He, no doubt, still held great respect for Saigō-sama.

Several more people entered the room and stood behind the speakers. Some wore kimonos but others were clad in their imperial army uniforms from the days when they had fought for the emperor.

'We should raise an army of our own,' somebody called. 'Make the government answer for their assassination attempt.'

The samurai looked at each other, excitement crackling between them.

Wasn't this what they had been training for?

'Our response needs to be clever and well thought through. If we raise an army now, there will be war,' said Beppu-san in a strong voice designed to quell the rising emotions in the room. 'We should go with a few people only, and we must think with our heads and not our emotions. We need wise and experienced men, such as Kirino-san, to lead us to diplomacy.' He acknowledged Kirino-san with a respectful bow of his head, and the other man bowed back.

'You are naive,' barked a clean-shaven, balding man in a kimono. 'What if they send more soldiers and capture Saigō-sama? We'd be falling right into their trap! I say we strike now and drive out the corruption!'

Murata-san watched on in silence, his face troubled.

The men stood in a group, their voices rising as they quarrelled. Keiichirō looked between them. Would they go to war? Would they emerge triumphant? Could they even hope to face the imperial army? Other samurai called out their opinions, although Keiichirō didn't add to the debate.

'We should follow the sea route and land on Tokyo's shores. Take them by surprise.'

'The whole city of Tokyo taken by surprise by us? Don't be a fool.'

'We could raise an army from across various strongholds. We have allies all over Kyushu.'

'There's no time for that.'

'So we have to rely on luck instead? That is not the samurai way.'

Saigō-sama took a pace forward and, one by one, his men fell silent.

Keiichirō swallowed, watching his superiors. Whatever Saigō-sama decided, they would follow.

'You all feel strongly about this, I can see. And so, if you will it, I will pledge my life to this cause,' Saigō-sama said, and a loud cheer rose.

That's settled, then, thought Keiichirō, who'd abstained from cheering. Diplomacy as a first approach had been tossed aside, and now it seemed they had just voted to go straight to war, and the imperial government would answer for their crimes through violence.

As he looked around at the committed faces of his dear friends, Keiichirō wondered why he wasn't sharing the sense of glee rapidly washing through the room.

*

News of the impending war spread through Kagoshima in mere hours. The corrupt new government must answer for its crimes, was the rallying cry. These crimes were plotting their leader Saigō-sama's death, infiltrating their *shi-gakkō* with spies, and stealing the Satsuma weapons under the guise of saying this was on the emperor's orders. Everyone seemed to be uniting to the samurai cause.

'How did you know?'

'Know what?' Isla said carefully.

'How did you foretell that the imperial soldiers were coming?' Nene pressed.

Isla shifted, uncomfortable. They were working in a field today, the winter sun strong in the clear sky. She turned from Nene and raked at random, not answering. She heard the other girl sigh crossly.

A cold shiver that had nothing to do with the weather ran through Isla. History was unfolding before her eyes. She had just borne witness that the devastating Satsuma Rebellion had begun.

Had she changed anything by making sure Keiichirō saw the approaching thieves, or would things have worked out this way anyway? If the soldiers had never been discovered, would things be different?

She had no way of knowing.

These people she now knew would be dead in a few short months. Toramasa Mori. Uhei Ikeda. Keiichirō Maeda.

There's a reason I came here. I know it. Now I just need to find what that reason is, Isla told herself.

Nene gave another huff of displeasure at her silence and stomped away.

Isla, now working with the unmarried women once more, was given another sack of food for her work, and this she gladly handed over to Kana. She couldn't conjure the words to apologise for having returned, so she simply bowed and went to her room.

She thought about Takamori Saigō's plan, which was still to march to Tokyo to speak to the emperor.

If history was to run its course, as she had read about what was going to happen, Takamori Saigō would never make it within a hundred miles of the capital. Isla had hoped that warning Keiichirō would have altered things, but clearly not.

She went to the river as the sun was setting, wishing she'd never come to Japan in the first place.

The falling-out with Will as their relationship crashed and burned, Isla would have got over in time if she had stayed in Scotland – he just wasn't worth the problems she had faced since they broke up.

And no matter how curious she had been about her own Japanese ancestry, she'd pretty much been a failure at finding out about this, and in any case the knowledge she had gleaned in no way made up for the pain and anxiety she had experienced in these unsettled times as the Satsuma samurai readied for war. She was hungry nearly all of the time – not that she was ungrateful to Kana and the others – and she was unhappy and unsettled. She didn't belong, even if there were things about this place she liked. Or, more exactly, people she liked.

As her thoughts turned to Keiichirō, Isla recognised his footsteps approaching in that frustratingly calm way of his. When he came to her side, she didn't look at him. She wanted to be stoical, to hide her feelings like he did so easily. But she was not him. She was impatient, passionate Isla.

'Why didn't you tell me about Nene?' Hating her weakness, she turned to look up at him.

'Nakamura Nene and I got engaged because our parents wanted us to,' he answered. 'I care about her as a friend. Our mothers were close, you see, and as Nene doesn't have any brothers or sisters she played with me and Kana a lot when we were small, and so the promise to each other didn't seem onerous.'

Keiichirō sighed. He looked to the sky, almost as if he was forcing himself to swallow his emotions. 'Father's death changed things then, and I felt differently about Nene, not as certain, although I didn't want to dishonour her. Then you arrived, and now she is upset with you, and with me. And I cannot make her feel better.'

Isla crossed her arms against the cold, digesting his words. He seemed to be saying he did have feelings for her, but that it was complicated. Well, complicated was her world now, wasn't it?

'Marrying me would elevate Nene to the status of samurai. Her father is a merchant, traditionally the lowliest class.' He gave a mirthless laugh. 'Her father makes more money than I do. I couldn't protect my mother from her illness, my father from his actions or my sister from being hurt,' he said, and Isla understood why he felt as he did.

Who was she to even for a second think about standing in the way of another woman's happiness – especially as, the moment she found a way to get back to her life in 2005, she'd take it at once?

Isla looked at Keiichirō. He was studying his sword, stroking the handle with his thumb, the tassel snaking through his fingers. 'I know that Nene would be better off marrying someone else, someone who loves her in all the ways that I never can, but she cares for me, and I can't bear the thought of hurting her.'

Something lurched deep within Isla as Keiichirō took her hand. 'I'm so sorry, Isla, if I hurt you,' he said, but she didn't hear. Her skin tingled where he touched her, her heart singing.

He stepped closer to her and, while she yearned for him to kiss her, she saw the white crest of the Shimazu clan stitched on his jacket at eye level, a sobering reminder of who he was. Where they were, and who she was, too. She stepped back and turned away from him.

They wandered the small garden, finding quiet sanctuary behind the house. No one was here but them and the skeletal trees.

'I was with someone I thought I loved very much,' Isla said softly, keeping her gaze on the crest on Keiichirō's *haori* jacket. 'I trusted him with everything I had. I thought we'd get married, have kids, all that stuff. We spent a lot of time together. He met my parents, and my friends.' Her chest tightened at the memory, but Keiichirō was here, he was warm and real, and in that moment she wanted to be vulnerable, for him to know. 'He was a student, a bit like you, Keiichirō.' She remembered Will's face: industrious as he studied for his PhD, handsome, friendly and trustable. 'But I was mistaken. And I found out I wasn't the only woman he was seeing – it shattered my world, and I felt so used.'

Keiichirō sighed. Then, despite their best intentions, Isla allowed herself to be pulled into a hug.

Isla relaxed against a chest that smelled of incense and cedarwood, of male strength. As Keiichirō's cheek pressed against the top of her head, all thoughts of Nene vanished, and she hugged him back.

It felt so long since anyone had hugged her, she had almost forgotten what it was like. When had the last time been? Hugging Mum goodbye at the airport months ago? She sighed against him, enjoying his warmth, his silent strength. Her heartbeat slowed, calm stealing over her as they stood among leaves blowing on the grass. She didn't want this to end.

But he pulled back eventually, his palm cupping her face. Isla sniffled, hoping he didn't want to kiss her and at the same time hoping he would. She looked at his full lips, at the little freckle near his mouth, and anticipation stole her breath. But he simply said, 'We're getting ready to leave. But before I go to help the others, may I ask how you knew the boats would come?'

Isla closed her eyes, but she owed him an answer.

'I can't explain in a way you can understand, Kei. But I know what will happen,' she said after a lot of consideration. 'This is a war you can't win.'

*

Keiichirō thought sadly that Isla may well be telling the truth. Certainly, it seemed that she felt she was saying to him what she believed would happen, and he didn't particularly care now how she had come by this opinion. The way she had spoken told him she was on his side, the side of the samurai, and that was all he needed to know.

'Whoever sent those men did not do that in support of the emperor or at his request. We have to trust our decision that he will listen to Saigō-sama when he hears the truth,' said Keiichirō.

Solemnly, they looked at each other, each aware of the other's position.

'You're still going to go with Saigō-sama to Tokyo,' said Isla. It wasn't a question. She knew enough now about the samurai to understand how they thought, and that promises and honour were everything.

'Yes, soon. It's thanks to Saigō-sama that the samurai have any sort of life left here. My father fought at his side, and it is an honour for me to be asked to go to Tokyo to help him.'

*

It felt like almost everyone resident in the Satsuma province wanted to follow Takamori Saigō to war. Samurai, farmers, cooks, women, even children. The town was alive with activity as men gathered weapons and spoke in hushed, excited tones about how brave they were going to be. And as preparations were made, the samurai of the *shi-gakkō* walked around with pride, swords at their sides and guns strapped at their backs.

Isla looked on apprehensively. She couldn't let them go. They'd all be dead in a few months, but it wouldn't help them or their cause if she voiced her concerns to anyone else besides Keiichirō.

After it became gossip-fuelled common knowledge that Hisao Nakahara had denied her involvement in any spying, Isla found that she was no longer the centre of attention in the town, and that suited her just fine. Even Nene treated her better.

'I wish we could stop them going,' Isla said to her as they wandered through the now bustling town. 'The imperial army is too strong. I fear they'll be massacred.'

But they couldn't stop an army. Maybe Keiichirō would listen if they pressed him enough, but there was too much passion in the people's hearts to try to convince them not to go to war.

'I don't want them to go, either.' Nene's eyes filled with tears. 'I don't want him to die.'

Isla was squeezed with something that felt suspiciously like jealousy, but she made sure to squash that sensation immediately. She wasn't going to risk upsetting Nene's marriage plans with Keiichirō. It might be an arranged marriage, but it was something Keiichirō felt honour-bound to see through. And this made Isla determined not to do anything that might affect Keiichirō's concentration in the upcoming days. He needed to focus wholly on the task that lay before him in Tokyo. Things were bad enough already without her behaving selfishly.

'At any rate, we can't let them go alone.' The thought of staying here with Kana and waiting for months on end to hear news she already knew sounded beyond terrible. She had an idea. 'Come on, Nene. Let's find Kirino-san.'

Hisa Kirino was gathering women who wanted to join the army. Until then, Isla had thought the men would insist they stay, but, whether that was the case or not, the stern woman didn't seem to care. Isla felt a rush of pride at the sight of them.

They were wearing straw hats and holding halberds and swords, with other weapons thrust through their obi belts. Others sat tying sacks and sharpening swords. The women she saw before her came from all walks of Satsuma life. The unmarried younger women she knew already had been joined by older women, and many with brothers or husbands or sons in the ranks had joined Hisa Kirino's group.

With their hair tied behind them and their wide hakama trousers, it would be difficult to distinguish them from the men, and maybe that was the idea.

'Kirino-san,' said Nene meekly as they approached Toshiaki Kirino's wife. 'We'd like to join you.'

Hisa Kirino's stern gaze swept over them both.

Isla fought a shiver. She always felt like the older woman was X-raying her.

'Are you not in our town under protection, MacKenzie-san?' she said sharply. 'This is not your war, remember.'

Several women turned to stare at Isla. She itched to snatch up a halberd or a sword, to prove to them she belonged here.

Had she not proven herself these past weeks?

Or would she always be a gaijin?

'All hands are needed in this great fight, and we want to help,' Nene persisted, stepping forward. She quailed beneath the older woman's gaze, and her voice trembled, but she kept going, showing a tenacity that impressed Isla. 'We want to help protect Saigō-sama, too. We are all part of the Shimazu clan, aren't we?'

'There is some sense in what you say,' said Hisa Kirino. 'Very well, but don't make me regret this. You may both join the ranks. We will dress as men, otherwise people will try to stop us. They mustn't know we are with them until it's too late for us to be sent back.'

Isla and Nene bowed their thanks, and then they dressed as instructed and found wide-brimmed straw hats to hide their faces. Isla made sure to hide her hair, terrified her red locks would give her away.

Later the women passed where the men were preparing themselves amid the scent of sweat and iron, and unobtrusively prepared themselves for a silent wait until they could join the march to battle.

This is it, thought Isla as Takamori Saigō's best-led battalions got in line to leave for Tokyo. And so we follow.

WAR

To win any battle, you must fight as if you are already dead.

Musashi Miyamoto

CHAPTER 12

The army moved in their platoons out of the town of Kagoshima. Shinsuke Beppu, the man who had been present when Isla first met Takamori Saigō, led the first battalion, thousands of samurai from the *shi-gakkō* following eagerly in his wake. The leaders rode horses, some soldiers holding long banners with the Shimazu clan crest painted in white. Some of the men wore lamellar armour, others thick jackets and wide trousers, swords pushed into sash belts around their waists. The ground almost shook with their synchronised steps, and the atmosphere was alive with a thirst for vengeance against those who had tried to hurt their beloved leader.

The air smelled of horse, too, a nostalgic scent for Isla, who had loved to ride on the Scottish hills, and she inhaled deeply to catch the musty, hay-like aroma beneath the traces of steel, grass and men.

Some of those watching the brave samurai shouted well wishes and cheers of encouragement, although others remained silent with their thoughts.

Shinpachi Murata was the chief of a second battalion. It was surreal, seeing these characters Isla had read about at the Museum of the Meiji Restoration, regal and mighty on their horses, faithful warriors at their backs.

They waited behind Toshiaki Kirino's battalion, and Isla spotted Keiichirō's cousin, Tatsuzō, talking with a woman and a little boy no older than three. 'Come back soon, Daddy,' said his son, and Isla was touched to see that the lad had thrust a tree branch into a sash at his waist, in imitation of his father.

'I will, Jin. And I'll bring you back a present from Kumamoto, all right? Be good and take care of your mother.'

Tatsuzō's wife held his cheeks, scanning his face as though to memorise it. Then her hands fell to her sides. Tatsuzō bowed to his family and turned to join his comrades. What unspoken words crossed between them? Had he said goodbye properly the night before, away from prying eyes?

Tatsuzō Maeda joined his fellow soldiers without looking back at his family. His usually jovial face was serious.

Another small boy, bigger this time, ran after Takamori Saigō, his sandalled feet kicking up dirt and his dog, the same Satsuma inu that had disturbed their meeting, yapping as it ran excitedly beside its young master. A ripple of laughter followed the barking dog and even Nene gave a small giggle of delight.

'Please, Father,' shouted the boy. 'Let me come, too.'

Saigō laughed good-naturedly, patting his little boy on his head. 'One day you'll make a fine samurai, Toratarō.' His hands moved to pet his dog, Tsun. The Satsuma inu's tail wagged so furiously it smacked Toratarō's skinny leg. 'But you can't come with me. You have to stay here and protect your brothers and sister. Can you do that?'

Toratarō stiffened, his little face screwing up with determination. He stood straight and nodded, though his lips were pressed hard together, like he was fighting back tears.

It was too much. Isla had to look away from these sights of goodbyes, tears welling for the families. These poor, dear children would never see their fathers again.

'There's Kirino-san's signal,' whispered Nene. 'We should go.'

The bulky layers of their clothes made them easily able to pass as men. And if any of the men noticed them, they said nothing. Perhaps they recognised the value of as many as possible swelling the ranks.

Isla and Nene carried heavy rifles, though neither of them had swords. Isla had no idea how to use the gun, and, by the way Nene held hers, she didn't either. Some of the men carried large ceramic bottles of *shōchū* to keep up their courage.

The marching pace was fast, and Isla was glad she was so fit these days. Nene struggled more, to judge by her deep breaths, but she never voiced a complaint as the sounds and scents of the town faded and, as one, the army headed purposefully towards the snow-capped horizon.

Isla remembered seeing these hills full of train stations and ryokan inns and roads filled with cars, every hot spring commercialised, every 'secret' spot pictured in magazines. Now, almost a hundred and thirty years earlier, they were wild, full of wolves and boars and more.

Which was better?

Isla couldn't decide.

Snow began to fall after a while, muffling far-off sounds. Isla felt mesmerised by the sound of so many feet crunching on fresh snow, distracting from the cold nipping at her ears and nose. She kept her eyes on Hisa Kirino marching ahead of her.

How many women would die alongside their men? Isla wondered. Would she be one of them? She hoped not, but if that were her destiny then so be it. It was easier to accept when she was surrounded by brave men and women. She had no idea where Keiichirō was, or whether he knew a regiment of women was with the samurai. She wondered whether her ancestor Hisakichi Kuroki was with them, although she had already resigned herself to the thought that she would never find out for sure.

Isla thought back to what she had seen at the museum. She had skimmed over the details of the journey to Kumamoto Castle, not paying attention to the finer details, and this was something she bitterly regretted. They would lose the battle at the castle, that she did remember.

Isla threaded her fingers through Nene's. At first, Nene's hand twitched in hers, like she wanted to pull away. But then Nene's small hand clutched her back, and they found comfort in each other's half-frozen, entwined fingers.

The army advanced north along the shore of Yatsushiro Bay towards Kumamoto, and at last they stopped to make camp for the night.

Isla heard whispers that it was expected they'd have free passage through Kumamoto and across the Shimonoseki Strait. The soldiers were confident in the emperor's honour and that he would grant them passage and listen to what his old friend had to say. Isla wished she didn't know that it wasn't going to work out like that.

'Did your father join the fight?' she asked.

Her lip trembling, Nene shook her head. 'He's a merchant, and I am ashamed that he said he had better things to do. He'll know I came by now. I was so embarrassed by his words I didn't tell him I was going. But he's not a bad man, and I am sorry now I didn't say goodbye.'

Would Nene die here, too? Had her father just lost his only child – his daughter who he would have been so proud to have seen betrothed to a samurai? It all seemed so pointless.

*

Kumamoto Castle was the nearest stronghold of imperial army soldiers, and their first stop before heading to Tokyo. It was controlled by a major general named Tani Tateki. Kono told Keiichirō that he had fought alongside Saigō-sama and Kirino-san only nine years prior. But now Tani Tateki stood against them, side by side with his former enemies.

Many of the soldiers in the castle were from Kumamoto or Satsuma. Would that work in their favour? The samurai following Saigō Takamori dearly hoped so. Surely anyone would side with Saigō's banner, and not the treacherous soldiers influenced by the Westerners and the *shinseifu* government. Or, like Tani, had they turned their backs on their shared history and were now fighting against them?

Keiichirō marched beside Toramasa. His family armour, still at home, was ungainly and rusted. He wouldn't know how to put it on and, besides, the lamellar armour wouldn't be much use against rifles and cannon fire. Most of the men around them, many of them not having samurai ancestry and thus having no armour to inherit, wore thick *nagagi*, warm outer layers of a kimono, hakama trousers and *haori* jackets like the one he had let Isla borrow. He caught sight, however, of some of Beppu's men wearing their armour with pride. The helmets, some with horn-like ornaments to make them appear taller and more threatening, looked heavy and uncomfortable.

Keiichirō had said nothing about the Scottish woman warning him of the imperial soldiers attacking the arsenal.

Too many of those whom Keiichirō knew would be like Taguchi, he feared: resolute in their belief that Isla was a spy, regardless of Nakahara Hisao's vehement assertion that she wasn't.

Would he see her again? He longed to, but he couldn't forget her warning of them losing the war.

Long, rectangular flags bearing the Shimazu clan crest flapped in the wind. Saigō-sama was at the front of the procession, carried on a palanquin. There were rumours of a disease that made it impossible for him to ride a horse. He wore his Western officer uniform, mighty and regal, so that when he met the emperor he would stand before him as a friend and not a rebel.

Toramasa took a hearty swig of *shōchū* and grinned at Keiichirō.

Nakamura Nene's father had filled Keiichirō's jug to the brim, waving away his protests. Keiichirō had grabbed his father's favourite blue *shōchū* cup last-minute as he said goodbye to Kana and Yura. He told himself that, once they had claimed victory at Kumamoto Castle, he would have his first drink of *shōchū* since they had left Kagoshima. Until then, knowing it was in his sack brought Keiichirō a measure of comfort he couldn't quite explain.

CHAPTER 13

Isla's heart beat a frantic rhythm. She marched alongside Nene as they drew closer to Kumamoto Castle.

They would lose this assault, but she had no idea precisely what would happen or on which date.

For days they had marched, stopping in the evening to dig into their rations of sweet potatoes and dried fish before collapsing, exhausted, to sleep. Now, they marched again, north, as more wind and snow pelted them.

The women camped in the middle, surrounded by samurai, farmers and merchants' sons alike. They talked quietly as they cooked above the fires or sparred, the firelight reflecting on their cheekbones and dark eyes. Isla yearned to reach out to someone, to tell them this was folly and they should go home, but she knew nobody would listen. The trust she had gained was far too fragile for anyone to believe her. Well, anyone other than Keiichirō, and he wouldn't say anything for fear of being thought disloyal to a great cause.

She wrung her hands as she sat alone, a chill at her back. What should she do?

The women slept in groups, sheets and spare clothes laid out on the snow, using each other's bodies and the fires for warmth. In the distance, men leaned against trees or rocks, hands on their swords or rifles laid across laps. Isla's legs and feet ached from the non-stop marching, and she grimaced as she massaged her sore calves. Her thoughts strayed to Hisakichi Kuroki. Keiichirō hadn't found any sign of him at the *shi-gakkō*. Maybe he hadn't been a samurai after all.

The second night after they'd left Satsuma, Isla had woken in the pitch black to discover Nene was gone from her side.

'Nene,' she whispered. But she wasn't in her sleeping spot. Fear spiked through Isla. The other women slept around them, their breathing slow, but Nene's blanket was tossed aside. Fresh footprints in the snow led towards a group of trees.

Maybe she should go look for her.

No... She was simply off to empty her bladder, surely. Nene wasn't stupid.

Isla rolled onto her back, looking up at the stars. The snow had settled, a white blanket in the night. It wouldn't be long before they reached Kumamoto and the castle where this regiment of samurai would lose horribly to the imperial soldiers.

She had no idea how to stop it. Samurai *wanted* to die in battle. So long as they thought their cause was just and they did it for their lord, in this case, Takamori Saigō, they were willing to throw their lives away. Thousands of samurai had done it before them.

But none would do it in the future. As of September 1877, the samurai would be no more. The thought was heartbreaking. It was one thing to read about it in a textbook or at a museum, but these people surrounding her were living, breathing soldiers. She talked with them, bathed and ate with them. Was history destined to follow its course? If so, what was the point of her being here? She was as powerless as a leaf being swept along by the river.

Isla listened to the steady breathing of the women around her as she tucked her clasped hands between her thighs, curling into a ball and listening to the quiet pop of the nearby fire. What if she approached Takamori Saigō directly? The museum had said he was *reluctantly* taken out of retirement to lead this rebellion. He had a condition that made it difficult for him to ride a horse, and he was nearing fifty. Surely he would rather be fishing and hunting and spending time with his children than marching through the snow to a war he couldn't win? Surely he didn't really believe he'd reach Tokyo without resistance?

The thought of approaching the leader personally, however, was intimidating. He was an imposing person, of great importance, loved by his followers. Shinpachi Murata had treated her like a dangerous wild animal when she had accidentally bumped into him. The foreign girl, an unwelcome burden who had sneaked to join them, likely wouldn't even be granted an audience. And even if she was, what could she say? 'I'm from the future, your soldiers will lose, and you will die on top of a hill near your hometown in September'?

She'd be ridiculed at best. At worst... well, those were real swords, and many of the older samurai had killed before.

Isla absent-mindedly massaged her neck as she glanced into the darkness, listening to the wind blow the trees. Fires flickered here and there in the camp to keep away wolves and *yōkai*. She imagined what it must be like to believe in fabled creatures like those, to suspect them of lurking in forests and rivers.

What if she approached Keiichirō? Somehow convinced him this was useless? If she could save him…

But there were thousands of people here, and it wouldn't be sensible to go looking at sleeping men's faces hoping to find him. Sighing, she settled to try to get some sleep, but then hurried footsteps reached her.

It was Nene. She lay down, not noticing Isla was awake.

Isla thought about asking her what she had been doing, but it felt too much like prying. Instead, she asked, 'The shrine, the one near Kagoshima. Why is everybody afraid of it?'

'I don't know much about it,' said Nene, 'but it's said that animals are sometimes found dead there. And people who stray inside go missing.'

Missing? Isla's heart flipped.

Could that mean what she hoped?

The next morning Isla felt as if she hadn't slept before the army rose to continue their march north.

They reached Satsuma's castle and bowed at the gates before passing through, but whispers ran through the army that the samurai lord didn't acknowledge them.

Isla kept her head low. Satsuma's feudal lord wasn't fond of foreigners.

Her heart was heavy. Kumamoto would be a disaster, bloody and pointless. But turning back alone was a thought more awful than pressing on.

*

Mid-February, they crossed into Kumamoto Prefecture. Despite the sometimes deep snow, it had taken them only a few days to march from Kagoshima to the town of Kawashiri.

The castle stood above the treeline, regal and elegant above a vast moat. If the rebels gained Kumamoto, all of Kyushu would fall to Satsuma forces.

Keiichirō joined the other samurai lining up cannons outside the castle walls.

'Most of Tani Tateki's soldiers are conscripts,' Kono reminded everyone, face twisted in disgust. 'He fought with Saigō-sama for the emperor, but now he's reduced to leading a pack of weak imperial conscripts. We'll show them a real fight.'

Keiichirō could see his fellow samurai were confident that their might, their warrior blood, would easily flatten the conscripts who'd stayed hidden in the castle as Tani, the major general, had barricaded them all inside, opting to defend the castle rather than meet the samurai in an open field.

Cowards, Keiichirō thought, this is why you are not samurai. Even if it was a smart war tactic.

Kirino-san and Beppu-san patrolled the ranks, telling them they were to stay here until they were given further orders. The leader of the second regiment asked if they had enough food. All the samurai had their own provisions and ammunition, though they were getting plenty of extra food from hunting. Murakami came back one evening with an entire sack of fish from the river, which he shared that evening with his closest friends. They praised their friend and all his ancestors. Tatsuzō spoke of his dreams again, which his friends poked fun at, and they swapped stories of their childhoods. It was almost pleasant.

Before the last of the sunlight died, Keiichirō found Toramasa sitting at the edge of the river, his *kamisori* razor in his hand.

'Unbelievable,' he said, laughing. 'You're shaving at a time like this?'

'Of course.' Toramasa slid the blade gently over his chin. 'Ikeda-san says I look good without facial hair.' He finished and patted his topknot. 'One of us has to keep up appearances. I want to look beautiful even in death.' He waved his razor, looking to Keiichirō, who was sporting a bristly layer of stubble. 'How about it, Maeda? They say I have a feather-like touch. You won't feel a thing.'

'I'll take your word for it.'

Several hours later, when the stars twinkled in the sky, Keiichirō was jerked to consciousness by someone violently shaking him. His fingers closed around the handle of his katana, which was nestled in the crook of his arm as he'd slept against the cold bark of a tree. He gave a start as his eyes opened, but it was only Toramasa, excitement gleaming in his eyes.

'Let's go and see the castle grounds up close.'

Blinking away sleep, Keiichirō rose with a rustle of cloth. He tucked his sword into his belt and followed Toramasa like a shadow in the night. Ikeda, unsurprisingly, joined them, as did Keiichirō's cousin Tatsuzō and their classmate Murakami.

'An army, those in the castle would see coming,' Toramasa said. 'But not a few of us.'

'What are you carrying?' Keiichirō noted the bulging sack at Toramasa's back. 'Where'd you get it?'

'One of the carriages. Hurry up, will you?'

Men slept back-to-back or against rocks or trees. Some were awake, but nobody paid attention to their small group walking past. Others stoked fires or polished their swords.

The stars lit their way, though the castle district was alight with lanterns. Stone walls surrounded sprawling grounds, the castle itself in its centre, glowing with lamplight and its roofs, several storeys high, sloped and elegant. The imperial soldiers stood poised at the gates, ready for any sign of attack. A silhouette of an enemy soldier, armed with a rifle, patrolled the wall.

They waited until he walked away and then sneaked near the moat before the castle wall, keeping low to the grass.

The samurai avoided the main gates guarded by imperial soldiers, and kept to the bushes. Someone's foot hit a stone and it rolled. They froze where they stood in the treeline, hands moving to sword hilts when an imperial soldier glanced in their direction, but only briefly.

They sneaked further around the moat and Keiichirō thought the walls of the castle looked impenetrable, which didn't bode well for the attack the next day.

Toramasa stopped and quietly put down a sack he'd been carrying. He knelt and fiddled with something. It was several feet long and resembled an arrow, except it was much thicker, almost the size of Keiichirō's arm, and it had metal fins.

'*Bō-hiya* I stole from the Somuda arsenal,' boasted Toramasa.

A fire arrow.

Keiichirō watched his best friend in silence as he slid the enormous arrow into the firing mechanism and aimed towards the top of the wall across the moat.

'Wait,' urged Keiichirō, 'shouldn't we use this in the battle? Beppu-san will want to use it.'

Toramasa replied, 'But this is so much more fun.'

'We are not here for fun,' said Keiichirō as Toramasa lit the fuse wrapped around the shaft and pointed it above the wall towards the storehouse.

'That'll make a noise when it goes off,' remarked Ikeda, his voice serene.

'Yes.' Toramasa laughed again. Then his mirth melted away and he suddenly looked alarmed. 'Oh, yeah. You're right.' He bolted from the cannon.

Keiichirō, Tatsuzō and Murakami all glanced at each other, then they ran, too.

They fled deeper into the forest, and there was a boom behind them.

Startled birds took to the air and the samurai heard an angry yell that echoed through the castle grounds.

Keiichirō looked to where they had been to see flames crackling on the other side of the wall, orange reflecting brightly in the moat. The fire arrow had hit a storehouse, and a fire was taking hold.

By the time Keiichirō and his friends reached the top of the hill where their fellow samurai were sitting up and rubbing sleep from their eyes as they wondered what had happened, a whole building was ablaze in the castle grounds.

'Toramasa,' said Keiichirō, 'you might have just turned the odds in our favour. But we can never let anyone else know that we were part of it.'

CHAPTER 14

The next day nobody mentioned the incident, though there were rumours that Kumamoto Castle's storehouse had been damaged, hindering the enemy's food supply. Any praise they might have gained for damaging the enemy's food or ammunition supplies would be overshadowed by the fact they had stepped out of rank and used a weapon that could have been reserved for the army. Not that the *bō-hiya* seemed like much compared to the cannons they rolled up to the castle walls when reinforcements arrived behind them the following morning.

After two days of watching and waiting, the imperial army attacked. Young conscripts in Western clothing opened fire on the samurai after the sun had passed its zenith. They were clumsy with their shots, and the samurai had their own weapons.

Keiichirō used his heavy rifle against soldiers running up the hill, the weapon smoking in his arms as conscripts screamed and fell. It was easy to forget, he found, that they were his kinsman when they were wearing trousers and buttoned jackets, pointing weapons at them. Somebody who looked like a farmer fell three metres to Keiichirō's right with a scream, a hole in his chest. Keiichirō clenched his teeth, willing himself not to look at his fallen comrade.

Never surrender.

An imperial soldier rolled down the hill, navy cap flying off his head before he came to a stop, groaning and bleeding. Keiichirō's gun fired, the explosion rattling his brain as smoke filled his nose.

Never be defeated.

The conscripts' platoon was left scattered and screaming, much to the samurai's delight, and a huge cheer rang out from the men.

'These conscripts don't stand a chance against the samurai!' Kirino-san bellowed, pulling out his katana sword and pointing it into the air. And then others copied him and thrust their own swords into gun smoke and shimmering sunlight that sometimes glinted gold on the blades. 'Let us take the castle and make the emperor listen!' yelled Kirino-san.

Keiichirō's shouts joined the others. Excitement coursed through his blood, victory roaring in his heart. The air around the samurai crackled with confidence and bravado, each remembering their *shi-gakkō* training, each feeling Saigō Takamori's teachings beating in their blood.

A cannon boomed and felled a wall on the outskirts of Kumamoto Castle, bricks and stone crumbling into the moat. The allies tried to force their way into the castle, but conscripts wielding rifles rained shells down on them.

The samurai attacked, many falling in the rain of bullets. Some crawled away or were carried off to be treated for their wounds as more samurai ran to replace them, firing their rifles at the men on the walls. Some screamed, bleeding as they fell into the moat with mighty splashes. The Shimazu clan's supporting cannons fired the castle walls to smoking ruins and many screamed as they died, red spraying as the air filled with the stink of gunpowder and blood.

At last the samurai could force their way into the castle grounds.

Keiichirō took several deep breaths to prepare himself, his rifle in hand, and then joined the others as they ran up stone steps towards the castle.

But something was wrong, and they couldn't breach the castle's entrance.

The charge, so heroic only moments earlier, crashed and burned, and then stopped. There was a yell of retreat, at which Keiichirō looked around for Toramasa and Murakami. Both had been at his side as they'd run up the steps.

Keiichirō's world stopped. It all ended in a brutal flash.

Murakami lay crumpled on the stone steps, a hole blown in his stomach spilling shiny, slippery organs.

Murakami's head lolled to one side as Keiichirō grabbed his nearest arm to try to drag him to safety. Thick blood oozed between teeth broken to bloody stubs. A desperate sound escaped Keiichirō, a howl of despair. He wouldn't be able to save him.

Instead, as the sounds of war and any sense of what the other samurai were doing slipped into nothing, Keiichirō sat down on a step and pulled his friend's head to his lap.

'You have been the bravest of samurai and the best of friends,' Keiichirō told him as he struggled with tears.

Samurai rushed past, some shouting to him to get up, but he barely heard them. Nothing existed now except the dying man cradled in his lap.

Murakami tried to say something but only coughed up more blood. He felt limp in Keiichirō's arms.

'Stop this, Keiichirō. Get up and save yourself,' the dying samurai managed at last, his words coming out alongside popping bubbles of blood.

But Keiichirō didn't move. His vision tunnelled as he held Murakami close. He talked about their childhood and the japes they'd got up to, and then Keiichirō promised he would make sure everyone knew back in Kagoshima that there had never been a braver, better samurai. As he spoke, Murakami gurgled and grew heavy, and Keiichirō looked down to see his friend's eyes glazing over. But although Murakami was dead, Keiichirō didn't leave him.

'Remember how you chased off the soldiers with your *obaachan*'s mochi mallet?' he chuckled, his tears mingling with his friend's spilled life.

It may have been seconds or hours. When Keiichirō came back to himself, almost all his comrades had disappeared in the retreat.

Toramasa was running back for Keiichirō. 'Leave him. It's time to go.'

Toramasa pulled away a blood-soaked Keiichirō from Murakami's corpse and, as they hurried away, a bullet chipped the stone step where Keiichirō had been seated a heartbeat before.

Toramasa panted as they ran to the other samurai, wiping his sweaty brow. 'You idiot! You could've died.'

'But you came back for me,' Keiichirō said, sense finally catching up with his grieving mind. 'I'll never forget it.'

*

Nene whimpered, clutching Isla so tight it hurt.

They had found refuge in a nearby copse of trees when the shooting and cannon fire had begun. Neither of them were fighters or were pretending to be. A wee bit of casual sparring hadn't prepared them for trained soldiers. When Nene had fled into the trees, Isla saw no reason not to follow.

'I hope he isn't hurt,' Nene sobbed.

The shouting and gunshots felt like they lasted a lifetime, but then, unexpectedly, the sounds of fighting faded.

Isla went to the edge of the trees and stared towards the castle.

She wasn't versed in warfare, but she could tell the samurai were in retreat. And she saw, too, that nowhere nearly as many of the samurai were heading back to camp as had set out. Isla's stomach tied in knots. How many had died?

Did Keiichirō live?

Was he hurt?

Had he died?

Nene came to her shoulder and they watched the desperate sight of the blood and faces twisted in pain, and tried not to breathe in the stink that wreathed them, iron and death.

Isla had known people would die, but experiencing it was something else.

She bent over and vomited as her eyes watered. Nene dragged her back and Isla wiped her mouth, trembling.

'Breathe, lass, breathe,' cried Mum's voice in Isla's thoughts, and she did her best to do what her mother would have wanted. She had never missed her mother so much. She felt helpless, devoid of all power and agency. Isla wished she was anywhere but here.

'It's all right,' Nene tried to comfort her, thin arms wrapping around her.

It wasn't all right. Nothing would ever be all right again. But Isla clung to Nene all the same.

The women had stayed on the outskirts of the battle, although Hisa Kirino had joined the fray, wielding her own samurai sword as mightily as her husband did his.

The returning samurai collapsed in exhaustion, and Isla and Nene quietly joined them so that they could tend to the injured.

The conscripts in the castle, knowing they were stronger if they stayed behind the castle walls, hadn't given chase.

Isla's heart jumped when she spotted Keiichirō by a weedy campfire, Toramasa at his side. A smudge of brown-red was across Keiichirō's cheek, a lost look on his face. Isla longed to go to him, but instead she lowered her head beneath her straw hat. She knew her place, and it wasn't at his side. That spot belonged to Nene, who nodded in relief when Isla pointed Keiichirō out.

They found a fire with a stew cooking above it, and silently they busied themselves helping a line-faced man with a bandanna around his head handing out bowls of sweet potatoes and dried seaweed. He barely gave the women a second glance as he worked in silence, his gaze distant. How many friends had he lost today?

'We'll stay here for now,' said Nene as she made sure she and Isla each had a bowl of food, once the samurai had taken their fill. 'There are orders the samurai should wait for reinforcements. I heard someone say there are more loyal fighters on their way.'

Isla let out a shuddering sigh and forced down some food. It was like chewing ash.

That night, Nene pushed her bed beside Isla's and they shared their warmth. As Isla slept she dreamed that cannons fired, men shouted and an army descended faster than a tsunami wave, cutting off limbs and marching through a path of blood. When they came for Isla, fire burst from their mouths.

When she jumped awake, Nene was coming to lie down beside her again, and Isla knew she had been to see Keiichirō.

'Is he okay?' she asked.

Nene nodded, and Isla pulled the blanket over her shoulder as Nene slid back beside her, bringing with her the scent of pine and silk.

As she lay awake and listened to Nene sleep, Isla thought once more of Hisakichi Kuroki and whether he was nearby, perhaps fighting off the cold and the memories from their bloody encounter just as she was. Or could he have perished on the battlefield, leaving a wife and children, Isla's ancestors, waiting for him?

She wanted to ask around but, when she looked at the samurai slumped on the ground, it didn't feel right to disturb their grief.

*

Keiichirō was exhausted, but every time he closed his eyes Murakami's toothless, dead face flashed before him.

Sleep felt nowhere near, so Keiichirō poured clear spirit into his father's beloved *shōchū* cup. He'd been saving his *shōchū* to do this in victory, but now simply dulling his mind was the best he could hope for.

'*Kanpai.*' He raised the cup in a toast to Toramasa, seated beside him, and to Murakami and their other fallen brothers. He raised it to his lips.

He gasped so sharply that several surrounding samurai glanced up, some snatching up their swords. Inside it was an enormous insect with long antennae, six legs and a fat black body. He reflexively slung the cup away. It cracked against a rock and split in two.

Nearby, Taguchi and his friends roared with laughter.

'Cockroach!' Keiichirō's heart pounded.

'*Bakamono*, calm down,' Toramasa said. 'It's winter. There aren't any.'

Of course Toramasa was right. Keiichirō went to his cup and saw someone had *painted* a cockroach inside. He held the pieces in his hands, embarrassment clashing with fury.

Taguchi had a grin Keiichirō didn't like on his face as he munched on an apple.

The broken pieces of his father's cup felt too personal. Keiichirō charged towards Taguchi.

'Don't.' Toramasa grabbed Keiichirō's hakama trouser leg. 'I have a better idea.'

Keiichirō lay awake that night, fighting to keep his temper under control. When everyone except he and Toramasa were asleep, they rose together. Keiichirō clenched his teeth so they wouldn't chatter in the freezing air.

They knew where Taguchi was sleeping.

The lights of the castle walls sat to their left. Tani Tateki's men had finally doused the fire that evening, nearly a quarter of the grounds blackened to ashes. Toramasa gripped his *kamisori* razor as he and Keiichirō crept to where Taguchi lay snoring propped against a large rock, his arms folded across his chest and his head leaning backwards, mouth open.

If someone caught them…

'It's all right. I have a gentle touch, remember.' Toramasa knelt before Taguchi and delicately shaved off half of his precious moustache, drawing back for a few moments when Taguchi's mouth twitched.

Toramasa offered the razor to Keiichirō in silent invitation. He hesitated. It didn't feel right, somehow, after everything that had happened.

Toramasa nodded in understanding, although this didn't stop him for good measure running the blade gently over an eyebrow. Taguchi looked so stupid they had to cover their mouths with their jacket sleeves to keep from laughing.

The next morning, Ikeda came to Toramasa, long hair blowing in the wind as he put it into a hasty topknot, his swords tucked into his belt.

Toramasa put down his bowl at once and bowed in greeting.

'Am I to assume you had something to do with Taguchi-san's new look?' asked Ikeda companionably, taking a seat beside Toramasa and accepting a bowl of fish and sweet potatoes. Keiichirō let out a slow breath; if Ikeda had worked out what had happened, it was likely Taguchi would too.

'See no evil, hear no evil, speak no evil.' Toramasa shovelled food into his mouth as a couple of samurai strolled past, smirking. A young boy who had joined their ranks ran past, giggling and telling everyone who would listen about Taguchi's missing eyebrow and half a moustache.

A half-hour later, Taguchi was stomping around. 'What's everyone laughing about?' he snapped at those who looked at him. 'We're at war, don't you know?'

He went to the riverside to wash and Toramasa held up his fingers in a countdown. A strangled yell made the three of them shout with laughter.

CHAPTER 15

Reinforcements arrived, fresh-faced and bringing food. Toramasa raised his bowl with a cheer. These newcomers looked alert and ready for battle, swelling the forces to a formidable number in the tens of thousands.

Across the camp spirits lifted, and then Saigō-sama addressed them all, his large hands clasped behind the small of his back.

His voice boomed out. 'Do not think that those in the castle are not demoralised by their losses back in the Shinpuren Rebellion! They are mere boys playing at war, and we are Satsuma samurai, the best warriors in the world! The emperor will listen to what I have to say to him.'

Keiichirō's cheers joined the rest. Once they took the castle, the emperor would be forced to listen.

This time the samurai attacked Kumamoto Castle in a pincer movement aimed at the ramparts. Two groups of warriors, rifles and remaining ammunition in hands, descended on the castle grounds.

But the imperial soldiers were waiting for them.

Men ran to their deaths, meeting gunfire from the soldiers waiting at the tops of the walls and inside the surrounding buildings. Wave after wave of samurai attacked the walls, but they were cut down, screaming as they fell, bodies littered with bullet wounds.

Keiichirō watched in horror as friends and classmates died at the walls of the castle, barely able to scramble halfway up, swords in hands, before firearms gunned them down in bloody pieces.

Toramasa jerked his head towards the bridge. 'Over there!'

Keiichirō looked and saw that, across the bridge, the gates were open. Waiting for a delivery of supplies, perhaps.

'They might close them soon. Let's go!' Toramasa shouted, and he, Keiichirō and Ikeda ran in the direction of the bridge.

'We're close to winning! I can feel it,' laughed Toramasa. Being the fastest runner, he was pounding across the bridge in front of the others.

The bridge exploded.

The force of the explosion threw Keiichirō onto his back. The breath was knocked from his lungs.

He lay for a moment in shock, struggling to breathe in as a piercing ring echoed around in his ears. With a tremendous effort, Keiichirō forced himself to roll onto his stomach, pain rippling across his torso, until at long last he took a huge gulp of dusty air.

A cloud of debris had risen, leaving still-fighting samurai as vague shapes. Time slowed. Sounds echoed. Nearby, Keiichirō could see Ikeda mouthing something, terror on his usually calm face. He dragged himself to his feet and looked around for his friend.

Where Toramasa had stood there was nothing but a smear of red. Something thumped beside Keiichirō, and he stared at it, the world falling apart around him.

It was a hand, a hand that was marred with a thin, pink scar from a clumsy sparring session.

Keiichirō lowered to his knees in anguish. Mori Toramasa couldn't be dead.

Sounds were muffled, movements slow. Pain blossomed in Keiichirō, a terrible grief sweeping over him, engulfing him like smoke. In this moment, nothing else mattered.

His best friend was gone.

Dead in a heartbeat.

*

Aghast at the punishment the samurai were taking, Isla headed down the hill, pulled there as if by an inexorable force. She found a dropped sword and picked it up with trembling hands. Heavy and ungainly, it took both her hands to hold it out in front of her. In her reflection, amid the red stains, her skin was pale as the melting snow, grey shadows beneath her eyes.

'It's so pointless,' she whispered as samurai ran for the walls only to be shot down, collapsing like sacks of bricks. The sword wasn't going to help her, and she let it fall.

But she was near to the castle gates now, and she could help the wounded samurai.

Then she stopped and stared.

The man before her was familiar.

She recognised his high cheekbones and his serious expression. Clutching his sword, he turned towards the castle, a fearsome, vengeful expression on his face. He stood there, holding something small. Isla couldn't see what it was.

She could barely square the aggressive set to his stance with the gentle man she had known.

'Keiichirō,' she cried. 'Kei!'

He was going to run to his death.

'No, Kei, don't go!' Isla screamed, and he paused but didn't look in her direction as he allowed what was in his hand to drop to the ground.

She wasn't certain he had heard her plea.

Isla ran past through gunfire, stumbled over a corpse and grabbed Keiichirō's *haori* jacket sleeve. She hung on tight as he took a step forward.

He tried to swat her away, but Isla gave a small shriek as she realised Keiichirō had been holding a *hand*, which was still spilling red as it lay beside them on the ground. A wave of nausea washed over her. She could barely register it enough to wonder whose it was.

Somehow the noise she made seemed to bring him to his senses. Or at least some of them. He still looked crazed.

'Isla?'

Keiichirō stared at her in disbelief. Up close, Isla could see that the sparkle in his eyes she'd liked so much had gone out. His face was grey from shock, with the blood of what Isla hoped was others speckled across it, and his brow embedded with profound lines that hadn't been there when he was back in Kagoshima.

He wasn't pleased to see her or deterred from what he wanted to do, and he tried to shake his arm free, but Isla clung on.

'Let me go,' he shouted, yanking roughly away. 'I've a wrong to right.'

Gone were Keiichirō's good manners, and now all she could see deep in his eyes was a raw and raging fury.

'No, please! Look!' She pointed at the walls, where samurai climbed and were met with bullets and blades. The gunshots popped in the air, Keiichirō's friends and classmates falling like rocks off a crumbling mountain. 'They're all dying, Kei. You'll die, too. Don't go, it's useless, can't you see?'

'I'm not a coward.'

'You're not, but—'

A screech filled the air, a girlish cry that made Isla's blood run cold. They both swung around to see an imperial soldier pointing a smoking gun at Nene, who cowered before him as she begged for her life. The imperial fighter laughed at her.

Keiichirō charged and plunged a blade into the solder's neck. His laughter turned to gurgles, and he fell to the ground with a thud.

Isla helped Nene to her feet. Nene's lip quivered, and she seemed to be in shock.

There was a dull bang behind Isla that made Nene scream. Isla saw a woman lying still in the dirt, her hat nowhere to be seen and half her torso blown away, cascades of her blood pumping into the mud. Nene wriggled away from Isla and collapsed next to the dead girl.

'Aiko-chan!' she sobbed, holding the dead woman to her. 'Aiko-chan!'

Horror filled Isla as she looked at Aiko's face, frozen in shock.

Nearby, a samurai cut down an imperial soldier holding a gun. Isla's insides felt like water; she wanted to collapse and sob, but she forced herself to grab Nene. Nene again wriggled from her arms like a petulant child, clinging to her friend.

'She's gone, Nene. There's nothing you can do.'

Isla pulled Nene away, and then she looked towards where Keiichirō still stood in the rubble of the bridge. He didn't run back to safety but neither did he join his friends who were being cut down.

Smoke burned her throat. Her arms screamed their protest as she pulled Nene along. Tears left tracks down her muck-stained face and her head pounded with the cacophony of war.

No heroics. No romance. They needed to get out of here.

*

Keiichirō's heart thundered like a frantic animal against his ribcage.

Ikeda crouched, his eyes glassy, staring at the place where Toramasa had died. He didn't seem to notice the fighting around him.

'Ikeda!' Keiichirō bellowed, wiping furiously at his burning eyes. 'Fight!'

Ikeda blinked and held up his sword. He ran at some nearby soldiers. Keiichirō ran after Isla and Nene.

'Come with me,' he growled to the women, putting his sword into his belt. 'And stay low.'

Keiichirō swept Nene up in his arms and together he and Isla ran back up the hill to safety.

'Stay here,' he instructed, as he ran back in search of Ikeda.

Isla wrapped her arms around Nene, pulling her close as they sprawled on the ground, Nene barely conscious and

Isla wishing she was likewise senseless, as the hideous sight behind her far surpassed her worst nightmares.

*

The fighting continued into the night, with thousands of shots fired and hundreds injured.

In the early morning, before the first rays of sunlight could kiss the sky, the remaining samurai shivered in the freezing cold. After everything, they had failed to take the castle. They had committed the cardinal sin in warfare of underestimating their opposition. Now they knew the odds were heavily stacked in favour of the conscripts and their general.

Supplies were running low. They couldn't keep wasting resources like this.

'Starve them out,' was the order that swept along the samurai. They dug into the freezing ground, sharing their food and spare clothes among them. They would starve out the soldiers there; force them to leave and then kill or capture any who did.

The samurai could hunt or send for more supplies. So long as they blocked reinforcements to the castle, Tani and his men would be forced out first.

Doubt flickered in Keiichirō's heart. Increasingly, Isla's doom-laden words echoed in his mind.

Don't go. It's useless.

So many of his friends had died. Kono had perished from a gunshot wound. Murakami was gone. And Toramasa – well, the cowards' landmines had made short work of him. It should have been Keiichirō who went there first.

Guilt settled heavy on his shoulders. He should have died along with Kono on the ramparts today. He would have if Isla hadn't stopped him.

But if he had died, then he wouldn't have been able to save Nene.

Both women were still alive somehow, for which he was grateful.

He had found them later, crouched in a ditch, shivering together. And as he looked towards them, Ikeda sat beside him, blood matting his hair to his face. He hadn't said a word since the landmine.

Keiichirō ignored a scratching pain in his arm caused by a bullet grazing him. The muscle burned when he flexed the arm, but he would survive.

'You're alive,' said Tatsuzō, hugging his rifle to his large chest as he sat beside Keiichirō.

'It's good to see you, Tacchan.' Keiichirō had hoped Tatsuzō would make it through the day. He had his family waiting for him back home, little Jin and his pregnant wife, Saki.

The next morning the samurai saw the imperial army had emptied the moat over the course of the night. And now, in the darkness and holding rifles to their chests, the soldiers headed down to get the dead koi carp inside. Guns poked out of every window and hole in the castle walls to cover them, meeting nearby rebels with gunfire. It was infuriating. As much as the samurai hated to admit it, the conscript soldiers with their Western clothing and foreign weapons had proven competent in battle.

'Only because they have a *castle* protecting them,' snarled a samurai when someone mentioned it. 'If this were a fair fight, they'd be flattened. They won't meet us on an open field. At least we burned their storehouse.'

Thanks to Toramasa.

'Saigō-sama is right. We have the castle surrounded. They'll be starved out in no time,' someone said.

'If we don't starve first,' muttered Tatsuzō.

Good news arrived for the battle-weary samurai. The samurai of Kumamoto had pledged to join Saigō Takamori's banner, throwing their support behind the cause and bringing some much-needed ammunition and food.

For the next few days, the samurai tried to breach the walls. Tried, and failed.

It was unknown how much ammunition Tani and his conscripts had left, but it was more than the samurai had. They had brought what they could carry, but they were running out fast. And now the samurai in charge of the battle strategy had begun to squabble.

'Saigō-sama, we must launch a full-scale attack on the castle,' said Kirino-san.

Murata Shinpachi agreed, supporting the idea of an all-out offensive.

'We must attack separately,' countered Nomura. 'A full-scale attack is admirable in theory, but we are more likely to succeed if we split.'

'Remember when we took over the castle in Aizu, Saigō-sama?' Kirino-san asked. 'They lasted a month before they surrendered. We can do it again.'

'This is not Aizu,' said Saigō-sama. 'No two battles are the same. Tani was better prepared. They have more supplies. The imperial army will be gathering reinforcements. We have to intercept. Shinowara-san, take Kirino-san and three thousand men and halt them.'

Keiichirō fought against rising dread at the command.

He would be leaving Isla and Nene behind. He'd not spent time with them since he'd helped them up the hill, as he had had too many other things to attend to. But he had to follow orders and hope the women would remain safe. Kirino-san's wife, Hisa, was protecting them, and she was a force to be reckoned with.

Together, Keiichirō and his cousin Tatsuzō prepared to leave as part of Shinowara's army, like the obedient samurai they were. They marched as instructed, and at night when they hunkered down in camps or trenches, Keiichirō, Tatsuzō and Ikeda talked about their lost friends. The world was a darker place without Murakami's smile, or Toramasa's jokes, or Kono's quiet counsel.

Isla's face swam before Keiichirō in the moments before sleep, and he hoped she and Nene had kept themselves safe. Why had Isla joined the ranks if she was so sure they would lose?

Keiichirō's sleep was fitful, full of memories of himself and Toramasa fishing together, laughing as they ran from the angry farmer, sparring with bokken sticks. When Tatsuzō shook him awake at the break of dawn, he felt he hadn't slept at all.

As the days passed Keiichirō wanted to be angry at the Westerners who'd forced open Japan's doors and instigated the shift of power. But maybe it had always been inevitable.

Now was the time of cannons and guns, not armour and swords.

The men of Satsuma and the imperial conscripts were simply caught in the middle of it, forced to spill each other's blood until there was nothing left but death.

They got used to waiting and, by the time a scout reported a battalion of imperial soldiers two kilometres north who were heading their way, Keiichirō felt defeated – before any combat had begun.

The samurai emerged from the woods to ambush the imperial soldiers. The path ran between two cliffs, the perfect place for an attack. Keiichirō huddled between a rock and a samurai. One glance and he suppressed a groan.

Of the thousands who had come here, the man next to him had to be Taguchi.

'If we're going to die,' whispered the hateful Taguchi, 'I want to clear my brother's name.'

So he had followed him. Keiichirō said nothing, just looking out over the cliff path where the imperial soldiers would come. The grass was cold beneath his prostrate form, and Taguchi's presence was like a bothersome mosquito buzzing around his head.

He kept his rifle pointed at the path. 'Speak, then, before the soldiers arrive.'

'My brother did not rape your sister.'

Keiichirō looked at Taguchi with a longing to ram his sword into the man's pathetic gullet. 'And you know this how?'

'Listen,' said Taguchi. 'Kana panicked when your father confronted her. She was sleeping with my brother willingly. She was sleeping with half the town.'

'Shut up,' Keiichirō snarled, breaking his gaze from the path to glare at the younger man. 'Keep her name out of your filthy mouth.'

'Maeda. Taguchi,' hissed a samurai nearby. 'You're here to fight imperial soldiers, not each other. Concentrate.'

Fury beat in Keiichirō's breast as he forced himself to ignore Taguchi's presence beside him. The early spring air was an icy kiss on his face. His front grew numb as they awaited their enemy.

An hour later the imperial men appeared, the leaders on horseback and wearing hats to stave off the frozen air. They bore banners with the imperial flag, the rising sun with bright red beams against a white background.

No one glanced up to where the waiting samurai hid.

Explosions and smoke burst through the air as the ambush began. Thousands of samurai descended on the battalion, slashing with swords when they got too close for guns.

It felt good to strike back, to let out some of the anger, and Keiichirō felt energised, in large part by Taguchi's words.

It couldn't be true.

Because if it were, his sister was a liar and his father had died for nothing.

CHAPTER 16

Tenderly, Nene helped a man sip some water. He guzzled noisily, not caring or noticing that women were helping him. He shivered, the bandage around his waist stained rust-red.

Sometimes wounded samurai succumbed to the elements in the night. It pained Isla that there was nothing she could do, and she hoped this samurai wasn't one of those. She hated to know that simple antibiotics could save many of them, if only they had already been discovered.

Nene did her best to find natural herbs to dull the pain – she had a real skill in this – but the freezing, still-wintry weather didn't allow many plants to thrive.

Isla couldn't stop thinking about the warmth spring would herald. She was tired of the frost and the cold, of her fingers numbing, of shivering at night as men moaned in pain around her.

She'd never expected that in her life she would see death like this, nor so much of it. It was visceral and repugnant, with none of the glory about it that the poets of yesteryear had so often promised. Death was a sad and lonely thing, one that left a black hole in her soul. To see the shell of a person, to know they once had worries and fears and dreams just as she did, but now to see their flesh brittle and hard, skin grey and their bodies unmoving, had changed her for ever. There was nothing heroic about death in battle.

These days she put all her efforts towards keeping the wounded alive; it felt like the least she could do.

Shouts jerked her out of her thoughts. A pair of samurai, bandannas around their heads stained with splashes of blood and bits of dirt, dragged two men along.

'What are they saying?' Isla asked Nene. This burst of sharp, quick Satsuma dialect was impossible for her to follow.

'They're prisoners,' Nene breathed back, her voice thick. She had been crying, as she did most days, clearly unable to forget the sight of Aiko dying before her.

The men in the samurai's custody wore simple kimonos, not imperial army uniforms.

Nene added, 'I think they sneaked out of the castle and tried to get past the Satsuma patrol.'

One of these men was shaken hard. He gave a sob and answered the question. 'Nunoda is my name.'

'Why have Saigō-sama's letters to the emperor gone unanswered, Nunoda?' shouted the samurai holding him.

'I don't know,' the man cried. 'I'd tell you if I did.'

This protestation of innocence, which looked to Isla very much to be the truth, didn't stem the samurai's anger.

Nene and Isla watched in silence, dull numbness across Isla's chest. The increasing casual and cruel violence was something she could never get used to.

Early the next morning, the sun still only a promise on the horizon behind the trees, Isla awoke to the sight of the two samurai marching past without a second glance, bulging bags tied to their waists.

'Nene?' Isla shook her companion awake and nodded towards the pair.

Sticking out of one of the bags was a tuft of black hair. Isla swallowed, her stomach curdling.

'They must have been spies, or sent out to get reinforcements,' said Nene in a dull voice.

Not long afterwards there was a sudden yell from behind the castle walls, followed by yelps of laughter that sounded closer.

Nene licked her dry lips. 'I think those samurai killed the spies, and then they threw their heads over the ramparts.'

Isla began to rock violently, hands clamped over her ears. She didn't want to hear any more.

Gunfire, sounding close, popped through the air.

Nene screamed and fell onto her back. A samurai ran to them, yelling something, and thrust guns at their chests, forcing them to grab the weapons.

'We have no choice. No hiding now,' said Isla as they rose to their feet.

Nene trembled, the weapon shaking in her hands. They were ushered forward towards the fighting. Adrenalin flared throughout Isla. Death could come for them at any moment but, now push had come to shove, she realised she didn't fear it. There had been so much that was strange in her life since she and Will had separated, and now Isla saw this turmoil had grown in her a strength and a resilience she would never have thought possible.

She stayed firmly at Nene's side, samurai stretching into the distance on either side of them. Nene sniffled quietly, moving forward with the crowd. Isla didn't know who was the most fortunate – Nene, who seemed to care too much about what was going to happen, or herself, who hardly seemed to care at all.

The castle walls loomed before them, the morning fog concealing the soldiers on the ramparts.

'You're firing our own ammunition back at us,' a samurai shouted, holding up a chipped piece of a bullet. 'What's wrong? Are you running out of ammunition as well as food?'

'They're out of bullets?' Nene said as whispers raced around their group. 'Does that mean we're winning? And we'll go home soon?' There was a happy sound in Nene's voice at the mention of home.

Isla stayed silent. Nobody would believe her warnings that this attack was doomed to fail. Samurai surrounded her, their body heat warming her up. The gun remained feeling foreign in her hands.

'How are *your* supplies doing?' a soldier from the inside the castle yelled back. 'We've got more coming from Tokyo. Guns, lots of guns. And more bullets than we can ever need to kill you all.'

'Not if we can help it! Your supplies – those guns and bullets – have to get past us first.'

Another samurai shouted, 'We're going to love turning them on you, as we eat the noodles sent with the weapons.'

Some of the men laughed, and Isla thought she heard a chuckle from behind the rampart. She watched in disbelief. Here they were, trying to kill each other, yet not above an exchange of playful banter.

Nene guessed what Isla was thinking. 'Some of our samurai have cousins or brothers in the imperial army, remember.'

The day's fighting commenced, and soon Nene and Isla were retreating under heavy gunfire. Isla didn't care if people thought them cowards. She had come for Keiichirō, and he had been sent away days ago. And now all she could do was to look out for Nene, his betrothed.

A pained whinny ripped through the air. A horse had been shot, its mouth open in panic, showing the whites of its eyes as it bucked and screamed in pain, red pouring from its side.

'Poor thing,' Isla couldn't help saying. She was fond of horses, and this faithful creature was in pain.

Nene crawled to Isla and wrapped her arms around her. 'I'm tired,' she whimpered. 'I'm scared.'

'I know.' Isla held her and rocked her like she would a sister, wishing she could close off her ears to the sound of the dying horse and dying men.

It was much later when Nene looked up, her eyes red-rimmed. She rose, brushing mud off her *haori* jacket. 'It's dead. Isla-chan, help me.'

'What are you doing?' Isla barely registered that Nene had used the honorific 'chan', for friendship.

Nene took out a dagger from her belt, a wakizashi blade she had taken from a fallen samurai. 'This is meat.'

After what she had seen, Isla never thought she would feel hunger again. But the dizziness and weakness was real, and she knew Nene was doing the right thing.

The horse, its hooves having long stopped kicking in the mud, lay lifeless, the locks of its mane lifting in the wind, black eyes empty, sightless orbs.

'We can prepare dinner with the meat,' said Nene. 'And the bones will make soup. Our warriors will be pleased to eat well.'

Isla didn't understand it at the time, but later it occurred to her that Nene needed to do something productive. Like her, she had come here to try to warn or protect Keiichirō, and they had both likely failed. And she was clearly grieving Aiko, her best friend.

Isla grimaced at the messy work, but what resulted was a meal that fed plenty of samurai. When Nene boiled the bones in water, it made a meaty broth, the taste reminding Isla of a sweeter version of beef. Her need to eat was stronger than her revulsion, and she couldn't help agreeing that it would be a shame to waste it.

*

'Ship incoming!'

Through the haze of torrential rain, a large vessel emerged heading to the shore. Imperial soldiers swarmed towards it like ants from an anthill. Keiichirō set his jaw. His rifle, damaged from water, was useless. He gripped his sword, water dripping from his hair. He couldn't remember the last time he was warm and dry. He could barely feel his toes.

'Defend Miyanohara! Protect the town!' Shinowara bellowed. The samurai yelled in response, a fearless war cry that sent tingles up Keiichirō's back and straightened his spine. Resolve filled him. It wasn't over yet.

Smoke from enemy gunfire thickened the air. A body thumped beside him. Without checking who it was, Keiichirō darted past and slashed at a soldier. He screamed and the gun fell from his grasp as a deadly slash from cheekbone to ribs. Keiichirō snatched up the fallen enemy's rifle and pointed it at a new enemy.

Fresh smoke blinded him as he threw himself to the ground.

'Shinowara-san. Get up!' a voice screamed.

Keiichirō's heart sank. Their leader had fallen.

Death and fighting surrounded him. Keiichirō struggled to reload, and gave a cry when a soldier almost stood on him. He lifted the gun and shot him before he could react, the man collapsing beside him with a ruined chest.

Scrambling to his feet, Keiichirō came face to face with a pinch-faced man wielding a sword. With a growl, Keiichirō threw aside his gun. Even in a matter of life and death, a fair fight was more honourable. He unsheathed his own blade. Theirs met in a fierce shower of sparks, rain and smoke blinding them. The man's eyes narrowed in rage. Keiichirō had the advantage in youth and training, but he was exhausted, hungry and soaked to the bone. His wet clothes made his movements sluggish. The man flicked his blade to the side and Keiichirō narrowly avoided being skewered.

With a snarl, Keiichirō brought down his blade in a sweeping arc, putting all his strength into the blow. His opponent screamed as the sword sliced through his wrist, and his hand fell to the ground with a thump. The soldier groaned, eyes bulging, and held the bleeding stump, backing away into the smoke.

Keiichirō breathed hard, his arms throbbing. This was a nightmare made real.

*

'Nene, you should think about going home. Whatever the samurai do, it will never be enough. You must see that.'

'I can't leave. Not when he's still fighting,' Nene answered. 'If he had died, I would feel it. And I haven't.'

Isla held her close. She was terrified Keiichirō was dead, too. They had to go back to Satsuma, to somewhere. Would the white torii gate ever reappear? Isla had almost given up on going home. When it had rained, she had ventured as far as she dared, hoping to catch a glimpse of the mysterious gate that might take her home... if it wouldn't take her even further into the past.

But she was sure now that the shrine near the town of Kagoshima was the key. That was where it had appeared, so why not again? Isla missed her family more than she could bear. She had seen death, far too much, had slept rough for weeks. She wanted to bathe, to wash the destruction and death she had seen from her body. She wanted to climb out of this hollow pit inside her soul that had made the world lose its colour.

She wanted to see Keiichirō again.

But she was so scared he was dead.

The next morning, Hisa Kirino gathered the women together. 'My husband has sent word he wants us women to retreat,' she called around the group. She stood straight, swords thrust into her obi belt, her face hard as her hair blew in the wind. Mud and blood covered the bandanna around her head and her robe. 'Those who wish to stay are welcome to do this, but there is no shame in returning to Satsuma. We leave in an hour.'

Isla could tell by Nene's quivering lip and crossed arms that she wasn't going back.

'I'll stay with you,' Isla promised.

*

The samurai had no chance. That was clear now.

'Maeda,' called Ikeda, and Keiichirō went to his side. Ikeda had a deep cut to his eyebrow and the rain was keeping the blood flowing down his alabaster cheek. 'They've sounded the retreat.'

Keiichirō hated that they had failed to defend the town of Miyanohara, but the thought of returning to Kumamoto Castle was heartening. He hoped Isla and Nene had made it through all this.

The samurai carried their ruined weapons and made for Kumamoto. The mood was dismal.

'I hope they have better news back at the castle,' said Tatsuzō. 'Saigō-sama will be standing at the ramparts to greet us, the Satsuma banner on a flag blowing in the wind.'

'Yes, and a feast awaiting us,' remarked a man who walked with a limp. 'Grilled fish and hotpot and rice.'

Tatsuzō groaned. 'Stop it! I'm starving.'

Ikeda smiled, but Keiichirō said nothing. Isla's words of failure echoed in his mind. They approached the village of

Uto as the sun was setting, overlooking a valley where several fires burned.

'Imperial soldiers,' whispered around the group.

Kirino-san told them they would attack at night. 'Let's spread confusion in their ranks. We can't kill them all, but if we pick off a few, steal their food, it will damage their morale.'

Keiichirō waited with the others, all sleeping in shifts, until the moon was high in the sky. A wolf howled somewhere. The wind rustled the branches of the trees as the samurai sneaked down the hill in silence, hearts pounding with excitement, inhaling the scent of grass and smoke. Keiichirō beheld a sense of power as they surrounded the unsuspecting camp. From here, he watched a young man polish his gun, still wearing his imperial uniform. A flag with the army emblem, the rising sun, sat at his feet.

As though the samurai were some foreign enemy, not the heart of Japan itself.

They waited longer until the camp was still. Only a few guards stood on duty.

Keiichirō sneaked forward, concealing himself in tall grass. He loathed sneaking about like a spy, but revelled in the mischief. On Kirino-san's signal, he buried his wakizashi blade into a young man's back. He clamped his free hand over his mouth, gently lowering him to the ground.

The sound of slashing swords and grunts filled the air. Several tents they left behind with dead men or on fire, their packs heavier. They came across a small troop of imperial soldiers and in the dead of night raided their camp, intent on stealing rice and dried fish.

Cherry blossom petals shone white in the moonlight as the samurai came and went like shadows, leaving a trail of death behind them. They showed no mercy to the sleeping soldiers.

CHAPTER 17

Nene and Isla wept with joy when the Shimazu clan banner crested the hill, signalling the return of a much more depleted group than Keiichirō had left with.

The samurai were thin and filthy.

Isla sought Keiichirō, and the longer she couldn't see him the deeper and darker her dread became.

Finally, she spotted him, and it knocked all the air from her lungs. He was bruised and exhausted, his topknot a mess and his outer jacket frayed with dirt and blood, but he was whole and alive.

As he walked by, his eyes met hers, and an unsaid confirmation passed between them, fleeting as a heartbeat. *You're alive.*

She and Nene waited until the weary soldiers had washed in the Tsuboi River, and had had something to eat. Men sat then in groups, talking quietly. Keiichirō looked up as they approached, the firelight reflecting in his brown irises. As Nene went to his side, Isla realised who was missing.

Toramasa Mori.

'Kei,' she said, her heart breaking. 'I'm so sorry.'

'You need to go,' Keiichirō said. 'It's dangerous here.'

'We *all* need to go. Otherwise we'll die,' said Isla.

'Then I'll die for our cause.'

Nene was staring at Isla. 'How do you know this?'

'Because I—' Isla decided it was time for the truth. 'Because I'm from a different time. I don't know why I'm here, but where I'm from, this all happened a long time ago.'

Nene gasped.

'What are you talking about?' Keiichirō asked.

'Come with me.' She led them both to the trees, away from curious eyes, Kumamoto Castle dark against the night sky.

'I didn't come to Japan by ship,' she said. She snatched up a stick and drew a shape in the dirt. She drew the torii gate that had led her here, then some numbers. 'I came a different way. A way that isn't known to you yet. I was in Kagoshima. I went to a shrine and...' She connected the numbers *2005* and *1877* with an arrow drawn in the dirt. 'There was a storm, and I stepped through a torii gate at the old shrine.'

'Are you saying you're from the future?' Keiichirō's eyes searched her face for a hint of a lie.

'I know it sounds impossible.' *It* is *impossible. At least, I thought it was.* 'But I came that night through the shrine. Somehow, I came here from the future, and I've been stuck here ever since.'

*

Nene looked as though she might faint. She sank onto a nearby rock and covered her face.

But Keiichirō considered the evidence. Isla had appeared in the darkness, terrifying Aiko-san and dressed in strange clothing. There was her odd dialect, her constant reluctance to talk about her past, her insistence the war was futile. In a world where people believed in *yōkai* and spirits, why not something as complicated and unknown as travelling through time? People had disappeared at that shrine, never to be seen again.

It explained so much. But it also explained nothing at all.

Nene looked at her in disbelief.

Isla said, 'I have things from my time. Things that use electricity, far more advanced than anything you've seen. The clothes I wore when I came here, have you ever seen anything like them?'

Isla pulled something from her obi belt. Folded, hard and the colour of a bruise. 'This is a *keitai denwa*.' She showed it to Keiichirō. He held it, fascinated. It was hard and of a material he had never seen, weighing heavy in his hands. There were little squares holding numbers and the hiragana alphabet, smaller than fingernails.

'I can talk to people miles away with it.'

'How?' Keiichirō asked.

Confusion flickered across Isla's face. 'I don't know how, I just can. But it's not charged right now, it's...' She tapped a small hole at the bottom of it. 'You put something in, and it charges it with electricity. It's hard to explain. Look.' She opened a folded, brown square made of leather. 'I have money from my time.'

Nene took a crisp note. *1000 YEN* was written on both the top right and bottom left corners and there was a sketch of a mountain, perhaps the famous Mount Fuji miles from here, drawn before a lake. Keiichirō took another and turned it over. There was an inked picture of a man with short, wavy hair and a moustache, wearing a Western jacket.

'This is money?' he asked. An otherworldly, eerie sensation washed over him. He didn't like this. But when he met Isla's eyes, he saw no lie, only fear. Fear he wouldn't believe her.

'Here.' She brought out a thick square of material. It was harder than paper, with neat, printed numbers and letters. She showed them both, and Keiichirō sucked in a shocked breath. Then Isla passed over a small unbending card, on which was a small picture of her, as lifelike and clear as though he was looking at her through a window. Her hair was longer, a serious expression on her face, which was fuller.

Keiichirō's eyes slid over the words *Government of Japan. Residence card.*

The address said she lived in Tokyo, but it was the *period of stay/date of expiration* that was the most interesting. October 2005.

Isla looked at Nene and Keiichirō carefully. 'I know how you must feel.' Her voice was soft. 'If someone came to me and showed me things they said were from the future, I wouldn't believe them. I'd think it was a lie or a trick.'

She took Keiichirō's hand, and he didn't pull away. Her fingernails were nibbled to nubs, her skin pale as fresh snow in the moonlight. The touch brought him comfort, the frustration at having them both here in danger melting away like frost at dawn.

'I think,' he said slowly, 'if you were lying, you would have come up with something more believable.'

Isla and he exchanged looks. Keiichirō was quite right.

'I'm sorry for not telling you before. I know the samurai despise lying, but... I was scared you wouldn't believe me.'

'We believe you, Isla-chan,' said Nene. She looked at Keiichirō. 'Don't we?'

Keiichirō glanced across at the woman he should be marrying.

Nene's hair, stained with dirt, was tied in a bun at the nape of her neck. Mud smeared her skin, and her cheeks were hollow. Her face was drawn with numb shock, and with the internal battle of someone who was cornered with a truth she didn't want to accept.

He said, 'I understand if Isla is here because she thought she could warn us. But why are you here, Nene-chan?'

'I am also worried for a man. It's not you, Keiichirō. I am sorry to have dishonoured you in this way. There is a farmer here, fighting for the samurai, and I care for him...' Nene twisted the material of her hakama trousers in her hands. 'He joined this army and... and...'

'Not for Keiichirō?' Isla blinked at her. 'But... but you were jealous, Nene. I don't understand.'

'I know, Isla-chan. I'm sorry.'

'Don't be.' Keiichirō smiled at her as Isla gaped. 'You and I... you're my friend, Nene-chan. I'm sorry I couldn't offer you something more.' He looked at Isla. She looked exhausted, but less tense. Like a weight had been lifted from her. 'Isla, do people in your time know Saigō Takamori's name?'

She nodded. 'Yes. There are *hakubutsukan*, monuments, statues. Everyone knows who he is, especially in Satsuma.'

Though he didn't understand some of her words, Keiichirō nodded, closing his eyes. He replied, 'Then nothing has to change. Samurai don't surrender.' He kept his voice patient. 'We don't run away. But neither of you should be here. Kirino-san sent his wife home with the women fighters. You can leave, too.'

'I'm not leaving,' said Isla, her voice steely.

CHAPTER 18

Nene was not in love with Keiichirō.

All this time they had been here, Isla had assumed Nene worried for her fiancé, just as she did. She had even been jealous. But Nene was in love with a farmer. Bittersweet relief swept through Isla. Nene was in love with someone else, and Keiichirō thought of her as a friend. Though Isla had never truly allowed herself to hope seriously that anything would come from her complicated feelings for the serious young samurai, a sense of guilt had followed her like a storm cloud all the time she and Nene had protected each other.

Now Isla and Keiichirō sat still as statues, waiting as the night deepened and the trees whispered their secrets. Soon Nene's soft footsteps sounded, and they saw a slender young man behind her. He wore a straw hat flecked with drying blood, a sword at his side. A bandage was around his left hand and his eyes were wide as he knelt beside them to bow in greeting.

Isla knew that Keiichirō's parents, thinking they were doing the best for Nene, had betrothed her to Keiichirō to elevate her to a better class. But all along, Nene was in love with a farmer's son.

'What is your name?' Keiichirō asked him.

'Kuroki, my lord,' the farmer said. 'Kuroki Hisakichi.'

His name hung in the air. Isla felt she was falling. Her hand slipped from Keiichirō's grasp as her heart rose to her throat.

Hisakichi Kuroki. My third-great-grandfather.

Isla swallowed, realisation sweeping through her.

She wasn't here to *change* the past.

She was here to ensure the future *happened*.

It wasn't to save the samurai, as she had believed, but to make sure Hisakichi Kuroki survived. That he married and raised Isla's great-great-grandfather.

Her eyes met Nene's.

Another powerful wave of emotion swept through her. *Nene is my third-great-grandmother.*

Her head spun, but she had to stay grounded. Had to find the right words to make sure her friend, her *ancestor*, survived this.

'Kuroki.' Keiichirō's eyes sought Isla's as he remembered the name Isla had been interested in, but she shook her head. Keiichirō kept quiet.

'Abandon the war,' Isla urged Nene and Hisakichi Kuroki. 'It's a lost cause that will kill you. But what the people of Satsuma will need after the war is food. Food grown by farmers like you.'

Hisakichi Kuroki had the same curve of eyebrow and round cheeks of Isla's much-missed grandfather, and he inclined his head at the truth of her words.

'Please go back to Kagoshima, both of you. You aren't bound by the same codes as a samurai is.' She took Nene's fingers now. They were cool and delicate. Tears threatened to spill down Isla's cheeks. Her own ancestor, here before her in the flesh. 'A farmer and his wife will not be convicted when the imperial army wins.' Isla clasped Nene's hand, and Nene squeezed back.

Hisakichi Kuroki bowed again to them both. 'I want to fight with Saigō-sama, but you are right. I am not a warrior. I only survived so far because of brave samurai protecting me. And Nene...' He glanced to her, his eyes softening. 'Will you come with me? I have relatives in Miyazaki. We can settle down somewhere safe and start a family, like we always wanted.'

A choked sob jumped from Nene's throat. She smiled, dimples deepening, and nodded.

'But what about you?' She glanced at Isla and Keiichirō. 'Isla-chan, will you come with us? Maeda-san?'

She was asking out of politeness, out of formality. Neither she nor Hisakichi expected, or perhaps wanted, the young samurai and the foreigner on their journey.

'No,' said Keiichirō. 'You two go. There is a road south of here. Take a horse. Go later tonight when the camp is asleep.'

*

Isla and Nene no longer bothered to hide the fact they were with the army. With the battles, death, injuries and dwindling supplies, nobody gave the young women a second glance. Isla sat beside Nene as they ate some boar meat Keiichirō and Tatsuzō had hunted earlier. Isla kept glancing at Hisakichi Kuroki.

She had so much she wanted to ask him. To tell him. Nene was not only her friend, but the great-grandmother of her own grandfather, who had never returned to Japan after falling in love with a Scottish woman.

'You own the farm near Kagoshima?' Isla asked Hisakichi as the sounds of quiet munching surrounded them, accompanied by the crackling and popping of the fire.

'My father owns it.' Hisakichi swallowed, wiping his mouth. Nene beamed at him. 'I heard he's been having quite some trouble with young men trying to poach his boars lately.' His eyes twinkled as they looked up to Keiichirō, who gave a guilty grin.

'It was never my idea to go there. Toramasa... he would always get me into trouble.'

He stoked the fire, sending several bright orange embers into the air that highlighted their faces. Isla watched her third-great-grandparents, the words catching in her throat. She couldn't complicate things further. If she told them the truth now, it might change everything.

'It's time to go,' she said quietly, before her resolve could crumble. She didn't know if Hisakichi Kuroki might have a sudden change of heart about leaving, but she didn't want to risk it. It was easy to find horses tied to trees in the darkness, as many of the riders had perished. Isla patted the silk-soft nose of one, sadness filling her. These beasts had seen as much blood and bedlam as she had, if not more. A white mare snorted and butted her gently.

'Goodbye, Isla-chan.' Nene hugged Isla close to her, biting back a sob. 'Take care of yourself.'

'You, too.' Isla held her friend, her *ancestor*, close, inhaling her sweet woody scent one last time. Their fingers brushed as Nene stepped back, tears in her eyes, but the dimples in her cheeks deepened as she gave a sad smile. Her gaze turned to

Keiichirō and she bowed to him. 'Maeda-san, thank you so much for everything.'

Hisakichi Kuroki bowed to them before helping Nene onto her horse and mounting his own. Isla's heart ached as they watched the young couple ride east towards the prefecture of Miyazaki, where they would begin their lives together. Have children, a son who would have his *own* son, who would then...

Have Isla's grandfather.

I'm not descended from samurai, Isla thought as Nene and Hisakichi disappeared over a hill in a fading rumble of hooves, leaving a chill in their wake. *Grandad would be disappointed.*

A shiver ran through her. If she hadn't come, if she hadn't stepped through the white torii gate, would Hisakichi Kuroki have died here, marking the end of his bloodline?

Was it always meant to be this way?

*

Keiichirō felt nothing but relief as he watched Nakamura Nene and the young farmer called Kuroki Hisakichi flee the army and go make their lives together. Nene was too pure to die here.

He grieved for those who had fallen. Toramasa's smiling face floated across his mind. Kono's. Murakami's. He clenched his fist, wresting control over his emotions. Already, the presence of Isla beside him was heating his body in ways he didn't recognise. There was a strange static between them, like the moment before a thunderstrike.

The unspoken request hung between them. He felt Isla's eyes on him, a silent promise. She would stay with him until the end.

'You were looking for him, weren't you?' said Keiichirō when they were alone. 'Kuroki Hisakichi. No wonder I couldn't find him at the *shi-gakkō*.'

'Because he was never a samurai,' Isla affirmed. They were sitting beside the treeline, looking out at the camp where the wounded lay bandaged, others helping them. Some people cooked fish above fires or drank from waterskins. All were grim-faced. Nobody talked or laughed. Isla glanced at Keiichirō. 'You want to know why I was looking for him? Because he's my ancestor and so is Nene. I just didn't realise it,' she went on. 'My grandfather always hoped he had descended from samurai. I did, too.' She gave an embarrassed laugh. 'He was a farmer all this time. But I'm happy they're my ancestors.'

'That's why you were close to your grandfather,' mused Keiichirō. 'This is... difficult to understand. If Nene-chan and Kuroki are your ancestors, which means your grandfather, whose shrine we made by the river...'

'Is their great-grandson.' Isla nodded. 'It gives you a headache to think about it, doesn't it?'

Keiichirō took out his sword to clean it, and Isla wondered if he had nervous energy, a desire to do something physical. 'I know it's a lot to take in, but... Thank you for believing me.'

He wiped a cloth along the blade and examined it for stains. 'Tell me about the future.'

Isla let out a breath. Where to start? The metropolis of Tokyo, chat rooms, planes, video games, maid cafés, vending machines, karaoke bars – it was a far cry from this little wood, men fighting and dying with swords, people hunting for their own food.

'Japan is peaceful and united in my time,' she said quietly. 'It's a country that benefits from trading with others, but everyone knows and keeps the culture and traditions.'

Keiichirō said, 'So, no matter what we do, the samurai are no more after this war.'

'I'm afraid not.' Isla leaned her head on his shoulder, unable to find the words to tell him how sorry she was. To know everything you have ever known, everything you've ever lived for, would all be gone would be a heavy burden to bear. She worried she had been too honest.

'Thank you for telling me. And if Nene-chan and Kuroki-san are your ancestors, that means you're Japanese, too. This is your history as much as it is mine.'

Keiichirō fell asleep not long afterwards, his fingers entwined in her hair, snoring softly as the fire died to embers. Isla lay awake and listened to the sounds around them: the rustling murmur of the wind in the trees, the crackling of dying flames, the low voices of friends nearby. Isla didn't want to move but her bladder insisted she get up.

Gently, she untangled from Keiichirō and eased off the ground. In sleep, she saw, the tension in his face relaxed, and he looked years younger. She wondered briefly what he might have been if he had been born in her time. A student, maybe, studying his family's history, like she was. Or a businessman in a suit, hurrying to catch a train to the city to work in an office.

She found a quiet place by the trees to pass her water. A breeze raised goosebumps on her skin and she shivered. As she peed in a quiet spot, she glanced to the horizon, to where hills kissed the sky.

Rain fell on a hill nearby. Isla watched it as she adjusted her clothes, curious. The rain collected there, falling only on the hillside, as though someone had torn a hole in the clouds.

Her heart rose to her throat.

A torii gate shimmered on the hill.

It shone in the moonlight, its wood slick with rain. It didn't belong there; there was no shrine nearby. Beyond the arch, Isla could see into it like a window.

She saw cars, city lights, trains, like a montage in a video.

It looked like her way home.

Exhilaration pounded through her.

The wind picked up, whistling about her and battering her clothes. A whisper, riding the wind like a prayer, unintelligible yet irresistibly familiar. Isla took a step towards the hill. Her fingers tingled, a strange sensation travelling up her arms. It felt just like her arrival, and her breath quickened.

Just a few minutes, and she'd be home. Back to her own time.

A laugh was lost to the wind. She gripped a nearby tree trunk to stop herself falling. What she had longed for was in front of her.

Isla glanced back beyond the trees to where the camp lay. The smile slipped from her face. Back there, Keiichirō was waiting for her.

No, she had to try to find 2005 again. Wasn't this what she had wanted? She'd been stuck in Kagoshima and the nineteenth century for months, embroiled in a war that was not hers, unable to change a thing. She had come here to save her ancestors, to ensure Hisakichi and Nene escaped. Her task was now complete. And her own time awaited.

She imagined Keiichirō waking up. Looking for her, calling for her, wondering why she had gone. Why she had left him alone without a farewell.

Agony tore at Isla. The gate beckoned. She could taste the rain, see the flash of artificial lights. She'd see her family again. Her parents waiting.

She stood rooted to the spot, torn between desire and love.

The rain pelted the hillside, the torii gate waiting on top. *Come*, it whispered in her mind. *Your task is complete. Come home.*

She took a step towards the hill.

Isla moaned. She couldn't do it.

She turned from the gate and collapsed against a tree. She couldn't abandon him. She wasn't ready to.

And the rain ceased, the gate disappeared. In its wake was a barren hill. And the tingling left her limbs.

Her face was tear-stained when she returned to Keiichirō. His eyes flickered open at her approach. He blinked, frowning, like he had just woken up.

'Isla?' he said as she lay beside him, her shoulders shaking.

She folded herself into his warm embrace.

'Shh, Isla. It's all right. I'm going to protect you. I promise.'

She trembled in his arms. Had that been her one chance to get home? Was she stuck here for ever now?

Lying in Keiichirō's arms, feeling his heartbeat, hearing his breath as he held her close, she couldn't quite bring herself to regret it.

CHAPTER 19

Isla knew nothing of the coming battles, only that the army would never make it out of the Kyushu region and the last of them would die at Takamori Saigō's side. It would happen on Mount Shiroyama, back in Satsuma, back where it had all begun.

Spring had finally come, the air mild as cherry blossoms flourished, seas of pale pink and white and then a flurry of petals drifting to the ground like snow.

Isla grew numb to the screams of the dying, to the blood, to the men who fiercely wiped away their tears when a friend or brother fell. She watched from a hill, a bloodstained *haori* draped around her shoulders. From here, the grounds of Kumamoto Castle spread before her like a painting. The ant-sized men ran around the ramparts, firing rifles at the samurai, who huddled in their trenches. For every man who died, no matter what side they were on, another piece of her soul slipped away.

Was Isla only here to ensure Nene and Hisakichi escaped alive? She looked at her hands, as though expecting to see herself fading. Her palms were calloused, nails dirty, fingertips marred with a faint dark stain no amount of scrubbing in the river had yet managed to wash away.

It was agony to wait. Isla had never been patient. But to run down the hill to try to find Keiichirō would be suicide. A stupid way to die.

She busied herself by counting the trees, collecting firewood, and singing songs she knew beneath her breath. It made her think of modern-day Japan, of her life as an international student in Tokyo. She and the other students had gone to karaoke together one evening.

A smile spread on her cracked lips at the memory of one of the students' horrible singing. He had given a drunken performance so full of enthusiasm everyone had clapped and whooped like he was a superstar.

Was all of that real? Had it all really happened? Or had Isla always been here, staring at death, powerless to stop it?

Keiichirō would come to her as the sun set, spilling golden light over the hills. His hair was tousled, new bruises and cuts on his arms and neck, his *haori* jacket more ragged than ever, but he was whole and alive.

Isla pulled him close each time.

One evening he said, 'I bring news. The enemy has seized one of our supply points near the town of Oe.' He stiffened, gripping her wrists. 'They forced us out of the way. We can do nothing to stop them. *Nothing.*'

'Saigō-sama will flee back to Satsuma eventually, I promise,' she whispered, cupping his face, 'and you must stay alive until he decides to leave.' Bristles on his cheeks scratched her palms as his light-brown eyes met hers. Some of the light in them had vanished.

They huddled together between some trees.

It was a rainless night, fires from the castle illuminating the ground below. A smoke-scented breeze played with Keiichirō's long hair, released from its topknot, as they enjoyed a moment of peace.

Keiichirō's lips found hers, a burning kiss that set her aflame. Her mouth opened eagerly to his, letting him taste her. A trace of *shōchū*, something masculine, a gentle but hungry caress that sent heat down to her core. They broke apart, their foreheads touching, their breaths hot and heavy.

It was the first time they had kissed.

'*Oi wa omansa ga wazze sujja,*' he whispered.

I adore you, MacKenzie Isla.

*

In mid-April, all endeavour to take Kumamoto Castle was abandoned. Kirino Toshiaki finally called for retreat so they wouldn't all be massacred. It was all exactly as Isla had foretold.

Keiichirō kept Isla close as they walked away from the castle. He had to protect her. She had tried to warn them and none of them had listened. Saigō-sama, as wise as he was, had vastly underestimated the might of the imperial army and the men who had defended Kumamoto Castle. Although they were conscripts, picked off farms and given uniforms and arms, they had superior firearms and an endless number of soldiers ready to replace those who had fallen. Not even the fact that many of them were from Kyushu had saved the Satsuma rebels.

But samurai were not ones to cower and go home after a defeat. Keiichirō caressed the handle of his wakizashi sword. He would die by the blade, either his enemy's or his own.

But for now, he had to look after Isla with every fibre of his being. She was no warrior. Kirino-san had put him in charge of the foreign girl when she had first arrived. But she was... from the *future*. That still made his head ache.

He glanced at her. She walked with her head down, the straw hat hiding her fiery locks. He only saw the tip of her nose as she walked. He had memorised the way she moved, and he could spot her in a crowd of a hundred. Perhaps she was his curse but, in the silent moments they could steal together, it felt as if she were his blessing.

They headed towards the town of Hitoyoshi. At least now there was no snow. Tree-covered hills surrounded them as they marched south. The cherry blossoms had already died, though some pale, dead petals lay on the ground, squashed into the mud by the samurai's wrapped, sandalled feet.

It took seven days to reach Hitoyoshi; they kept having to stop and fight the pockets of imperial soldiers that tried to decimate their numbers further. The samurai army dug in to wait for an imperial army offensive and built a campsite. Keiichirō assisted in chopping wood and hunting, and at night everyone swapped stories and memories of loved ones. On the nights they had caught wild boar or deer, the mood touched on jovial.

Ikeda Uhei didn't say much, but sipped *shōchū* as he stared into the fire, the nervous chortles bouncing off him. Keiichirō did not know him well, it was Toramasa the older man had spoken to the most, but he could tell something had vanished within Ikeda. A flame snuffed out when Toramasa had died.

It was a relief not to struggle to get warm. At night, they counted the stars and told stories of its constellations.

The days began to crawl by, monotonous when peace reigned, yet quick and bloody when they were attacked. If anyone wanted to go home, they didn't mention it. Their orders were that they had to wait for further instructions. For them, the war wasn't over. There was only one way this could end: when the rebellion was squashed and Saigō-sama lay dead.

The men tended to their wounds and took turns keeping watch. The days stretched on, and the samurai passed their time playing *shogi*, a board game that used twenty pieces, which the men fashioned from pebbles and a flat river stone. It helped, but only a little.

Isla and Keiichirō stuck together, sleeping near each other, and Keiichirō encouraged Isla to hide, but she whispered to him one night that she hated waiting, listening to the nauseating shouts and screams of pain and slashing and steel, wondering if he would ever return to her hiding place to get her or if she would find his corpse on the battlefield.

'Your Japanese is improving,' he said one night, and a smile flickered on Isla's face in the moonlight.

'I haven't spoken English aloud since I met the Dutch traders.'

'Teach me some of your language,' he asked.

She giggled, a sound that warmed his heart. 'All right.'

The moon passed over them, blurred by the occasional cloud.

An hour later, Keiichirō had mastered several phrases, including 'aye', 'wee' as in small, and 'bonnie lass', the last of which made Isla dissolve into peals of delighted laughter. She had to bury her face in her hands to stifle the noise. Her mirth was like music. Keiichirō thought it a spark of hope in the darkness.

'You are a treasure.' Keiichirō pulled her close.

Sunlight flooded the camp the next morning, and shouts jolted them awake. Isla pulled away from his arms and looked around. By instinct, she rammed the straw hat onto her head as Keiichirō rose, blinking the sleep from his eyes and snatching up his swords.

'Intruders!' a samurai hollered.

Blood-chilling gunshots filled the air as Isla flattened onto her stomach.

'Be careful!' she cried after Keiichirō as he ran to the edge of the camp. Bushes and trees surrounded them, so he shinned up the nearest tree and took in what was happening.

Imperial soldiers were running riot through the camp.

Ikeda felled a soldier nearby and snatched up the gun he dropped. From his vantage point Keiichirō saw Taguchi, hiding behind a tree with his sword before him, square jaw set. An imperial soldier, sneaking forward on his polished boots, didn't see the samurai until he was upon him. Taguchi gave a shout and a hard swing. The young soldier's head spun from his shoulders. It rolled in the grass as his body crumpled.

Keiichirō dropped from the tree and ran to Ikeda, who was firing at soldiers. When the gun was empty, he threw it to the side and ripped out his sword. Keiichirō fought at his back. He felt Ikeda's laboured breaths against his own spine as he fought off an incoming soldier.

A shot rang through the air. Taguchi fell beside Keiichirō, his eyes wide open and a gaping hole in his belly. And although Keiichirō hated Taguchi, he sought the culprit; a thin-faced man with a beard. Before the enemy could reload his cumbersome rifle, the samurai darted to him and smacked him in the face with the pommel of his sword, breaking his nose with a sickening crack. Then Keiichirō sliced open the soldier's chest with his shorter wakizashi blade. The conscript collapsed, choking on blood.

Taguchi's eyes widened as his very life bled out of the gunshot wound in his belly. He grabbed Keiichirō's robe. His eyes beseeched, begging Keiichirō to believe his brother had not raped Kana.

Keiichirō began to doubt his sister for the first time as Taguchi shuddered into death, letting out a final, bloody cough before slumping, his sword slipping from his fingers.

For a samurai didn't lie, and especially on the point of his extinction. Keiichirō had seen no deception in Taguchi's eyes, even when facing the cold, permanent beckoning of death. He closed Taguchi's eyes. It was what anyone would do.

A cheer rang out as the attackers ran for the hills, leaving dropped rifles behind.

Keiichirō did not join their celebration, even when Isla ran over, relief on her face to find him alive.

If Keiichirō were to die in this war, he wanted to know the truth about his sister, to know whether his father's death had been in vain.

They had lost only three of their own in the attack: Taguchi and two farmers Keiichirō didn't know. They buried them all by the treeline.

'Let's go to Satsuma,' he said to Isla after the appropriate words had been said for the dead men. 'There's something there I need to do.'

Isla looked at him, her warm eyes softening. 'The fight will go to Satsuma eventually,' she said. 'Let's head back before that happens. We've been here six weeks and it's time for us to move.'

They left that night, sneaking out of the camp. As they walked, Keiichirō felt stronger with Isla at his side.

At night, he held her to him, inhaling her scent and nuzzling into her soft hair. His heart was heavy with the burden of his question, but he felt better with Isla in his arms.

He longed to do more with her. To kiss her and touch her; but for them to do more out in the wilds like this would be foolish. It didn't stop his desire, however, and he held her from behind one night, his aching need pressing into her plump backside.

'Sorry,' he mumbled, fighting to rein in his desire.

There was a smile to her voice. 'Don't be.'

She turned her head to him, her lips finding his. Heat rushed through him at her silk-soft touch, and his mouth opened at her invitation. A shudder of lust ran through him as her tongue traced over his, her feminine scent wreathing him like perfume. She faced him, her warm hands tracing his torso, running lightly over his robe. Their breaths quickened, warmth between them, as she slid his robe off his shoulder. She kissed his neck, her lips leaving a burning trail down to his chest.

He wanted her so much. Wanted to touch her, let her touch him, to fill this aching longing. His fingers traced her neck and found her breasts, warm and soft and inviting. One tug, and the robe would fall away, exposing her beauty.

A rustle startled them both.

Keiichirō sat up, his robe hanging off his shoulder. They had settled down for the night beneath some trees in case of rain.

The branches above them barely moved, no wind tonight. Yet Keiichirō was convinced he'd heard the snapping of a twig. That there was something here. Something alive.

An enemy.

'What is it?' Isla whispered.

Keiichirō laid a hand on her arm to silence her.

Then he saw it. A pair of cold yellowish eyes, irises catching the moonlight, staring at them from the brush.

Keiichirō snatched up his sword, which was never far away. The hairs on his neck stood on end. How many surrounded them?

A low growl erupted from the beast's throat, sending icy fear through him. He remained silent and still, focused on those eyes.

His words were barely a breath. 'Stay here.'

The wolf emerged from the brush. It was slight and thin, lips drawn back in a snarl.

Keiichirō let out a loud yell, jumping to his feet in a rush of cloth. Perhaps he could frighten the creature away. He brandished his sword, slits of moonlight from the branches above catching silver in the steel. Judging by the matted fur and skinny limbs, it was a runt. But even the meekest of wolves could be deadly.

'*Oi!*' he bellowed again as he rushed at the creature, hoping it would run.

The wolf challenged him, paws smacking the dirt. It snapped at his leg. He whipped his calf out of the snarling jaws' reach and slashed his sword at the creature. It whined and backed off, saliva dripping onto the soil. Keiichirō's heart hammered. He had never fought a wolf before.

The beast darted forward again as Isla screamed. Keiichirō slashed upwards, hoping to catch the beast mid-jump, but he mistimed it.

Pain pierced his shoulder as the wolf tackled him to the ground, its teeth digging into his collarbone. Snarls and growls rang in his ear. It stank of fur and filth.

Keiichirō struggled to push the beast away, his shoulder in agony as the wolf angled its jaws towards him. It shook and snarled, its weight heavy on his chest, seconds from tearing out his throat.

Isla sprang forward with a stone in her hand, which she brought down on its head as hard as she could. Keiichirō pulled out his wakizashi blade and stabbed the wolf in its side, his blade meeting meaty flesh and matted fur.

Keiichirō needed to find its neck, and he found the space between its ear and its shoulder and sank his blade into the fur with all his strength, giving a growl of his own through clenched teeth.

Blade met bone again and again, as Isla and Keiichirō both kept up their attacks and the beast squealed, relentless. The wolf gave a high-pitched whine and, finally, its jaw slackened. Keiichirō tossed its body aside. But Isla was not finished; she hit the creature over and over, its blood spraying her.

'Isla,' Keiichirō panted, trying to focus as black spots filled his vision. 'It's all right. It's dead.'

He collapsed.

'Kei!' She rushed to him and pressed her hand against his bleeding shoulder to staunch the blood, and he forced away the dizzy blackness. 'Did it get your neck?' she asked.

'Just my shoulder, I think.' Keiichirō clenched his jaw against the pain pulsing against Isla's palm. Isla was pale as she stood and looked around, still holding the blood-splattered rock with her free hand.

'It was alone,' Keiichirō managed to say as he sat up. 'But let's move, just in case.'

The wolf, its skull broken, lay with its jaws open in a silent snarl, pink tongue hanging out, mouth stained with Keiichirō's blood. They gathered their satchels and made their way slowly along the road.

Once they were a distance away, Isla used her obi belt to wrap his shoulder. 'Are you going to be okay?' Her voice was anxious.

'I've been hurt worse on the battlefield. It's barely a scratch.'

'Are you sure?' Isla had seen the puncture marks in his shoulder.

'I am sure, bonnie lass.' He took her hand. 'I never lie.'

CHAPTER 20

The town of Kagoshima emerged at last in the quiet hour before dawn. Mount Sakurajima stood as a black silhouette against the sky, a trail of smoke snaking up to meet the clouds. Keiichirō's heart ached at seeing his hometown again, with its sloped roofs and neat, narrow streets. When the town awoke in a couple of hours, it would be mostly women and children wandering the roads, many of the men having thrown their support behind Saigō Takamori's cause. Now, however, the town was dark and mostly empty. Only a few houses were aglow with lamplight.

He could not wait to slip into a hot spring, to sleep on a futon with a roof over his head. The height of summer would be here soon, and he had no desire to continue sleeping outside at the mercy of mosquitoes. His shoulder flared with each movement of his arm, and he ached all over, but he made himself enter, back straight and proud.

'Dawn will be here soon,' he said as they reached the place he and Taguchi had brawled all those months ago. A dull pang squeezed his chest at the thought of his fallen rival. Soon enough, he would know whether Taguchi Hanzō had been telling the truth. But not yet, and Keiichirō took a moment to stop and inhale the familiar scents of his home. Wood, the sea, the faint traces of miso. Even the grass smelled different here. Clean and fresh. Or perhaps it just seemed that way without the tang of blood seeping into everything, the awful odour he and Isla had become so used to.

She stayed close to his side, relieved that they were almost at their longed-for destination. They would settle into the house, greet Kana and play with Yura, bathe in the hot spring… Wonderful.

Side by side, their shoulders brushing against each other's now and again, they started to walk the last mile, their pace picking up.

'Shh,' said Keiichirō suddenly as he threw out an arm to stop Isla. A movement in the streets below had caught his attention, and he pulled her into a patch of deep shadow. 'Conscripts,' he hissed.

Sure enough, when Isla looked she could see two men carrying rifles, in hats and Western uniforms, gold buttons glistening in the light of a lantern as they patrolled the hill. A shot of loathing ran through him.

'How did…?' Keiichirō's question trailed off. 'By ship. Of course.'

They stared beyond the town to the seafront, where in the faint first hint of dawn, now they knew what they were looking for, there was the heavy bulk that indicated a dozen ships anchored at harbour.

Saigō-sama hadn't left any samurai to defend Kagoshima; all the men had wanted to follow their leader. Now the emperor's soldiers strolled about as if they didn't have a care in the world, probably harassing the townsfolk and upsetting them with untruths about Saigō-sama and the samurai.

Keiichirō wanted to leap from the shadows and cut down the patrol, but what would that do? They were only men following orders.

But there was something horrible about seeing their enemy here in his hometown, like finding ants in your rice.

'How much of Satsuma is under enemy control?' Keiichirō whispered.

'I don't know, but we'd better be careful. Come on,' Isla murmured, and they set off again, making as little noise as possible.

Guilt suffused Keiichirō for leaving the samurai behind. In some ways he felt he should be there with them, fighting alongside his cousin Tatsuzō and Ikeda and the others who still lived to fight another day. But he had to know the truth about Kana and Taguchi's brother, and this might be his last chance to know for sure. And he'd wanted to get Isla to safety, although it didn't necessarily look like Kagoshima was going to offer her sanctuary after all.

'Isla, I have to ask my sister a question,' he said when they were safely by the riverside, heading towards his home, keeping to the shadows and eyes peeled for more soldiers. 'You should know I may not like the answer, and there could be some shouting. It won't be anything about you.'

'I understand. I'm here if you need me, or if you want me to help in any way,' she answered. 'Always.'

And for Keiichirō this answer felt like sinking into a warm bath. Isla made it fine for him to face things both good and bad. She gave him strength, and belief in himself. He hoped he did the same for her.

He took her hand, revelling in their short time alone to show a small portion of the affection he felt for her in his heart. Her warm fingers squeezed back, and resolve filled him.

*

When they slid open the front door, quick footsteps came to them. It wasn't Kana but Yura, the little girl wearing a child's lightweight yukata, her black hair spilling down her back as she sucked her fingers. She had grown in the past six months, was surer on her feet, and some of her baby fat had left her face. She stared at them, long eyelashes fluttering as she blinked.

'Hello, little darling.' Isla crouched before her and spoke quietly. 'You're growing up so fast.'

Yura edged back to the wall, unsure.

'Yura?' said Kana's sleepy voice.

'We're back, sister,' called Keiichirō.

A squeal preceded Kana sticking her head out of the sliding door to her room, her hair tousled. She gasped as her eyes landed on Keiichirō's bloodstained shoulder, at the mud marring his clothes. 'You're hurt.'

'It's only a flesh wound,' Keiichirō tried to reassure her.

Isla may as well have been made of air. Kana grabbed Keiichirō's hand, barely giving him time to kick off his sandals, and ushered him to the sunken hearth, where she lit a lantern with trembling hands.

Kana acknowledged Isla then, and she raised her thin eyebrows pointedly at the dire state of them both.

They looked down at themselves and then at each other, before glancing at the spotless room with its neat, square cushions and dark polished floors.

They were so used to seeing grime of all sorts and old blood staining their clothes and hair, and to their grubby skin and dirty fingernails, that they had ceased to notice any of this, nor how they smelled. But Kana's face told a different story.

Yura pottered about, babbling to herself, while Kana insisted on looking at the wolf bite on Keiichirō's shoulder, removing Isla's hastily wrapped bandage with an impatient sigh.

'Nasty. Go and clean yourself in the hot spring, brother, and then I'll dress this properly for you,' Kana told Keiichirō, and he nodded and left the room, while Kana went to prepare some food.

Left to her own devices, Isla stayed standing where she was, not daring to sit on anything in her mucky clothes. Kana had given her soiled hands such a look of horror that Isla knew she wasn't going to be allowed to help get a meal ready. She doubted Keiichirō would say to his sister that his shoulder injury had been caused by a wolf, as this would worry her.

Yura looked up with eyes full of interest, and chuckled when Isla took off her hat, pointing at her hair. Isla wanted to pick her up and hug her – she had become fond of the girl when they had all lived together – but instead she knelt on the floorboards, wincing as she imagined leaving a smudge on the wood beneath.

'Ayya,' said Yura.

Isla smiled. Even though they had been apart for a long time, Yura recognised her, and this made her feel warm inside.

'Ayyyya.' Yura ran forward and flung her arms around her. Isla pulled the little girl close. Her innocence melted something in Isla's heart.

'Yura, she's dirty. Stop it,' Kana exclaimed from behind Isla.

'It's true,' agreed Isla, and stood.

They could hear that Keiichirō had now finished with the *onsen*, so Isla went outside for her turn, stripping off her clothes with delight and washing first with water from a bucket. Kana followed a few minutes later with a towel, a clean robe and a pair of sandals for her.

Isla looked down at herself. Her body was thinner now, even though she had built muscle in a way she never had before; months of eating nearly nothing meant her ribs stuck out, her legs were pale sticks. Three meals a day, sugar and coffee were a distant memory now. It had been brutal, but Isla had learned to appreciate the small, simple things in ways she could never have done in her old life in Scotland.

It took a while to scrub away the dirt and old blood. When only bruises marred her skin and her hair clung to her neck, wet and clean, she slid into the heavenly depths of the hot spring. She dunked her head under again and again – the warmth felt so good on her scalp. Hot water like this was a definite benefit of living so close to a volcano.

She didn't dare linger too long in case this made Kana cross with her, and so with great reluctance she climbed out and got ready to go back inside.

She found Keiichirō intently watching Kana dress his wound, the slightest twitch betraying his pain. She carefully stitched the bite with black thread, not flinching at the blood. Isla was relieved to see the injury wasn't deep. She dreaded to think what would have happened if the wolf had reached his throat. As she expected, Keiichirō was non-committal when Kana enquired how he had hurt himself.

'You're thin,' he remarked to his sister.

'There isn't much food,' said Kana irritably. 'And what I do have, I give to Yura. You don't look any better.'

Keiichirō glanced at his niece, Isla following his gaze. Yes, she looked healthy, and she knew he'd be doing the same as Kana if their positions were reversed.

Kana stirred something in a nearby pot in the sunken hearth, glancing at the inside. 'It's ready,' she announced.

The scent of the hot miso soup made Isla's insides groan, and soon they were all sipping meagre portions. Isla sat quietly, closing her eyes and savouring every mouthful. After weeks of eating whatever they could get, the salty taste almost overwhelmed her.

'We saw patrols on the way here. The imperial army?' Keiichirō asked.

Kana nodded. 'Three imperial warships came a few weeks ago and took all the gunpowder in the town. And now there are soldiers everywhere.' Her voice cracked, but she carried on. 'They took Father's biwa lute, and I remembered how I loved to hear him play it, and you, too. Said they needed to confiscate it, although I can't see what good it's going to do them. I hid the armour beneath the loose floorboard by the door and they won't find that.' She gestured towards an unremarkable section of the dark floorboards close to the entrance. 'But it never occurred to me that they wouldn't let us keep a musical instrument.'

As Kana took Yura back to one of the tatami mat rooms to put her to bed, Keiichirō's gaze met Isla's.

She could see he wanted to ask Kana the question he had mentioned. Would he want her here, or should she leave? His face was half cast in shadow, and, though he said nothing, she could feel he longed for her presence, and she wondered what the question was. It hadn't seemed that important as they were heading to Kagoshima but, to judge by Keiichirō's serious expression now, maybe it was. Isla was glad he'd reassured her the question wasn't anything to do with herself.

They all went to the room where Ujio Maeda's urn stood in an alcove, mercifully overlooked by the patrols. The space was empty without the armour.

Isla sat beside Keiichirō, an inch between them, and Kana's lips pursed slightly as she saw Isla as near as she was to her brother, but she positioned herself before them, legs tucked beneath her. It felt surreal to be here, in this calm, clean house, after the chaos and death they had witnessed. Kana's hair was neat, her robe free of wrinkles.

'There is something important I wish to ask you, Kana.' Keiichirō's voice was calm, though Isla sensed a gathering storm. 'As samurai, we do not lie. I expect the sister and daughter of samurai to adhere to the same rule.'

Kana didn't move, but Isla saw her cheeks pale.

'Taguchi Hanzō told me something that I didn't want to think was true. It was about his brother, Taguchi Gorō.'

Kana stared at the floor, but Isla thought she slumped a little. Whatever was coming was upsetting his sister.

With a resigned look on her face, Kana stared at her brother. Isla was sure now that she knew what was about to be said, and this wasn't something she was looking forward to.

Keiichirō continued. Isla listened with growing concern as he described how this samurai, Taguchi Hanzō, who had fallen right beside Keiichirō as they battled the imperial soldiers, had been the brother of the man named as Yura's father. The person Kana had accused of forcing himself on her when their father found out she was carrying a child.

'Father killed the man you named, Kana. He was called Taguchi Gorō,' said Keiichirō, his voice quiet. 'Father slit his throat as he slept, knowing all the time it was a coward's murder, and yet he did it anyway. And for this, our father, a good samurai, had to commit seppuku. What is the truth of what happened, Kana? You told Father that this man forced himself on you, but did you say that at the time out of fear? He doted on you, but a stricter father there never was. I believe you panicked. You didn't want to tell him the truth, and so you lied.'

Something tightened in Isla's chest.

'The consequences of your lie were more terrible than you predicted. Before Yura was born I believed you, and I went to war hating Taguchi Hanzō for being the brother of your attacker. But when Taguchi was dying and looking into my eyes with his final breaths, he insisted you had gone to his brother's bed willingly. I changed my mind and thought it must be he who was telling the truth, for samurai never lie. Am I wrong, Kana?'

The lengthy silence after Keiichirō stopped speaking was intense.

Although she wasn't the subject of the interrogation, Isla felt fear spike at Keiichirō's grave words. Heat blossomed in her chest, fear that made her skin tingle.

Kana's eyes dimmed as Isla silently begged her to deny everything, to insist she had told the truth and it was Taguchi Hanzō who had lied. For, if it were Kana who had done so, her cruel claim had cost two men their lives.

'Well?' Keiichirō's voice was firm.

Isla clenched her fingers, her pulse racing.

'Did you sleep with Taguchi Gorō willingly? Did you lie to our father?' Keiichirō spoke louder now.

Kana's lower lip trembled as she nodded.

Isla closed her eyes. This was horrible.

Kana's shoulders shook and she let out a heaving sob.

Keiichirō moved in a sudden flurry. He raised his hand, and Isla flinched in alarm. Kana covered her head, cowering. For a moment, they all froze, Keiichirō's hand raised, fury on his face. Then he sighed and lowered his arm, sinking back beside Isla, his body and legs clearly touching her now.

He sighed, all the heartbreak in the world in that simple sound.

'I was scared.' Kana's curtain of black hair hid most of her face, and Isla had to strain to catch her words, she was speaking so softly. 'I thought Father would kill me and my baby if he knew the truth. I couldn't let him harm my daughter.'

'He wouldn't have hurt her.' Keiichirō's shoulders were rigid as he glanced at the urn. 'Or you. You know that. He would have shouted, but no more.'

Kana fell forward into what vaguely resembled a bow, her sobs turning to wails. But Isla saw no tears coming from her eyes, like her despair was all for show. It was uncomfortable to watch.

'I'm sorry, brother, I was scared! I didn't know Father would kill him.' Kana pressed her face into the floor, her shoulders shaking as her cries were muffled into the tatami mat. 'Please, I beg you. Grant me permission to end my life!'

Isla didn't believe Kana was serious in this request.

'Get up,' said Keiichirō in disgust. Sniffling, her eyes red, Kana slowly straightened, patting her hair.

'Kana, you don't deserve the luxury of killing yourself. Who will take care of your daughter?' Keiichirō had a tremor of anger to his voice Isla had never heard before. She wanted to reach out to him, but it wouldn't help. 'I never touched or held Yura because of how I thought she came to be born, even though she is completely without blame. Because of your lies, Father is dead and Yura has no father or grandfather.' Keiichirō turned to Isla. He had regained control, but that storm raged behind his brown eyes. 'I'm sorry, Isla. I need to be alone with my sister.'

Isla swallowed, understanding. She couldn't look at Kana. She didn't know how he wasn't angrier, how he could restrain himself. But she could tell by the way his jaw was clenched and the fire in his eyes that he was only this calm on the surface. What sort of tempest raged in his heart? Isla couldn't try to understand. Instead, she fled to the garden. She left behind their whispers, Kana's pleading, his anger, as if the room was full of wasps.

Outside in the garden, it was humid, mosquitoes buzzing in the grass.

Pity stirred in her for Keiichirō, and for Yura too. The little girl had had no one in the world except her mother, and now Kana was shamed. How could someone lie about something like that? How had the guilt, knowing her actions had led to two samurai's deaths, not torn Kana Maeda to pieces?

But her stiffness, the way she was suspicious of Isla and her strange behaviour. Maybe she was carrying around that guilt. Perhaps in time it would be a relief for Kana to have her older brother finally know the truth.

Would Keiichirō ever forgive his sister? It was difficult to say. The one who would suffer the most for this was the little girl now sleeping soundly in the house.

Isla thought of Nene Nakamura and Hisakichi Kuroki. People of her own blood, if only they knew. They would be safe now, and soon would give birth to their son, the next Kuroki, and Isla's great-great-grandfather. Then in several decades, their family would welcome baby Yoshitomo. The young couple who had fled the war had no idea their legacy would lead to Isla's birth.

She wished Grandad was still alive. Alive in her own time. Isla no longer knew if she would ever return to the twenty-first century but, if she did, she would have wanted to tell him all about this bizarre adventure and how she had witnessed history unfold, powerless to avert its course.

How she had saved her own future by convincing Nene and Hisakichi to leave the war behind.

How she had fallen in love with a samurai and would rather die than leave his side now.

Keiichirō came into the garden. The whites of his eyes were red, as if he had been crying. She went to him and enfolded him in a strong embrace. She didn't care if Kana saw them. She held him close, feeling the steel of his muscle through his robe, and soon their touches became heavier, his lips finding hers as they stood alone together in the starlight.

No words were needed as they shrugged off their clothes, standing in front of each other in their nakedness, no hint of embarrassment between them. Isla's breaths grew heavy as she took in his slender, muscular form, tendrils of his black hair resting on his neck, healing wounds from the past months scabbed and scarring.

They laughed and then slipped back into the hot spring water, standing eye to eye for a long time. His gaze roamed hungrily over her body. It was the most erotic moment of Isla's life.

At last, Keiichirō's strong, gentle hands ran up her arms to her shoulders, taking in the sight as her nipples pebbled anew beneath his gaze and her breath caught. The changes in him were subtle; the slow intake of breath, the fire lighting in his eyes as they rose to meet hers, the pressure of his fingertips as they traced the curve of her back and pulled her closer. His hardness pressed against her hip, warm and demanding, and her legs weakened as Keiichirō guided her from the bath, water running down their skin.

They lay on the grass, wrapped in towels Keiichirō had brought outside with him, and under something that resembled a mosquito net that hung from the branch of a nearby tree, protecting them from insects.

It felt like they were hidden from the world, the hot spring's mist concealing them in their own private haven. Isla reached out and traced Keiichirō's jaw with her damp fingertip, taking in his serious face, the high cheekbones, the eyes that held sadness and regret and desire.

'Are you sure this is what you want?' she asked. Keiichirō had been so upset with Kana that she didn't want to force anything, and there was a part of Isla that thought they should wait for a time when they weren't worn out, and harsh words hadn't been said between brother and sister.

'I have never been more sure of anything,' said Keiichirō, and Isla's doubt fell away.

Isla inhaled sharply as he took her hand in his and kissed her palm. His soft lips left a trail of kisses up her wrist. Heat flushed through her.

Keiichirō's touch reached her shoulder, his hair tickling her cheek, his mouth leaving tingles on her damp skin. Heat rippled through her as he looked into her eyes. She gazed at the curve of his lips, the freckle near his mouth. His gaze made her feel beautiful.

He was intoxicating. And Isla wanted to feel him inside her, to hear his sighs and murmurs of love, for them to lose themselves in each other.

A long strand of Keiichirō's hair fell past his eye. She tucked it behind his ear, her heart igniting when he leaned in close, whispering, 'Bonnie lass.'

His mouth pressed against hers, strong hands wrapping around her waist as he pressed her to the ground beneath them. His passion left her breathless, heat rushing to her thighs as they lay among the scent of grass and steam. And Isla wanted him so badly she could barely breathe. All the emotion of the past months made every bit of her yearn for this, and Keiichirō's eyes told Isla he felt the same.

Keiichirō pulled her on top of him, her knees pressing into the grass, his eyes boring into hers as their breath quickened. When his heat slipped inside her, she groaned into his shoulder, losing herself to him. Each thrust sent a new wave of pleasure through her as she caressed the steel of his chest, fingers running over scars. His arms held her like he'd never let her go, pushing inside her faster and deeper until he sent her over the edge, and she had to bite her lip to stop from screaming. He spilled hot and fast into her, clutching her back so tight it hurt, their bodies and souls one.

They lay spent, his fingers entwining with hers, damp foreheads pressed together. Isla's heart felt tight and full, bound with ribbons. How could she ever let Keiichirō go now?

It would be impossible.

CHAPTER 21

Keiichirō would have given anything to be happy, to marry Isla and find somewhere quiet for them to settle. But each day that passed that he was away from Saigō-sama and his army carved more guilt into his soul.

At night, Keiichirō caressed the wrapped handle of his katana sword, glaring into the dark. At this point of the war and back in Kagoshima, he was not a true samurai, a warrior his ancestors could be proud of. He had abandoned the battle and left his friends to die.

Keiichirō drank in the sight of Isla's sleeping face, wishing that they could go where Nakamura Nene had gone, find somewhere to farm, and leave the war far behind.

But it wasn't an option for him. If that were to happen, then every day a small piece of him would die. He would be as cowardly as Kana.

He could not abandon the *bushidō*, the way of the warrior.

It was his life.

His very existence.

He blew air onto his forehead. Even at night, the humidity was stifling.

Morning came, bringing another sweltering day. Summer had arrived in full force. Cicadas buzzed in the trees as people flocked to the river to cool off. The women of Satsuma, now wearing thin-layered yukatas, harvested blueberries by the basketful. Kana and Yura came home many afternoons with a bag full of the little blue fruits.

'Kirino Hisa made it back safely,' said Isla, pleased, as she set down her own basket of fruit. 'She's back working with the unmarried women, as before.'

'The soldiers still patrol,' said Kana. 'I don't think it's safe for you to go out there, big brother. Not with your swords.'

Kana had stopped treating Isla as if she were a nasty smell, though there was still a strained atmosphere between them all, and as far as Isla knew Keiichirō had said nothing to his sister about himself and Isla, although their relationship was obvious now and they slept together in Isla's room every night. Keiichirō told her privately that Nene had decided to marry a farmer.

Keiichirō glanced at Yura and patted his leg. Yura hesitated, then toddled over to him and placed herself in his lap. She was warm and soft and so fragile. Carefully, she plucked the proffered berry from his hand and shoved it into her mouth. She smiled, and he offered her another one.

What he wouldn't give to be able to forget the war and flee, like Kuroki Hisakichi had. But he would never forgive himself. He couldn't abandon his brothers, abandon Saigō-sama.

One hot night, Keiichirō slept fitfully.

He dreamed of Murakami, his face covered in blood as he shouted through broken teeth, 'Where are you, Maeda?'

Toramasa glared at him, shouting about betrayal before he exploded, body parts flying. Beppu-san and Murata-san, mighty leaders both, regarded him with disgust, blood seeping from bullet wounds as they called him traitor. His friends fell to gunfire as Kirino-san ran into a burning forest, his sword held high above his head. All of Satsuma burned while Keiichirō was eaten alive by wolves.

He gasped awake, his face damp from sweat and tears. Isla sat up beside him, her eyebrows creased with worry. But even her touch couldn't quell the guilt that threatened to tear him apart from the inside.

He had to fulfil his duty as a samurai. It was his burden.

With no lute to play, Keiichirō picked at a hangnail as he sat on the porch overlooking the riverside, watching the imperial soldiers patrol until the sun rose and bled the earth.

'Brother.'

He didn't look up as Kana knelt beside him. They had sat like this as children, watching people fishing, or wondering aloud whether Mount Sakurajima would one day erupt and cover the whole world in ash. For just a moment, it felt to Keiichirō like they could go back to that time if they sat here long enough; smell their mother's cooking, hear their father's laughter.

'I know you won't forgive me,' Kana murmured, 'but I have something for you.'

On Kana's outstretched hand was their father's favourite *shōchū* cup, the halves Keiichirō hadn't been able to throw away newly mended. Keiichirō smiled to see the picture of the cockroach still inside. It seemed fitting somehow.

When the sun reached its zenith, Isla and Kana worked under dark parasols to shade themselves from the heat as they picked fruit, and Keiichirō shaved weeks of bristle from his face, smiling sadly at the *kamisori* razor in his hand. When his face was smooth, he showed Yura the fishing boats in the harbour and watched her run around on the grass nearby with other children, picking flowers, stopping her just in time as she tried to eat them. He was sorry he hadn't been as good to Yura in the past as he could have been, but it was enjoyable making up for it now.

It was bittersweet. Perhaps if there had been no war to return to, he and Isla could have had a child together. In his mind's eye, he saw a chubby little boy, light-brown hair catching rust-red in the sunlight, laughing as he ran with a wooden stick, begging his father to teach him swordplay.

But the guilt would tear him apart. Maybe at first, he could convince himself it was best as he left his swords behind and started a new life as a farmer. But the guilt would catch up to him, only in his dreams at first, then in every waking moment, sapping any life and happiness he managed to find with the woman he loved.

His hand automatically went to brush the swords at his hip, but they weren't there. Leaving them in the house had been like leaving a piece of his soul behind. He was anxious, but two-thirds of Kagoshima was controlled by the enemy. It was odd, watching the children play and laugh, oblivious to everything happening around them.

'Kei-chan?'

A slender woman approached, hair tied in a neat bun. A little boy clung to her leg and she held a bundle in her arms.

Keiichirō caught sight of a chubby cheek in the cloth. It was his cousin Tatsuzō's wife, Maeda Saki.

He bowed. 'A healthy birth. My congratulations.'

'A boy.' A smile played on Saki's face as she gently rocked the bundle. Yura came running up and Saki knelt, showing her the baby. Yura gently touched the silk-soft cheek and the baby burbled.

Saki glanced at Keiichirō. 'Would you like to hold him?'

He held out his arms for the child, and a paternal ache ran through him as he gazed down at the large brown eyes and the tuft of midnight hair. 'When was he born?'

'The beginning of April, as the cherry blossoms were falling. His name is Haru.'

Keiichirō cradled little Haru, his own blood. Saki's older son, Jin, ran off with Yura to play, and she shrieked with laughter as she ran after him. Then Saki asked the question he knew was coming.

'Is Tatsuzō coming home, too?'

Keiichirō met her eyes. He had not seen his cousin since the battle in Kumamoto months ago. 'I don't know if he still lives. He was alive when I left, but the battles are many and the imperial soldiers are strong. Many of us have perished. I'm sorry.' His voice cracked as his friends' faces flashed before his eyes.

Saki took back her baby, her mouth firm. No samurai's wife would show her emotion, least of all in public to a man who was not her husband.

Keiichirō looked over to where his cousin's son Jin was playing with Yura, hiding his face behind his palms, then crying out, '*baa!*' to make her laugh. Yura's giggles were like sunshine, but even that could not penetrate the dark storm cloud that loomed over them both.

'Why did you come back?' Saki asked. Her words were soft, but they were like needles.

Keiichirō knew the real question behind what she said, and it was a fair one. *Why are you here in Kagoshima when so many others have died and there is still a war to be fought?*

There were so many ways he could answer that question. *Because I needed to ask Kana something. Because I knew I would die otherwise. Because I'm a coward.*

He let a slow sigh escape his lips and blow away on the summer wind. His gaze travelled to the hilltop, where two soldiers in Western imperial uniforms were coming to speak to him, guns at their sides.

One of them pointed. Shouted.

'Jin! *Jin!*' Saki called after her son, who came running back. Yura followed, her hair flying behind her, giggling and unaware of the danger.

'I'll take her,' she said under her breath as the soldiers came close. 'I'll pretend she's mine. You'll be faster without her. Go. Now!'

Saki snatched Yura's hand as Keiichirō fled, his waist feeling empty without his swords. Cold fear for Saki and the children flooded him and Keiichirō glanced back, but the soldiers had run past them after him.

Keiichirō crossed a stone bridge over the river and headed towards the town, narrowly avoiding colliding with a carriage pulled by a horse. An old man grumbled something. He took to the alleys that he and Toramasa had made their own as children.

'Stop!' yelled one of the soldiers, and an elderly woman cried out as Keiichirō shoved past her, racing around a corner and past a soba noodle shop, jumping over a pile of foul-smelling trash. He took a turn, then another, and pressed himself against the secluded wooden wall of a house, hiding in the shadow of its low roof, his chest rising and falling as he listened for the soldiers' shouts.

'O-samurai-san?'

Keiichirō glanced around to see a familiar little boy. His straw sandals were a touch too small, and his own wakizashi sword sat at his hip, thrust through his belt. It was the child he had given the fish to all those months ago.

He put a finger to his lips as shouts echoed on the next street. The boy nodded.

'I'll distract them,' he said bravely. 'So you can escape.'

Keiichirō's breath caught with emotion, and the boy moved past him into the alley and out of sight.

'Hello.' Keiichirō shrank against the hard wall of the building at the sound of the youngster's voice. 'Could you help me? I'm lost.'

'We're busy, child, looking for a samurai.'

'A real samurai?' The boy's voice rose as if in awe. 'Oh, I'd love to see a samurai. My mother tells me one day I will, but the day never comes.'

'Tsk,' muttered a soldier. 'They are not all they are cracked up to be.'

The footsteps retreated and Keiichirō let out a breath. When he was sure they were gone, he slipped between some trees and took a long route home. The sun was descending by the time he stepped through the sliding doors.

'Where have you been? And where's Yura? You've been gone for hours,' Kana snapped.

Keiichirō quickly explained, adding, 'Yura is with Saki. The soldiers were right behind me and I wouldn't have escaped if I had kept her with me.'

Kana looked stricken, gripping her robe as the remaining colour drained from her face. Keiichirō looked at her, the sister he loved yet now almost despised for her mistake. But the terror on her face, the way she anxiously glanced towards the door...

She really loved her daughter.

'She's safe. Saki would die before she'd let anything happen to her,' he assured her.

Keiichirō found Isla sewing in their room, a light sheen of sweat on her face and wearing one of Kana's old yukatas, dulled and frayed at the edges. He knelt before her, holding his swords.

'I can't stay any longer,' he said, tucking the blades into his belt at his side. 'I need to be with my men, with Saigō-sama.'

Isla glanced up from her work with strained, tired eyes. 'Yes,' she murmured. 'I thought you might say that.'

'I hate this cowardice. The hiding.' He clenched his calloused fingers in his lap. He wanted to cut his own throat, to thrust his wakizashi blade into his belly and spill out his insides for his cowardice. 'I shouldn't be here. I need to be with my men. With Saigō-sama.'

Isla moved close, her scent of earth and pine wreathing him. Her presence was like perfume, intoxicating and warm. He felt at home with her, like he could finally drop the mask he wore for others.

'I am a samurai,' he sighed, something crumbling within him. 'I must live like one. Die like one.'

Something hot and wet splashed onto his hand as his shoulders shook. The dam was broken. He could no longer hold it all back. Isla's warm arms wrapped around him as he spilled his grief, the sorrow he had kept inside all this time. He held her back, sobbing into her shoulder, wishing everything could be different. Wishing he wasn't a samurai. Wishing Saigō-sama had never gone to war. Wishing for death.

'I will leave,' Keiichirō promised when he had dried his eyes. 'First thing in the morning. I will rejoin the fight—'

Knuckles pounding on wood made them spring apart.

'This is the imperial police!'

Kana looked in, her face ashen. 'They're here. Quickly, under the floorboards.'

*

Isla and Keiichirō slithered beneath the hidden floorboard as quietly as they could and crouched in the uncomfortable, cramped space next to the Maeda family armour.

Rapid, sharp Japanese accompanied heavy footsteps above their heads as the men stomped about.

Yura, back now, screamed, '*Haha-ue! Haha-ue!*'

'What are you doing with my baby?' Kana cried.

'So she *is* yours?' said a deep voice. 'Our soldiers saw a samurai with this girl earlier today. What have you got to say about that?'

Keiichirō crouched beside Isla, gripping the handle of his sword. Slits of light fell onto his face. It was unbearably hot, and Isla was certain she could hear both their heartbeats, pounding frantically as one. A trickle of sweat made its way down her spine. The air was muggy and thick, and she resisted the urge to wipe her brow.

A shadow fell over Keiichirō's face, casting the lower half in darkness. His eyes hardened.

'The samurai is here, I am sure of it,' said one of the policemen as Yura wailed for her mother. 'Where are you hiding him?'

They'll find our belongings, Isla thought desperately. *We'll be discovered.*

'Give me my child!' Kana shouted.

A slap, loud as a clap of thunder, resounded through the room.

There was a thud as Kana fell to the floor. Yura screamed louder.

It was too much for Keiichirō.

Isla tried to grab his robe, but he burst from the floor as fast as a whirlwind.

Before the officer could shout in surprise, there was a meaty slice as Keiichirō's sword went right through him. There was another thump and a strangled groan, blood seeping through the floorboards above Isla, the coppery scent filling the air.

She scrambled out of the floor as the other officer roared his rage, dropping Yura and pulling out his own sword.

Isla ducked through the chaos and grabbed Yura. She buried the little girl's face into her chest and reached the garden, cradling her.

'*Haha-ue!*' Yura wriggled in Isla's arms as she held her close.

'Wait, little one.'

Yura kept screaming. Heart in her mouth, Isla peeked around the corner. Keiichirō was helping up his sister, who was groggily coming to. The two police officers were lying in bloody pieces at their feet.

Isla rushed to Kana and handed her Yura, who clung to her mother, both of them wailing.

'We need to go, now,' said Isla as Keiichirō flicked his sword, flecks of vibrant red flying off the steel.

Keiichirō sheathed his katana into his belt, his chest heaving, as he said, 'Kana, take Yura and everything you can carry and go to Maeda Saki's house.'

Kana, holding Yura's face against her chest, nodded, her left cheek bright red from where the soldier had struck her.

Keiichirō turned his gaze to Isla. The blood seeping across the floorboards and onto the tatami mats turned her stomach. She forced her gaze away from the men's shocked, lifeless faces. Blood, again. So much blood. She would never get used to the sight.

'I'm coming with you, Kei,' she said. 'My place is at your side.'

They snatched what they could from their shelves, not knowing who had heard the screaming and who would come running next. A cockroach scuttled along a shelf, but Keiichirō barely seemed to see it, too busy grabbing pots and bowls from the shelves and glancing inside them.

Isla pressed all the food she found into Kana's free hand. Yura lay against her mother's chest; whether she was oblivious to the carnage or simply too little to take any of it in, it was impossible to tell.

Isla and Keiichirō changed hurriedly out of their blood-splashed clothes, and Isla made sure to get her phone and her wallet. They were all she had left of her old life.

Outside, Yura stretched pudgy hands towards her. Isla gave the little girl a quick hug and kissed her silk-soft cheek.

'Are you coming with us, Isla?' Kana asked, and for the first time there was no haughty dislike in her tone. Only writhing fear of what fate awaited her brother.

Isla shook her head. The thought of running to hide with the other women while Keiichirō went off to die was nauseating.

'Brother, I'm sorry.' Kana bowed to them both, difficult with her daughter in her arms, and ran off into the darkness without further ceremony.

Isla and Keiichirō fled Kagoshima and the two dead men at home and headed for the trees of Mount Shiroyama. Cicadas buzzed in the leaves, their trilling calls masking their fleeing footsteps.

'Saigō-sama is coming back to Satsuma,' Isla said. 'He'll go to Mount Shiroyama, and the imperial army will give chase.'

Keiichirō let out a breath. 'Then that is where I must go.'

'We.' Isla took his hand, and Keiichirō grasped hers back. 'Where *we* must go.'

*

Ikeda Uhei and the others were outnumbered seven to one.

In his opinion, there was no better way to die. A sword in his hand and blood on his robe, like his ancestors had. The dousing of blood he had suffered meant the fabric had been dyed to the colour of rust, and he had long since forgotten what it was to be clean.

The imperial army had them surrounded on the slopes of a mountain of which Ikeda Uhei did not know the name.

Saigō-sama had left with a party of the uninjured. Ikeda had joined the shouts for him to go, to escape the clutches of General Yamagata and his men. The war would end when Saigō Takamori was dead, and Ikeda was determined that this would not be today.

Ikeda himself did not rank among the uninjured.

He had been shot in the hip, and he couldn't walk, a buzzing numbness now spreading from the injury down to the toes of his right leg. He stilled as he heard the thunder of thousands of feet running up the hill towards them. The frantic buzzing of the cicadas was almost drowned out by the racket.

'It has been an honour to fight at your side, Ikeda-san,' said Maeda Tatsuzō, who had remained there because of a nasty slash at his chest, and was next to Ikeda. Every wheezing breath was a chore. Blood ran down his chin, his teeth crimson.

'And at yours.' Ikeda looked down at the short wakizashi blade in his hand, where dark brown stained some of the steel. It had saved his life on several occasions these last few months. Now, it would end it.

'Are you ready?'

The roar of boots on the mountainside grew, shaking the ground like an earthquake. Some of their comrades had surrendered, but the thought of treason, of cowardice, had barely crossed Ikeda's mind. Farmers, merchants, commoners, they could do what they wanted. Let them beg the emperor's men for mercy, and pray they found some.

Samurai did not surrender in the face of defeat. There was only one way it could end.

'It's a pity I could never see my second child be born.' Tatsuzō inhaled hard through his nose, fighting to struggle upright. His whole body shook with the manful effort, before he finally settled on his knees. 'If he was a boy, we were going to call him Haru, for spring.' Tatsuzō's entire left side was bloody, sweat beading on the parts of skin not drenched in red.

'Haru will grow up knowing his father was a brave samurai,' said Ikeda. 'Goodbye, my friend.'

As a warm, fresh-smelling breeze washed over his dirt-stained face, Ikeda's final thoughts were of a handsome young samurai. How quickly and unfairly he had perished, his beautiful body blown to pieces on a bridge without any kind of warning.

Mori Toramasa would never smile again, would never blush in that charming way of his when Ikeda looked at him.

Ikeda fought back the tears that threatened and propped himself up on his knees, despite his shattered hip. The pain was excruciating as he pulled aside his undershirt to expose his firm stomach. From the slopes below, men emerged from the trees like insects, their imperial uniforms dishevelled, clutching rifles as they called to each other, struggling up the slope.

There was no choice. It was either commit seppuku now or have gunfire rain down upon them.

A grunt and the meaty sound of a dagger thrusting into flesh told Ikeda that Maeda Tatsuzō had done it, and he looked across to see veins in Tatsuzō's neck bulging and a rictus look on his face as fresh blood poured from pale lips.

Bolstered by Tatsuzō's bravery, Ikeda held his breath and shoved the dagger deep into his own belly. It felt like a punch to the gut more than the cold kiss of sharp steel. Before he could faint or lose his nerve, Ikeda wrenched the blade sideways, ripping open his abdomen. And then it hurt to breathe, like inhaling knives.

There were shouts and the tramp of feet as Ikeda's vision blurred and agony burned across his stomach. Wet, hot blood and something warm and slippery spilled on to his knees and out across the grass.

The shouts faded as an image burned in Ikeda's dying mind. A memory of him and Toramasa at a hot spring. They had sneaked away from class together to breathe in the steam of the *onsen* bath, and then their bodies had moved as one, each lost in ecstasy. It was the happiest day of Ikeda Uhei's life.

He thought he could hear Toramasa calling. His smiling face appeared before him now, and Ikeda died in rapture.

DEATH

Revere Heaven, love mankind.

Takamori Saigō

CHAPTER 22

Summer rain fell on Isla and Keiichirō, beading like stars in their hair. It masked their footsteps and laboured breathing as they ventured towards the place where it would all end.

In Isla's time, the foot of the mountain was home to a road, cafés and a statue of Takamori Saigō.

Now, it was a dark and lonely hillside covered with trees and bamboo stalks, a whole world away.

Contrary to Keiichirō's fears that they wouldn't find their allies, it didn't take them long at all to seek out the samurai army, hidden in the trees on the slopes of Mount Shiroyama. They slipped into its ranks and, when they rose in the morning, no one remarked on their appearance, though several samurai cast tired glances at Isla.

It had been easy to find the army. Too easy, Isla thought. She looked to the sky, and, though she had never been much of a believer, she couldn't help thinking there was some omnipotent force guiding their steps.

She accepted that the reason for her being there – if there was any reason at all – was to meet Hisakichi and Nene and convince them to abandon the war.

But what had been the point in all that when she was destined to die here anyway?

Perhaps the gate appearing on the hillside shortly after her ancestors' flight had been her chance to go home.

But she had chosen Keiichirō.

Not that she regretted this choice for a second.

Maybe the point hadn't been to save herself, but Hisakichi Kuroki's other descendants. There had been four generations between him and Isla, dozens of Kurokis who had lived their lives and perhaps made a difference in the world.

Or maybe there was no point at all.

Either way, she had met Keiichirō, had stayed with him.

They grieved their losses together, for the families they would never see again.

Even so, Isla felt her life had never been richer or more fulfilled.

Meanwhile, the army hid in the trees of Mount Shiroyama. When word came that Takamori Saigō had returned, the samurai ran to their leader and bowed low before him, expressing their delight that he was with them, was alive. He told them he had escaped his enemies' grasp by fleeing through forests and mountains.

'Ikeda isn't here,' Keiichirō said to Isla. 'Neither is my cousin, Tatsuzō. What became of them?'

Saigō regaled them with tales of the past weeks as they sat around a fire. 'They chased us out of Miyakonojō. They tried to trap us in a pincer attack, but we escaped.'

'That must have angered Yamagata,' a warrior remarked, and laughter rippled among the trees.

Yamagata was a general of the imperial army, and he had doubtless torn apart his beard in frustration when Saigō avoided him yet again.

Isla sat among the trees in silence beside Keiichirō. It was so strange to hear laughter these days.

Takamori Saigō's warm eyes met every man in the group around him, the fire reflecting in his midnight irises. 'We made a stand on Mount Eno Dake. I burned my uniform and papers and slipped through the fingers of the imperial army yet again, but the injured stayed to commit seppuku. These men you see before you are, as far as I know, the only ones who remain.'

He gestured around at his war-beaten men, some wearing old bandages, all with robes or lamellar armour stained bloody.

It seemed a pitiful number of men, and Isla remembered the many who had left to go to war, and the many reinforcements who had joined the fray later. She had known it would be the case, but it was sad all the same.

Keiichirō tensed beside her. Ikeda and Tatsuzō had died, then.

Isla had known it, they both had, but it was a terrible blow all the same.

Her hand found Keiichirō's in the darkness and she gave him a comforting squeeze. His fingers felt like ice, despite the balmy weather.

Shinpachi Murata, his beard and moustache bedraggled and too long, sat tall at his leader's side, silent and strong as they all grieved the brothers and friends who had fallen to this rebellion. There was Shinsuke Beppu, too, kneeling beside a forlorn Toshiaki Kirino.

'I can run no more,' said Saigō. He shifted in place, his thick eyebrows furrowing to a frown of pain as he adjusted his position. 'My body is weak and sick. This will be our final stand.'

There was a long silence as his audience absorbed the meaning of his words, and understood they were facing certain death.

*

One evening several days later, long after the cicadas' buzzing had died down, Isla approached Kirino-san. Foreboding swamped her breast as she stood in front of the man whose face she had seen in museums and textbooks.

'Foreign girl. You're here.' He didn't sound surprised or shocked, but Isla thought that probably not very much took him aback these days.

There was an old cut along his cheek, and grey bruising along his neck that suggested he had narrowly avoided being strangled to death. His robe was filthy, his hair now shoulder-length and a dirty tangle. He worked at building a fire, jaw clenched as he fought a tremor in his hands.

'I just want you to know that your wife is safe,' said Isla quietly. 'Hisa-san is working with the other women in town, as always. She's making them all work hard, and spar too, just as she did when I arrived.'

Kirino-san's lips pursed. He didn't respond. Isla hesitated, then rose. As she left a few sparks ignited some of his poorly piled twigs, and Isla heard him murmur, 'Thank you, foreign girl, that's good to hear. She liked you, thought you determined. She wasn't often wrong.'

Isla turned and bowed, and as she went to find Keiichirō a tear slipped down her face that the old warhorse that was Kirino-san would never see Hisa-san again.

A blanket of grief lay heavy on Isla's shoulders.

With the endgame of the war drawing ever nearer, the knowledge of what was to come left her numb. There was no respite, no ray of sunshine as to their situation.

The reality was there was no ammunition, no supplies, no reinforcements, nobody on their way to help them. Everyone had lost a brother, a father, a son or a friend. The men's clothes were ragged, hanging on their thin bodies. Although they had all fought bravely, it had all been for nothing. In the months since the samurai had left Kagoshima, they hadn't made it within a hundred miles of Tokyo, and the emperor had never spoken with Takamori Saigō, his old friend.

The samurai had been on a lengthy fool's errand, and now it had destroyed the spirit of many of Saigō's loyal supporters. Increasingly, there were divisions in opinion.

Some samurai wanted to return to their hometown and were happy to risk being caught by the imperial patrol. Others wanted instead to make one final desperate stand and die taking down as many enemy soldiers as they could. Isla thought that each of these options were as bad as the other one, and she never heard anyone suggest that, as she had seen in the museum, one day the emperor would pardon Takamori Saigō, even though that was what would go on to happen. The history she knew had never felt so far away.

Days would pass with nothing of note happening, and the long hours crawled by. Other times, endless conscripts attacked, arriving in Kagoshima via ships to the bay, the imperial supporters bolstered by fresh ammunition and arms, and an unremitting commitment to rooting out the last of the rebels.

After a while, Takamori Saigō and what remained of his army fled farther up Mount Shiroyama as more warships sailed into view on the horizon. The mountain overlooked the town and the sea beyond, where lay the almighty volcano, Mount Sakurajima.

There was no going back now.

As the samurai, many of them nursing injuries or limping, ascended the slope towards the summit, Isla took Keiichirō's hand.

He grimaced, a flicker of pain crossing his stoic face.

'Is it your shoulder?' she whispered. Several times she had caught Keiichirō examining it when he thought she wasn't looking.

'I'll be fine,' he insisted. The words 'are you sure?' caught in her throat before she heard his response in her mind like an echo. *I am sure, bonnie lass. I never lie.*

But Isla chose not to challenge him, and instead looked up to where Takamori Saigō limped ahead, Shinsuke Beppu on one side and Toshiaki Kirino on the other, tenderly helping their leader when he struggled to walk.

The army had abandoned Saigō's palanquin long ago, and now he had to be half-carried up the slope. Saigō was wearing a yukata now, his enormous shoulders slumped. He was injured, or sick, or simply too old for this sort of arduous exertion. It was clear he wouldn't last much longer.

She had known that already, but it was still a terrible thought.

To the Isla of her Scotland days, historical figures had always felt distant and not quite real, known only for their mighty deeds. They weren't remembered for the way they jolted awake from nightmares or their murmured inside joke to a friend that sent them into guilty chuckles. Now, she didn't feel Takamori Saigō was distant or unreal. The charismatic man she knew was real to her with every fibre of his being; close to fifty, slowly dying, yet proud and ready to offer a smile and a word of thanks to his men as they made camp near some caves. She had seen the sadness swim in his eyes when he stared into the fire of an evening. Maybe he was thinking about his family and the son he promised would become a fine samurai one day. Or perhaps he was thinking he had led this rebellion only with a great reluctance, and now many of those he cared for would perish, if they hadn't done so already.

Isla found she had to avert her gaze.

This hill, this place, she thought, was in the twenty-first century an observatory, a viewing spot for Mount Sakurajima.

How could it have become a place where you could spend a hundred yen to peer through the binoculars and eat ice cream cones? How could it have a tarmac road and benches? How could people visit here as a fun day out when it was the place the samurai tradition died? Did people have no sense of gravity, of veneration, of heart?

Keiichirō stood at Isla's side, strong and increasingly silent.

The mountain was surrounded, with ships waiting on the sea, and a thousand men or more guarding all the main paths.

Saigō had escaped and outrun them so many times, they were determined to finally corner him. General Yamagata had thrown his entire force at the mountain and wouldn't stop until the rebels were dead.

Even if Isla hadn't known what would happen, it was still clear as a winter sky.

Rain came and the samurai huddled in the caves. The men talked quietly in groups. No one played *shogi* or laughed now.

Isla and Keiichirō found a quiet corner and leaned against each other for comfort as someone lit a fire at the mouth of the cave.

Isla ran her fingers over her thin, mosquito-ravaged arms. Her skin had greyed, the veins beneath her skin stark. She had stopped feeling hungry days ago. She didn't know if she would ever desire food again. Keiichirō's face was sunken, but what was worse to see was grief sapping the spirit from him. Isla put her head against his good shoulder, closing her eyes. The fire crackled and popped. Men talked quietly. It was almost peaceful, and for a moment Isla could convince herself it was.

Beppu-san sat nearby, his face hard. He had lost weight, too, his muscles bulging, his skin stretched over high cheekbones and his goatee matted with old dirt. He gripped the sword at his left hip as though ready to pull it out at a moment's notice. His chest moved with every breath, his glaring look not leaving the cave wall.

'My brother is down there,' said Saigō eventually, but then he didn't say anything else. He sat at the mouth of the cave, and when night fell he was a wide silhouette obscuring the stars.

No one attacked them, though the imperial army knew they were here. They could feel it, hear the occasional call between soldiers. And the imperial army didn't need to attack, as they could simply bide their time until the samurai died of thirst or starved to death.

To Isla, the worst part about all this was that the men down there were not their enemies. Not really. This wasn't a war of good versus evil. This was a battle of necessity, both sides feeling they had to defend themselves against the other, but without a tangible reason for doing so. One side stood for the honour of the samurai, the other for the honour of their emperor.

Saigō stayed sitting in silence, his large shoulders increasingly slumped. Thousands of men had followed him to war and their deaths weighed heavily.

*

Keiichirō mourned the friends he had lost. He hated that he hadn't been able to reunite with Ikeda or Tatsuzō. He had never had the chance to tell his cousin how proud he was of him, never thanked Ikeda for his wise counsel. Why had he waited?

They had died gloriously, upright and with swords in their hands as every samurai should, but it still hurt Keiichirō that they were gone. He thought of Tatsuzō's wife, Saki, of their new baby Haru. At least he and Jin would grow up knowing their father had died a warrior's death.

'Isla,' Keiichirō whispered, late that night in the cave. 'Who is alive? Who survives all this? Do you know?'

She looked at him, her eyes sad.

Keiichirō knew that Isla had predicted all those months ago that they would die in this battle, and it had all happened exactly as she had said it would. It had been months of fighting, of dwindling supplies, of trying in vain to save the way of the samurai.

But despair wasn't crushing his heart; his only regret was that Isla had chosen to stay and to die alongside him. Keiichirō had thought about making her leave, but where would she go? Nene was long gone with her lover. Kana might take her back, but Isla would not want to grieve in a strange town where she didn't belong and no one really trusted her.

'Kirino-san's wife, Hisa, she lives. So do a few others,' Isla said softly.

'And Saigō-sama?'

She met his eyes with a tortured expression. 'Would he want to be saved?'

Keiichirō shook his head, knowing this was the truth. 'I heard someone say before that their cousin is part of the imperial army. And Saigō-sama's own brother fights for the emperor. It all makes no sense to me.'

'Me neither,' Isla said, and a tear, glistening like a star, ran down her cheek and on to the *haori* jacket she used as a pillow.

'Do you hear that?' Murata-san's loud voice made all eyes turn to the cave's mouth.

Keiichirō and Isla expected to hear the rustle of enemies in the grassland, or gunshots, perhaps. Keiichirō followed the others outside, Isla moving behind him with a whisper of cloth.

Moonlight bathed the mountainside, bamboo trees clacking against one another in the faint wind. There was a light sheen of sweat on Keiichirō's skin. The moon was a full silver orb hanging above the ocean.

Music reached them on the wind.

As one, the samurai stood and listened in awe. It was exquisite, and tears freely ran down many faces.

Keiichirō couldn't remember the last time he'd heard music, save his own strumming on the biwa lute. Isla stood beside him, sniffling, the music catching their ears with every sigh of wind. It was an accordion, playing a song Keiichirō had heard before but did not know the name of.

'They're playing for us,' Isla said.

For this brief moment of respite, the war was on hold.

As the full moon shone and the animals of the forest fell silent, those below knowing that come dawn they must fight once more, someone had summoned an accordion to offer the last of the samurai some comfort before their end.

Keiichirō felt tears, something he'd always pushed down, brim in his eyes. They burned, his vision growing hazy. As their men, many limping or shuffling from old injuries, passed them to better hear the music, Isla's hand slipped beneath his sleeve and gripped his arm.

Keiichirō had never feared death but, now the cold hand of mortality wrapped around his throat, he found himself grieving. Never had he thought when he first met the strange foreign girl that he would feel anything for her. He had felt his destiny was with Nakamura Nene, but now she was far away, safe, with her lover. He wished Isla was there with Nene. This brave redheaded woman didn't deserve to die in a foreign land and a foreign time.

When the music died on the wind and a cloud obscured the moonlight, their moment of peace was over.

'I suppose it is time.' Kirino Toshiaki held up a ceramic bottle that sloshed with *shōchū*. Several samurai cheered and the men took turns drinking the clear spirit. There was enough for one sip each. Keiichirō savoured his, letting the liquid run over his tongue and coat every corner of his mouth. The spirit burned its way into his stomach and abated the tension. Oddly, he found himself thinking of Taguchi, insisting to his death that his brother was innocent, and how he had been proven right. Keiichirō looked towards Isla, and her solemn face suggested she was having equally sombre thoughts.

Not caring who saw them, Keiichirō pulled her into a deep hug.

'Get some rest,' said Saigō-sama when the *shōchū* bottle was empty.

*

Isla didn't sleep. On the dirt of the stony ground, the air stifling, she lay as close as she could to Keiichirō. Every heartbeat was one beat nearer to the morning when everything would come to a swift, bloody end. Nothing mattered now except that she was close to her lover.

Keiichirō didn't sleep either, although he kept his eyes closed. He wore his hair down to sleep, and Isla curled a lock around her finger, feeling the silk of it against her fingertip.

Isla was thinking that she had seen so many people die. Had experienced the horrors of battle and how quickly someone could fall and breathe their last. There was no glory, no romance, no excitement. It was over in a blur before it could sink in, messy and manic. All one could do was try to survive. Whenever Isla closed her eyes, she saw men falling with screams, holding their own entrails or clutching bloody eyes or throats. She could still smell the tang of blood, feel the rattle of gunshots through her bones.

Isla was forever changed, but at least she had saved her family's future. Nene Nakamura and Hisakichi Kuroki would go on to have children, who would eventually go on to sire her grandfather. He would travel to the United Kingdom, marry her Scottish grandmother.

Isla would be born again in the future. The thought brought her some small measure of calm. She had lived a decent enough life in her time. She'd worked hard, made it to Japan, made her parents proud, enjoyed her life. Maybe that was enough. She hoped they would be able to find some peace even after her disappearance. She wondered what it was like to die. She hoped she would face it bravely.

Her fingers moved from Keiichirō's hair to his chest, tracing over his robe stained with dirt. His strong hand reached up to grip hers as his lips found her mouth. Emotion welled inside her at the silent plea, the desperation his embrace held.

In the darkness, surrounded by their fellow doomed samurai, Keiichirō cast caution aside and moved to lie on top of her. His breaths turned frantic and heavy. Her heart filled with equal measures of love and agony as she pushed aside his robe, Keiichirō's scars gleaming white against the darkness.

He entered her with urgency that made her gasp. Grief and ecstasy mingled as one as he moved inside her, filling her world. A groan, perhaps a sob, tore from him as he buried his face in her neck, clutching tight. She held onto him as her heart wept.

'When does it happen?' he whispered later as the sky outside hinted at the coming daybreak.

She didn't need to speak the answer, and he nodded gravely.

Outside, an explosion rumbled, shaking the mountainside.

CHAPTER 23

'Hide, Isla. Go, please! If you love me, don't make me see you die. And don't you watch me – I want you to remember me like this, alive and in love with you.'

Keiichirō's plea was so desperate Isla couldn't say no.

They had left the darkness of the cave behind a long time earlier. Men fell all around them, bodies littering the forest floor, the heavy bombardment a cacophony in which they crouched. An orchestra of chaos and death playing a deadly tune.

Blood sprayed, limbs flew, and the scent of smoke and copper assaulted the air. Shouts echoed up the mountainside, agonised screams cutting off to gunfire.

But Keiichirō and Isla were only looking at each other, their faces filling their whole world.

As the soldiers crashed nearer, Keiichirō pushed Isla into a nearby bush beside a cluster of bamboo trees. In his final moments, he was determined to do what he could to protect her.

The sun was rising, the sky pink and bringing light to the world.

Isla breathed hard, watching her final dozen friends stand among the dead, swords raised. Someone yelled a battle cry, a fierce scream concealing his despair. Any samurai left alive bellowed back an answering war cry with a passion that made the hairs on her arms stand on end in pride.

Isla hid in the brush, not daring to wave away a mosquito that buzzed constantly around her head. For the first time she could remember, she forced herself to be patient.

She heard imperial soldiers cresting the hill, shouting orders. The samurai fell on them like an avalanche, swinging swords and screaming for blood.

Keiichirō moved with the grace of a dancer from a lifetime of training, murder in his eyes as he stabbed a soldier in the chest and threw his body to the ground. Isla had no sword, no way to help. All she could do was watch him fight, terrified that, if she looked away, the man she loved would fall.

*

Keiichirō defended both his love and Saigō-sama with all the determination of a wounded animal protecting its young. He ignored the agony flaring in his weakened shoulder. What did it matter when his enemies were killing those he cared for? How could they hurt someone who had accepted their fate?

Blood bathed him, hot on his skin. His sword shimmered with it, a painting of silver and crimson. A flow of imperial soldiers, their hair cut short, pretentious moustaches on their faces, attacked at close combat with the frightened hesitation of men only trained with guns.

Keiichirō pushed away the fear in favour of confidence in doing the right thing, Beppu-san fighting at his side, Saigō-sama ahead with Murata-san. Their leader was hunched, in pain, but he held his sword aloft and Keiichirō was inspired by Saigō-sama's bravery. He would happily die at this man's side.

'Fall back! Retreat!' came the cry.

Teeth clenched, Keiichirō turned and joined his fellow samurai heading back to the caves.

He would find Isla, he would—

A gunshot.

The shocking sight of Saigō-sama on the ground, pain on his round face as he clutched his stomach.

'Saigō-sama!' the men roared.

Keiichirō ran to his leader, blood screaming in his ears, as he helped him stand. 'Saigō-sama, get up! Get—'

Pain exploded across Keiichirō's back.

*

Isla sobbed her relief when she saw Keiichirō with Beppu and Murata, their combined strength holding up Saigō's giant frame.

Then Keiichirō sagged against the cave wall, and Isla knew something was desperately wrong.

She burst from her hiding place and ran to him. She turned him onto his side. His eyes were shut tight as he sucked in ragged breaths. A whimper burst from Isla. His *haori* jacket was torn to shreds, his back a gory mess. How was he still breathing?

'He was shot,' said Beppu, not looking up from Saigō's side.

Isla glanced up, her eyes burning. Saigō held his belly, blood seeping from between his fingers. Which of them was Beppu talking about?

'Is... la...' Keiichirō moaned.

'I'm here,' she cried.

Keiichirō groaned, forcing himself up to sit against the rockface at the mouth to the cave.

Beppu and Murata knelt with their heads bowed, like a great weight had fallen on them. Saigō lay with his eyes closed, the wound in his stomach not bleeding any more. His hand was on the handle of his sword and his face, stained with flecks of blood, held a serene look of peace. He was dead.

The sun rose higher, the mountain set aflame.

Keiichirō's chest moved with rapid, shallow breaths as he stared at his fallen leader. A tear trickled down his dirt-stained face, leaving a track.

Isla reached out and wiped it away.

He turned to look at her. His face was soaked in sweat and dirt, splashes of blood on his skin, but he had never looked so handsome. That expression she knew so well, the strength that only melted away when he was asleep, adorned his face. And in his eyes, sorrow and affection. Grief and love.

Beppu withdrew his own sword.

Isla knew Beppu meant to cut off Saigō's head, but nothing could have prepared her for the meaty slice and the thump. The few samurai left prostrated themselves, bowing for the final time to their fallen lord. Isla helped Keiichirō join them, and she bowed alongside him, their foreheads touching the ground.

Beppu picked up Saigō's head, and announced he would hide it.

'Come.' Murata rose to his feet, fighting trembles as he rallied his comrades. 'Let us take our last fight to them.'

Then something slammed into Isla from behind.

She shrieked and fell forward. For a moment, terror gripped her as she thought another fresh barrage of cannon fire was coming at them.

But it was wind, howling and warm and carrying the promise of rain, and a branch ripped from a tree had felled her. Large drops of water began to splat on the ground.

She turned, Keiichirō mirroring her. He winced as the pain in his back screamed. She took his hand.

On top of the mountain at their backs, an impossible storm raged. Rain and wind battled, encased in a bubble mere metres away from them like it was wrapped in an invisible cocoon. Flecks of rain fell on her, soft as kisses.

And at the peak of the mountain Isla could see something that made her freeze.

A white torii gate.

A gate that hadn't been there moments ago.

'Isla.' Keiichirō's voice was weak.

Hope bubbled up through Isla. She could save him, she could.

Any second now, Beppu would order the samurai to run to their deaths, to draw their swords and take down as many soldiers as they could before the darkness took them.

Even now, the warriors were starting to rise to their feet, shaking off injuries and readying themselves. Murata, tall and regal, held his sword, his eyes shining with tears. Beppu was returning, wiping his face. Kirino Toshiaki, Hisa's husband, cast a final glance at Saigō's headless body.

'Come with me, Kei. I can save us.' Isla was desperate.

Keiichirō's face twitched. 'I can't.'

'You can.' Her voice was hoarse. 'You don't have to die.'

'Isla. You told me Saigō-sama is known in your time. He is remembered. This is how it happens.'

The samurai gathered, leaving Saigō's headless body to rest, Beppu in the lead. He glanced over at them, a silent question in his eyes.

Will you join us, Maeda Keiichirō? Or will you live like a coward?

Isla didn't need Keiichirō to explain why it was impossible for him to survive this day. His fellow samurai had fallen around him, given their lives to this cause. Even if he survived the horrific injury to his back, if he lived, he would hate himself until the day he died.

'He is known,' she said. 'Everyone knows his name. There are statues. Books. Movies…' She closed her eyes. 'He's remembered as a hero.'

Keiichirō lifted her face, and her eyes opened. Peace had fallen on him, his face relaxed. 'Then that's enough. But Isla, you must survive. You don't belong here.'

The words stung. Her gaze fled to the storm on top of the mountain. It had come here now, in her final moments, a last chance for her to escape. To go home.

Her being here wouldn't make a mark on history.

Keiichirō would stay. She had sworn to remain at his side.

But she was so afraid to die.

'Not any longer.' Keiichirō tottered on his feet; whether from emotion or his injury, it was unclear. 'Please live, Isla. Go back to your own time. Continue Saigō-sama's legacy. That's enough for me.'

'Maeda, it is time,' Beppu growled as the last samurai stood for the final charge, holding up swords, shaking off injuries and spitting blood. Shouts from the bottom of the hill erupted. A gunshot cracked in the air.

Keiichirō kissed Isla, his lips barely brushing hers. 'Goodbye, bonnie lass.'

Staggering, his back in tatters, strands of midnight hair spilling behind him, he stumbled to his brothers. 'Go!' he yelled back at Isla over his shoulder.

Her heart shattering, Isla ran.

She took a step after the samurai, and then she turned the other way and charged up the hill and into the torrent of rain.

Isla exhaled heavily as the warm deluge hit her, soaking her at once. Hair sticking to her neck, the water soaking through her robe and onto her skin, she staggered up the hill towards where lightning flashed, illuminating the torii gate at the top of the hill. Her muscles burned, rain blinded her, her soaking robe increasingly heavy; she grabbed tufts of wet grass to stop her falling back, pulling herself up.

Only when she had almost reached the gate did she turn back.

Trees obscured her vision of the hillside below, but through the rain she could see the ships in the harbour. Cannons and gunfire boomed through the air, smoke choking the trees. Hitting the last warriors. Killing them as they ran to their deaths.

Rain pelted her down to her bones. Isla's vision swam. She fell to her knees. Part of her wanted to throw herself off the hill, to join Keiichirō's fate.

But the torii gate didn't stop calling to her, like the sweet hum of music, and promising the way to her time. Her home. Wind rushed around her, pushing her, encouraging her to step through and leave all this behind.

Isla closed her eyes and put her hands over her ears.

Whispers surrounded her, mingling with the falling rain.

When she opened her eyes, beyond were city lights, passing cars, people with umbrellas and jackets, scowling against the downpour.

So familiar.

So alien.

Thunder rumbled, the wind pulling her into her own time and away for ever from the man she loved. The brave samurai she would never see again.

Her tears mingling with the rain, Isla stepped through the gate.

CHAPTER 24

Her limbs fizzed and shook. Rain made her scalp sodden. Her clothing clung to her skin, her freezing hands losing all feeling. Isla faltered as she ran, confusion assaulting her senses. She slipped and fell, dizzy, as though she'd downed a whole barrel of *shōchū*. She was in the shrine. Wind chimes jangled. Wood banged. Rain pelted her face. It made no sense. Was Keiichirō nearby?

She dragged herself upright and lurched past statues and stone walls, hands sliding across slick rock surfaces as she struggled to keep her balance in the roaring storm. She could still see Saigō's headless corpse in her mind, imagine the samurai rushing down the mountainside with their swords held high, *haori* sleeves flapping behind them. Keiichirō with them. Her heart felt broken.

A cannon boomed through the night, making her duck, fresh terror surging through her. No, not a cannon, but wooden doors that banged against the wall, sucked open by the wind.

An old woman cried out in shock as Isla almost crashed into her, her umbrella knocked to the side. Isla shivered as she ran. There were so many lights. So many people. Men and women dressed strangely, in suits and jeans and everything else from a half-forgotten life, stopped to stare. A bicycle bell rang in alarm as a cyclist narrowly avoided hitting her. Dizzy turmoil swam in her mind, memories slipping away as she reached for them, as elusive as trying to grab smoke as it coiled through her fingers.

What was happening?

A man swore as she knocked into him. She pushed away from a tangle of limbs and fell into the road. A car honked in warning.

Pain sliced up her arm and along her ribcage. Cold rain fell on her face, icy shards on her skin. Too many lights and voices surrounded her. She struggled to breathe. The sound of an opening car door, a shout to call an ambulance.

'*Oneesan*, can you hear me?' a voice echoed as the shadow of a man knelt above her.

People gasped and backed away. A man in overalls stood nearby, flashing a bright orange baton to redirect traffic. Isla lay on the cold, hard ground as she squinted against the downpour.

'You've been hit by a car. The ambulance is on its way. Don't move. Where does it hurt?'

She groaned. She couldn't move even if she wanted to. Bile burned in her throat as her head spun. How ironic if she died here, a million miles away from the man she'd sworn to stay with.

The man cursed. '*Kuso*. Uh…' Isla caught sight of a waving hand as the man searched for English phrases he knew. 'What's your name?'

'Isla.' Isla groaned into the rain. 'MacKenzie... Isla.'
And then, merciful blackness.

*

Maeda Keisuke stared at his bedroom ceiling. Rain hammered his window.

He had been dreaming for months about the same thing. An old village under the shadow of a volcano. Robe-clad samurai, endless war, gruelling death. A redheaded foreign woman, the very same who had been on the news a few months ago when she had gone missing. He had met her in January at the café, had chatted with her. Yet since she had disappeared, he had seen her every night in his dreams.

He knuckled his eyes, sighing, then rolled off his futon.

The scene was the same: a katana sword, heavy in his hand, sweat sticking his long hair to his neck. Fighting imperial soldiers, the low boom of gunfire, the stench of smoke and gunpowder and gore as swords chopped apart bodies and cut off limbs, leaving men screaming in the dirt. The foreign woman had been his friend, his lover, and they had parted ways at the foot of a mountain.

'Bonnie lass,' he muttered, the words foreign on his tongue but bittersweet and familiar. MacKenzie Isla. For a second, he felt their final kiss still burning on his lips. Sometimes Keisuke didn't know what was real, this life in Kagoshima as a medical student and part-time barista, or the life he returned to when he closed his eyes.

It was the middle of the night, early autumn rain beating against his window. The fan hummed as it blew cool air, wonderfully comfortable this humid season.

But right now, he needed to get out of his cramped little apartment.

Keisuke pulled on a rain jacket and slipped on his shoes. Pulling his hood up, he ventured out into the night and set off down the street, going nowhere in particular.

The dreams flashed before his eyes whenever he blinked, like strobe lightning. Running into earth-shattering explosions of cannon fire, choking on smoke, thinking only of the foreign girl who had run away from the battle at his command. No, he hadn't commanded her. He had begged her, desperate for her to live on, not die in a foreign land surrounded by enemies. His guilt at leaving his friends to die, his sense of retribution as he ran to his death, sword held aloft, bleeding from his injured back.

Keisuke could even feel the agony of bullets striking him, the scent of grass and earth as he collapsed to the ground, breathing his last. He felt these images were more like memories than dreams, as if the torment and grief for friends he never knew were part of himself. He rubbed his chest beneath his jacket, as though expecting to find the ghosts of bullet holes or scars from knife wounds.

He reached the main road not far from the path leading to Mount Shiroyama, where the famous statue of Saigō Takamori immortalised the fabled leader. A leader he had met in his dreams.

An ambulance, its lights flashing amid the rain, blocked half of the road. Keisuke watched in curiosity as some paramedics, calling to each other in their clipped, professional manner, rolled a stretcher towards the ambulance doors.

And on the stretcher a young woman lay, red hair roping in wet strands, dressed in traditional garb. Her eyes were closed and she was pale as death.

Keisuke froze, insides clenching.

It was *her*!

The woman he had dreamed about for the past nine months. He would know her anywhere. He had touched her, kissed her, made love to her. He had screamed at her to leave the fight, to save herself.

Keisuke stepped forward but was stopped by a traffic warden holding a glowing baton. Rain dripped from his cap.

'I'm sorry, sir. The road is closed. We apologise for the inconvenience.'

Keisuke watched as they packed MacKenzie Isla into the ambulance. Was she all right? She didn't look it. What had happened? A car stood in the middle of the road, a harried-looking man clutching an umbrella and talking to the police.

None of this made any sense, but Keisuke had to find out what was going on. He had to speak to her, to work out what all this meant.

*

Isla was dimly aware of a crisp English voice as she lay in a hard bed. The strong smell of disinfectant hit her, stinging her nostrils and turning her empty stomach. When she opened her eyes, she was in a dimly lit room, clean and plain and stark white. Raindrops dotted a window to her left, though it wasn't night-time any longer and the storm looked to have passed; glimmers of sun struggled through the clouds.

'British exchange student Isla MacKenzie has been found alive after going missing in Kagoshima Prefecture, Kyushu, at the beginning of January this year, and she is currently undergoing tests in hospital,' said the news anchor on the television.

English sounded almost strange to Isla now. She could understand it, of course, but it was like her brain needed time to adjust. Her body felt weak and malnourished, her right side tender and her arm in a cast, and when she blinked, her eye wrinkled with pain. Her head felt heavy and, as she soon discovered, pain shot across it if she moved it.

A low groan escaped her lips.

I shouldn't be here. I need to get back to Kei. He needs me, she thought.

A heart monitor beside her beeped as she stared at the television, squinting at the artificial brightness. An old, grainy photo of herself on the screen, cropped from a family picture of a Scottish holiday, her hair long and a huge smile on her face.

'No, absolutely not. She's not awake yet.'

Isla's eyes drifted to a white door. Voices echoed beyond.

The door opened and a middle-aged male doctor appeared, almost unnaturally neat and clean. Isla stared at him, catching a glimpse of a Japanese police officer in the hallway.

The doctor's coat was far too white, his face clean-shaven and free of scars. 'MacKenzie-san, it is good to see you're awake,' he said in crisp English. 'I am Doctor Iwasaki. How are you feeling?'

Isla had no idea how she was feeling.

Part of her didn't want to face everything that was surely to come. The police, the press. How widely known was her case? How many hundreds of people had been involved in her disappearance and were now waiting to ask questions? Questions she couldn't answer?

'Take your time,' said Doctor Iwasaki gently when she didn't respond. 'I am here to tell you that you fractured your right arm in two places and one of your ribs, but we expect you to make a full recovery. We hope to make a psychological evaluation and then the police want to question you.'

She let him speak on, staring at the wall. So meticulous, so different from the samurai spitting blood and insisting they were fit to fight when their bodies were ready to collapse. She felt foolish in her cast and tucked into bed.

'Your parents will be here tomorrow morning.'

Isla glanced up at that, then immediately wished she hadn't; pain jackhammered up her skull. But her heart lifted. Mum and Dad would be here tomorrow. Tears filled her eyes. She'd finally see her family again.

'Thank you,' she managed to croak.

The happiness at this news clashed with her broken spirit. When she closed her eyes, she was still on Mount Shiroyama, surrounded by dead or dying samurai, clinging to the man she loved before he would disappear for ever. She could still imagine his scent of cedarwood, his warm eyes, the way his fingers ran across her skin, leaving gooseflesh in their wake. She felt alien in this sterilised little room.

'Oh, and a nurse has brought you some menstrual pads. She reported to me your period started last night.' He bowed to her and left, closing the door quietly behind him and leaving her alone with the steady beep of her heart monitor.

The information took a moment to sink in. A second, smaller punch in her chest accompanied her grief. Fresh tears welled up in her eyes. What had she expected? Hoped for? That her passion-filled nights with Keiichirō would lead to pregnancy?

Maybe she had hoped, at least a little bit. Keiichirō was dead, but perhaps if she had been able to bring something back of him, a *piece* of him...

She closed her eyes. It was a silly thought, but she allowed herself to grieve for the child who would never be. To wallow in disappointment for a lost impossibility.

A nurse came by later to take out the IV drip attached to her arm, and she put a tray of food on Isla's lap. Isla took in the little bowl of rice, steaming miso soup, grilled salmon with grated radish, a tiny helping of pickled vegetables, and a bowl of fruit, served with a plastic fork.

She was starving, and she began to shovel food into her mouth, not caring about being polite. The nurse busied herself with arranging towels as the stark, strong flavours coated Isla's tongue. She barely chewed, swallowing great mouthfuls.

She balked. Her throat bulged. Nausea ran up her gullet and she choked. She vomited, rice bursting from her lips. The nurse appeared at her side, patting her back and holding a cardboard receptacle beneath her chin.

After Isla had calmed down, the nurse brought her a fresh bowl of cut-up fruit and a spoon, on a new tray, beside a little paper cup of water.

It was late afternoon when they finally left her alone, and Isla was exhausted. She climbed out of bed and wavered on the spot for a moment, and then took several wobbly steps to her shower room. Struggling with her broken arm, she managed to slip off the hospital gown and switch it on. Steam filled the tiny room.

It was paradise. Clean, fresh, perfect-temperature water spurted from a shining showerhead, soaking her in seconds. She groaned with pleasure as she leaned against the wall, inhaling steam, keeping her cast out of the flow. She wanted to stay here for ever.

It was heaven to lather shampoo into her hair, and to pat herself dry with a towel. She almost cried when she found a toothbrush and a little tube of toothpaste waiting for her beside a tiny sink. Firmly avoiding looking at her reflection, Isla brushed for five straight minutes.

Back in bed, fresher than before, she switched off the television and sighed. She lay back on the bed to stare at the ceiling, shouts and the clashing of swords still echoing in her mind against the sounds of the hospital and the traffic outside. Keiichirō's lips brushed hers in her memory, as if his ghost lingered. Her ears, attuned to listening for danger, caught far-off sounds. Footsteps and voices around the hospital. The steady hum of the air conditioner. The sigh of the wind. Sirens.

She didn't know where they had put her yukata, and she didn't want to call a nurse to find out. The old robe would lead to awkward questions. Her wallet, however, was safe; it lay on her bedside table next to the now empty paper cup, folded and tucked beneath her dead flip phone. The 1,000-yen notes were still in there, the little plastic card with her photo that she had shown Keiichirō and Nene in one of the pockets. It felt like several lifetimes since she had come to Kagoshima in winter, hoping to find information on Hisakichi Kuroki.

But you did find him, flashed across her mind.

She gave a snort, which turned into a giggle. The absurd ridiculousness of it all made her burst into laughter, and she clutched her pillow, burying her face into the cotton.

It took a while to calm down and, when she had wiped her eyes, she gingerly pushed herself into a sitting position.

She had indeed found her third-great-grandfather, but when she had come looking for her ancestor's history she hadn't expected to walk right into it.

If she had known what would transpire, would she have ever wandered into those shrine grounds? Would she be here right now, thanks to Hisakichi and Nene escaping the war, if she hadn't?

The door slid open, and Isla lay back down, closing her eyes. She didn't want to talk to anyone, least of all a police officer who might have forced his way in. Soft footsteps reached the side of her bed and a metal tray rattled as the newcomer placed it on her bedside table.

The voice was soft. Male. Not the doctor. 'Isla?'

Isla's eyes shot open. For a moment, she thought she was dreaming.

High cheekbones, long hair tied in a knot behind his head, and a serious look that melted into a smile of recognition. For an insane moment, Isla thought it was him.

But he couldn't be Keiichirō. Kei had died over a century ago. The young samurai had not worn a rain jacket.

She gripped the bedclothes. The spicy scent of clove wreathed him, and a memory found its way to her hazy mind. The man before her had served her a cinnamon latte at the coffee shop when she had visited Kagoshima back in January.

What was he doing here, in her hospital room? Why did she look so much like the man she had loved and lost? Was she hallucinating?

Her head felt heavy, and her eyes travelled along his chest, to the twenty-first-century clothes, and bitter disappointment burned in her for him not being Keiichirō.

'Isla? Good evening.' The café barista perched on a stool beside her bed. He was too close, too familiar. 'MacKenzie Isla? Do you remember me? We drank matcha *tapioka* together once.'

She raised her eyes to meet his. The resemblance was eerie, though there were differences. His jaw was more square, his hairline lacking the distinctive widow's peak Keiichirō had. But the way he looked at her now captured her attention.

In her confused and bruised mind, she felt in that moment that it was Keiichirō gazing at her. It was foolish – she wasn't so far gone not to think that – but she clung to the feeling.

'Who are you?' she murmured.

'This might sound odd,' he said, his warm brown eyes, a freckle near one of them, moving over her hair, to her mouth, and back to meet her gaze. 'But I know you. And you know me.'

'Been on the news…' she muttered as a well of emotions threatened to engulf her.

'No, it's not that.' The man pulled his chair closer. 'It's *you*, isn't it? Bonnie lass?'

Isla gasped in shock.

'I know this is strange.' The man took her hand, his fingers warm. She glanced down at his hand, not wanting to pull away. 'For months now, I've been dreaming of you.'

EPILOGUE

'This is where you grew up, *Okaasan?*'

'Yes. See how there's a huge volcano on the water over there?'

'Wow! It's so big.' The little boy's eyes widened in wonder as he took in the mighty Mount Sakurajima.

'There's a lovely *onsen* nearby we'll visit later, and I can tell you all about volcanoes. Would you like that?'

Nene held her son in her arms, Hisakichi at her side. It had been four years since she had last been to Kagoshima. Her father, with whom she had been exchanging letters ever since they had settled on the farm in Miyazaki, couldn't wait to meet his first grandson.

Now they strolled along the riverbank towards the familiar town, the sea sparkling beyond the sloped roofs. The *sakura* blossoms were blooming, and a cherry ceiling shielded them from the spring sunshine. Pink-white petals fell like snow, and little Ichirō giggled when one landed on his nose.

Despite her excitement, nerves jangled through Nene. Hisakichi didn't meet her father before they married. Her parents had dreamed of her marrying a samurai, but the noble warrior class was no more. Nene had married for love, and they now lived on a farm that she and her husband owned. It was everything she had ever dared to dream of, and more.

Hisakichi sensed her apprehension and scooped their young son into his arms. Hisakichi's skin was darkened by working in the sun. He wore a simple robe on his shoulders. Their work on the farm was hard, but Nene had never been happier. Now they were together properly, instead of her having to sneak over to his farm or send Aiko-chan to pass letters between them like spies.

A dull ache weighed in her stomach at the memory of her dear friend, of holding her in her arms as she had breathed her last. It was something she would never forget. So many people Nene loved were gone. Hirayama Aiko, Maeda Keiichirō, MacKenzie Isla. Even after four years, she missed them all more than she could bear. She wished she could have introduced her son to them.

Keiichirō's sister Kana had told her through a river of tears that her brother had perished on Mount Shiroyama alongside the last of the samurai. It was a brave death. Nobody knew what had happened to Isla. Her body was never found.

Isla's claims that she was from a different time felt almost like a dream, and Nene wasn't sure she believed it. Perhaps her Scottish friend had finally made it back to her homeland. Nene liked to believe that MacKenzie Isla was alive, somewhere out there. Maybe they would even see each other again someday.

Now, it was strange to return to where she had grown up, helping her merchant father sell fine cloths and farmer's tools, thinking her path held a marriage with a young man she considered merely a friend when in fact her future had held something quite different. The town of Kagoshima still reeled from losing so many of its men in the war. Nene was glad her father had not joined the conflict that was swiftly becoming known as the Seinan Sensō, the War of the Southwest.

Just like Isla had tried to warn, it had been a massacre, a rout. The samurai had been doomed as soon as their great leader had departed from Kagoshima.

The town seemed emptier, somehow, without Saigō Takamori. He had been known and liked by even the lowliest of peasants. Although he was branded a traitor by the country, the Satsuma people's love for him would never die.

'Look at that,' said Hisakichi as they came to a grassy slope that edged the river. Ichirō wriggled until he let him down, and the boy ran off on his chubby legs.

'Be careful! Don't get too close to the water,' Nene called. Men liked to do rough and tumble with their sons, to teach them to fight and be brave from the moment they could walk, but Nene would wrap Ichirō in linen and hide him from the world if she could.

Ichirō stayed an obedient distance from the water's edge, collecting fallen cherry blossoms. Nene followed Hisakichi's gaze to see what he was staring at.

It was a little shrine made from stones, a primitive version of a grave, yet oddly charming.

Nene knelt to peer at it. Her merchant father had taught her to read and write, making it safe to send letters to the farm under the care of her illiterate fellow women. The two kanji characters carved clumsily into a long, flat river stone made her brow furrow.

'It says Kuroki.' She glanced up at her husband. A few petals had landed in his thick hair. 'I didn't think you had more relatives in Kagoshima. Did someone you know make this?'

Her husband crouched beside her and examined the etchings. One long finger reached out to trace them. The first character, *black*, and the second, *tree*, spelled their surname. 'I can't be the only Kuroki around here, I suppose.'

'We'd better pray, just in case.' Nene rose to her feet and bowed to the little shrine. She didn't know why, but it gave her a strange feeling.

Hisakichi mirrored her and, after chasing down Ichirō, they got their little boy to show his respect to the strange monument, too.

Nene stayed for a moment longer as Hisakichi chased their giggling son, who wanted to go the far end of the grass. Above her head, a warbling white-eye chirped in a branch.

She thought of her fallen friends and made up her mind to pay her respects to their graves too while she was here. It felt like the least she could do.

'Wait up!' she called to her family, who had raced ahead along the riverbank, cherry blossom petals floating in a trail behind her son's chubby fist.

She took one last glance at the lonely little shrine before breaking into a run. She wasn't sure why, but the memorial made Nene smile.

AUTHOR NOTE

With a new passport and finally with money of my own, I first came to Japan in 2011 at eighteen years old. I cried when it was time to leave, and just a few months later I was back in Tokyo as a study-abroad student at Toyo University.

I came back after graduation and have lived here ever since, first in Nagano, then in Tokyo, and now near Enoshima Island in Kanagawa. I'm so glad I could combine my love for this wonderful country with my hopes of becoming a writer.

Japan entered a state of *sakoku*, or isolation, in 1603 and didn't reopen to foreign trade until the arrival of the Americans in the 1850s. During this period of isolation, no foreigner could enter the country and no Japanese person could leave, making it one of the most self-sufficient and uniquely developed countries in the world.

You understand, then, that, wanting to write about a romance between a European woman and a Japanese samurai, my options were somewhat limited.

I've always been fascinated with Japanese history. It's one of the major reasons I had wanted to move to Japan since I was a kid. I had tremendous fun researching the Satsuma Rebellion of 1877, named after the Satsuma province (now Kagoshima Prefecture), where the samurai made a final, dramatic stand against imperial soldiers intent on crushing the old way of life for ever in favour of the Japan we know today.

It is a sad history, one that became the setting for Isla and Keiichirō's story. Though Keiichirō Maeda is fictional, there were many young samurai just like him embroiled in the rebellion who gave their lives for their beloved leader. Real historical figures, such as Toshiaki and Hisa Kirino, Shinpachi Murata, and Shinsuke Beppu, also make appearances in the story, and are portrayed as close to real life as possible.

The Satsuma Rebellion was the final rising against the fast-developing modernisation and Westernisation of Japan to compete with international powers. The rapid changes sent a shockwave of violence throughout the country as the samurai class ceased to exist. Takamori Saigō was brought reluctantly out of retirement to lead the rebellion, and, with inferior manpower and weapons, he and his people were doomed from the start. It all ended with a last, bloody battle on the slopes of Mount Shiroyama.

Seinan Sensō: The Battle of Japan that Changed its History is a manga comic-style book that provides a stunning account of the rebellion. *Samurai Castles* by Jennifer Mitchelhill also provides fascinating information about various castles still standing in Japan, including Kumamoto Castle, a major setting of the conflict. Visiting Kagoshima was an amazing experience where I learned a lot more about the rebellion and walked in Isla's footsteps.

Takamori Saigō's statue stands in Kagoshima today as a sort of mascot. Anyone who visits can see the caves in which the samurai hid in their final days. I am pleased to set Isla and Keiichirō's story in such a rich part of history.

ACKNOWLEDGEMENTS

You would not be holding this book in your hands right now if it weren't for some very special people who helped bring *Gate to Kagoshima* to life. My mother, the best mom in the world, who has read everything I've written and has always given her helpful, unfiltered advice. You have always supported my dream of being a writer, and I'm forever grateful.

My amazing UK agent, Edwina de Charnace, and US agent, Jason Yarn, who were some of the first people to give this book a chance and whose infinite enthusiasm has made this journey a joy from the very beginning.

Mr. Tierney, my fifth-grade teacher, who wrote in my school report that I had talent and should pursue my dream.

Lexi Cooper, Sarah Karwisch, Alice Creangă, James Reid, SJ, and Julie Golden, thank you for being early draft readers who gave me the feedback and encouragement I needed to bring the book to its full potential.

My lovely editor, Sara Nelson, for her personalized touch and enthusiasm. Edie Astley, Amy Baker, Doug Jones, Megan Looney, and the rest of the fantastic team at Harper Perennial who have brought *Gate to Kagoshima* to life in America. It's an absolute dream come true to work with you all.

I also want to thank Michele Matsunaga, who set me up with a guided tour in Kagoshima. The tour guide, Kiyoko Tokunaga, who tirelessly answered my many questions about Takamori Saigō and the Satsuma Rebellion. And Hiroshi Wakamatsu, a descendent of Takamori Saigō's wife, who kindly gave an endorsement for the book and expressed his delight that I was writing about his family history.

To my husband for his love and support, and my son, Jack Valentine, who was a newborn when I started writing this, and who is an endless source of joy and inspiration. I love you all.

HISTORICAL TIMELINE

October 1873: Takamori Saigō, who would come to be known as the Last Samurai, retires from government and returns to his hometown of Kagoshima with Toshiaki Kirino and their soldiers.

June 1874: Saigō establishes the first *shi-gakkō* (military) academy.

December 1876: The Meiji government sends Hisao Nakahara and fifty-seven other policemen to Satsuma to pose as samurai students and spy on Takamori Saigō's academies.

January 30, 1877: The Meiji government sends a warship to Kagoshima to remove the weapons at the Kagoshima arsenal. They are discovered and driven off by angry samurai from the *shi-gakkō*. Nakahara is discovered and confesses under torture that they reported local disdain for the government and planned to assassinate Saigō.

January 31–February 2, 1877: The samurai attack the Somuta arsenal and parade the weapons around town.

February 12, 1877: Saigō announces he's going to Tokyo to question the government.

February 13–14, 1877: The army is organized into tactical units.

February 14, 1877: The Satsuma vanguard cross into Kumamoto Prefecture. Thirty thousand Satsuma soldiers join the rebellion.

February 15, 1877: About four thousand men under the command of Shinsuke Beppu leave Kagoshima.

February 19, 1877: The army reaches Kagoshima in just four days despite extreme cold and snowfall. A fire erupts in a castle storehouse, destroying much of the castle's food supplies.

February 21, 1877: The conflict officially begins. Satsuma troops fight off an imperial attack, driving them to seek refuge in Kumamoto Castle.

February 22–24, 1877: The Satsuma soldiers attack Kumamoto Castle, many throwing themselves at the walls in suicide-like waves.

End of February 1877: Toshiaki Kirino suggests a full-frontal assault on the castle but is overruled in favor of the army splitting up.

March 3, 1877: The imperial army attacks and the Battle of Tabaruzaka begins.

March 19, 1877: The Satsuma forces fail to protect the town of Miyanohara. Heavy rainfall damages most of their guns, forcing them to fight with swords.

Late March 1877: As the Satsuma forces reach the castle, opposing soldiers exchange lighthearted banter. The moat is drained so those in the castle, rapidly running out of food, can eat the carp inside.

April 8, 1877: A force from Kumamoto Castle gains the upper hand.

April–May 1877: The Satsuma forces, demoralized, retreat from Kumamoto Castle. Over the course of the next few months, they are defeated in major battles at Hitoyoshi, Noboeka, and Miyakonojo. They rapidly run out of supplies and men.

July 24, 1877: The Imperial Army attacks Saigō's army. The Satsuma forces cut free and escape.

August 17, 1877: The Satsuma army's numbers have dwindled to a few thousand soldiers. They make a stand on Mount Enodake. Most of the remaining forces commit ritual suicide (*seppuku*).

August 19, 1877: Saigō burns his uniform and papers and slips away to Kagoshima with his remaining soldiers.

September 1, 1877: Saigō receives a letter demanding surrender and rejects it.

September 2, 1877: Fewer than three hundred combatants remain.

September 8, 1877: By this time, the Imperial Army has surrounded Mount Shiroyama in five brigades. General Yamagata is determined not to let Saigō slip away again.

September 24, 1877: General Yamagata orders a full-frontal assault. By 6 a.m., only sixty Satsuma men are still alive. Saigō is mortally wounded and perishes (historical sources vary on whether he committed *seppuku* or died of his wounds). Shinsuke Beppu cuts off his head to preserve his dignity, and the surviving men charge down the mountainside to their deaths. The rebellion ends at 7 a.m.

February 22, 1889: Emperor Meiji posthumously pardons Saigō. Today, he is seen as a tragic hero.

BY THE NUMBERS

- Takamori Saigō opened his first *shi-gakkō* academy in June 1874. By 1876, there were 12 schools in Kagoshima and around 120 throughout the Satsuma territory. The total enrolment was about 7,000 students.
- Thirty thousand Satsuma troops went to war with Takamori Saigō. Upon leaving Satsuma, each man had about a hundred rounds each, a rifle or pistol, and their sword (their primary weapon). Only a few hundred survived the rebellion, having fled or surrendered.
- More than sixty thousand imperial officers fought in the conflict. Around sixteen thousand of them died.
- During the siege of Kumamoto Castle, which lasted fifty-four days, the imperial garrison lost 186 soldiers and police officers, with 584 wounded.
- Unlike the rebels, the Imperial Army was able to replace its lost men and ammunition with little trouble, ensuring victory from the beginning.
- Crushing the rebellion cost the Japanese government an equivalent of eight million pounds, forcing them off the gold standard and onto paper currency. It more than doubled the country's national debt.

FAMILY TREE

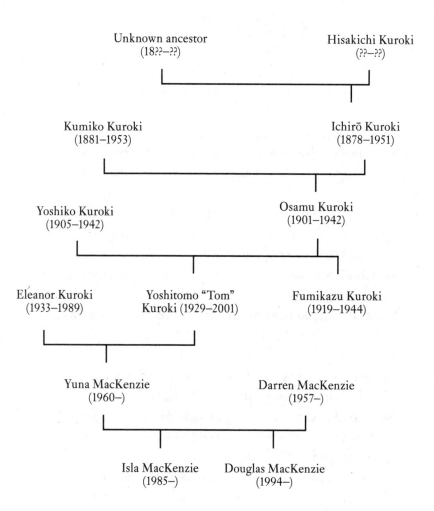

Unknown ancestor
(18??–??)

Hisakichi Kuroki
(??–??)

Kumiko Kuroki
(1881–1953)

Ichirō Kuroki
(1878–1951)

Yoshiko Kuroki
(1905–1942)

Osamu Kuroki
(1901–1942)

Eleanor Kuroki
(1933–1989)

Yoshitomo "Tom"
Kuroki (1929–2001)

Fumikazu Kuroki
(1919–1944)

Yuna MacKenzie
(1960–)

Darren MacKenzie
(1957–)

Isla MacKenzie
(1985–)

Douglas MacKenzie
(1994–)

CHARACTER LIST

FICTIONAL CHARACTERS

Isla MacKenzie: A young Scottish woman with a Japanese grandfather, Isla travels to Kagoshima City in Kyushu Prefecture during her year abroad to research her ancestors' history.

Yoshitomo Kuroki: Isla's grandfather. Originally from Kyushu, he moved to Scotland and married a Scottish woman, much to the dismay of his parents.

Keiichirō Maeda: a low-ranking samurai who fights in the Satsuma Rebellion.

Kana Maeda: Keiichirō's younger sister. She lives with him and her daughter, Yura.

Yura Maeda: A toddler and Kana's daughter.

Toramasa Mori: Keiichirō's best friend and a samurai at the *shi-gakkō*. He is in love with Uhei Ikeda.

Nene Nakamura: A young Japanese woman who helps Isla work and train with the unmarried women.

Aiko Hirayama: Nene's best friend.

Hanzō Taguchi: A Shimazu Clan samurai and a member of the *shi-gakkō* school. He holds a grudge against the Maeda family for the death of his brother, Gorō.

Hisakichi Kuroki: Isla's third-great-grandfather, a young man during the Satsuma Rebellion. Isla travels to Kyushu to find out more about him.

Uhei Ikeda: A skilled samurai at the *shi-gakkō*, a lover of Toramasa Mori.

Tatsuzō Maeda: Keiichirō's cousin and a samurai.

Saki Maeda: Tatsuzō's wife, originally from Fukushima Prefecture, though she hides this as best she can.

Jun Maeda: Tatsuzō and Saki's first son.

Haru Maeda: Tatsuzō and Saki's second son.

Keisuke Maeda: A barista and medical student.

Kono: A middle-aged samurai of Satsuma and a friend of Keiichirō.

Murakami: A young samurai of Satsuma and a friend of Keiichirō.

REAL CHARACTERS

Saigō Takamori: The leader of the Satsuma Rebellion. Once a general for the Imperial Army, he was brought reluctantly out of retirement when a plot was uncovered to assassinate him.

Toshiaki Kirino: Saigō's close friend who fought alongside him in the Restoration War. He commanded battalions during the Satsuma Rebellion and was with Saigō until the end.

Hisa Kirino: Toshiaki's wife. She led the female auxiliary troops in the march. She survived the war and lived until 1920.

Shinsuke Beppu: A samurai of the Satsuma Domain who cut off Saigō's head after he died.

Shinpachi Murata: A retainer of the Shimazu Clan and a close friend of Saigō. They fought together during the Meiji Restoration.

Hisao Nakahara: A spy captured by Shimazu Clan samurai who admitted to spying on the *shi-gakkō*. He was involved in a plot to assassinate Saigō, and was severely tortured and forced to write a confession. He was rescued by an Imperial delegation.

Toratarō Saigō: Takamori Saigō's twelve-year-old son, who pleaded with him not to leave. It was the last time they saw each other.

GLOSSARY

Arigatou gozaimasu: a polite way of saying "thank you"

Bakamono: idiot, fool

Bō-hiya: fire arrows

Gaijin: foreigner, literally meaning "outsider"

Hakama: wide pants worn over a kimono

Haori: a wide-sleeved jacket worn over a kimono

Inoshishi: a Japanese wild boar

Kamisori: a traditional type of straight razor used for shaving

Kanpai: "cheers" said before drinking

Katana: the longer sword used for fighting

Ndamoshitan: Kagoshima/Satsuma dialect meaning "oh my," "what?" or "seriously?"

Noren: fabric curtains used as dividers, often painted with words when used in restaurants or shops

Ohayou: an informal way to say "good morning." Adding *gozaimasu* makes it more polite

Oi wa omansa ga wazze sujja: Kagoshima/Satsuma dialect meaning "I like you a lot"

Oniisan/oneesan: friendly, polite terms used for a young man and young woman, respectively

Onsen: a natural hot spring

Sensei: teacher, instructor

Seppuku: ritual suicide

Shinseifu: the new government, established after the Meiji Restoration in 1868

Shōchū: an alcoholic beverage distilled from barley, rice, or sweet potatoes

Wakizashi: shorter sword used for close-range combat and for suicide

Washi: handmade decorative paper used for walls

Watashi wa anata no koto ga daisuki desu: standard Japanese meaning "I like you a lot"

Yōkai: a spirit or ghost of Japanese folklore

POPPY KUROKI was born in Scotland and grew up in England. She has been living in Japan since 2016, where she works as a writer and freelance editor. She lives in Kanagawa with her son. *Gate to Kagoshima* is the first in the Ancestor Memories series set in Japan.